MW01257863

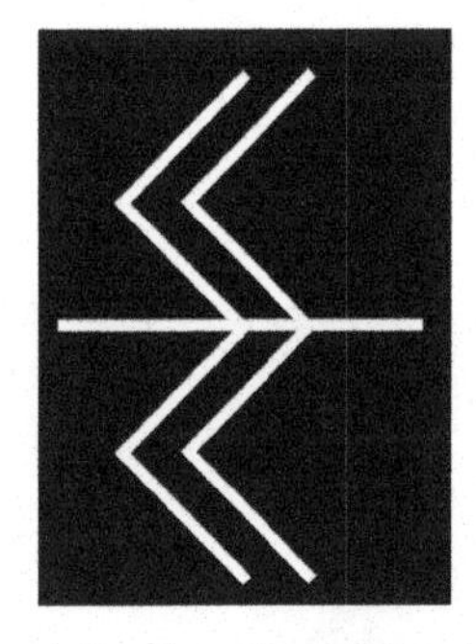

A Broken River Books original

Broken River Books
10660 SW Murdock St
#PF02
Tigard, OR 97224

Interior design by J David Osborne

Special thanks to Michael David Wilson & Charlene Bowles

ISBN: 978-1-940885-35-3

Printed in the USA.

CHUPACABRA VENGEANCE

STORIES

BY

DAVID BOWLES

BROKEN RIVER BOOKS
PORTLAND, OR

Dedicated to Álvaro Rodríguez,
for being there.

TABLE OF CONTENTS

BLEAK BORDERS

AZTLÁN LIBERATED

From the rubble of war-gutted Juárez they emerge: el Chamuco and his rumble-fish clique. La Güera is at point, machete and Glock in hand, wheaten hair bound in a bandana. Next comes Einstein, hairnet askew, Stacies badly in need of a shine, knapsack full of battered books and gadgets. Payaso brings up the rear, droning a constant comedic monologue despite the devastation.

El Chamuco mourns his fallen *carnales*, victims of the Pocho-Zeta War, but grins victorious. The four *pachucos* have avenged their *barrio*, following the only code that yields survival in this apocalyptic desert: kill or be killed.

The vultures wheel overhead. Life slithers on.

La Güera raises her blade to signal a sudden stop. Her Glock dips its glittering barrel. There on the shattered blacktop a vehicle looms unexpectedly, an army green jeep bearing the US flag, its forty-two white stars mocking. Against a knobby tire a soldier sits, legs splayed, guts gleaming red in his cupped hands. His comrades appear to be missing.

Choop attack, el Chamuco surmises, and he steps forward, eyes scanning, AK-47 raised.

The yank is Latino. He lifts a pained gaze at the gang, sighs. "*Bueno*." He gives a ragged cough. "Kill me."

"You're already dead." El Chamuco kneels close. "The hell you're doing in Aztlán, yank?"

A rivulet of blood dribbles down the soldier's chin. "Scientists. They figured it out. How to end the goddamn chupacabras. Found the queen. Meteor that hit near Las Cruces? Choop ship. The other goatsuckers were advance troops. Now they're plugged in. Hive mind."

The yank—Chávez, his uniform declares him—bumps the jeep with his head. "A nuke. In back. Their defenses scramble guidance. Got to take it in person. There's a detonator in the cabin."

"Fucking yanks," Payaso mutters. "Them and their nukes. *Cabrones*."

Wheezing, Chávez extends a bloody hand and seizes el Chamuco's tattered flannel. "You all are just *cholos*. Probably don't got it in you. But there it is."

His eyes glaze, and Holy Mother Death takes him.

"*Chale*," Payaso spits. "Like we're gonna forget fifteen years. *Putos* put up a wall, trapped us inside with the Choopi-choops, grunts ready to shoot your ass if you try to climb to Mother Mex or Gringoland."

Einstein shakes his close-cropped head. "Yeah, but we wouldn't just be saving them, *ese*. We'd be liberating Aztlán, from Brownsville to Tijuana. Free to build a permanent home for *la raza*."

La Güera scoffs. "Whatever. I just want to gank me some goatsuckers. Using this bomb means a shitload of them die, I'm all for it."

El Chamuco regards them all, bravest souls he's known.

"Then we do it. We go together as far as Las Cruces, then one of us drives the bomb to the crater's edge and hurries back fast as shit. Got to be far away when we detonate." The silence burgeons with implications no one will voice. "But right now you're in charge of the bomb, Einstein. Payaso drives. Güerita, gather any weapons the yanks left, get them working. *Nos vamos en diez.*"

As Einstein retrieves the detonator and a military satphone, el Chamuco drags the soldier to the dunes, douses him, and sets him alight, leaving nothing for the alien horde. The sun settles redly into a jade-swathed horizon. The cholo lowers his tattooed face, mumbles a prayer.

Darkness encroaches as they head north. Rusty remains of cars loom as if to snatch them from the road. Amid the windy silence comes a chittering whine. The four heft weapons, ready for the attack. Thudding impacts send the vehicle swaying back and forth. Large, glowing eyes and stiletto teeth loom at windows. Claws tear at sheet metal. El Chamuco sprays the roof, his tactic met by shrieking cries. Then the enemy redoubles its efforts. The *chupacabras*, their purpose as ineffable as ever, berserk against the gang.

A haze of smoke rises as barrels blaze. Payaso steers blind, plunging across obscure sand. Through a sharp-edged hole, Einstein is taken. Bursting from the jeep, la Güera screams as she fires. Like a fury she drives the monsters before her. Spiny backs sprawl in the dim starlit dunes. Einstein howls in pain, his arm shattered, and with it the detonator. They dress his wound, crouch near an outcropping of rocks, awaiting the sun, thinking somber thoughts.

As dawn drags itself into the sky, Einstein uses his good hand to scrounge through his knapsack. In short order he has kludged together a strange system, battered keyboard and cracked tablet jury-rigged to the soldier's satphone.

El Chamuco watches for a while as the barrio genius pecks at the keys and tweaks. "What you up to, little homie?"

"A sat-hack, *ese*. Gaining access to the net by bouncing a signal off a military satellite. Got to figure out how to manually detonate the *pinche* bomb."

Someone draws in a sharp breath, but no one argues. The choice is clear.

El Chamuco addresses his sibs. "We always knew. To get this nuke near the crater at Las Cruces is suicide for one of us. Now someone else gots to die."

Einstein nods. "I know how to activate it. Just need someone to drive. I've lived a life. Read a lot. I'll go."

"Shit, I ain't letting this *pendejo* get all the credit." Payaso grins, his eyes bright. "I got the wheel."

"*Pobres mensos,*" mutters la Güera. "The minute the choops attack, y'all are gonna wish I was there."

Their leader looks at each, looks down into their hearts. They nod at him. His chest aches with pride.

"*Órale, pues.* Time to show the haters what's what."

Einstein nods, points at his gear. "*Simón.* That's exactly what we're gonna do, *jefe*. I just set up a streaming feed. Bounces video of everything we do from here on out off that yank satellite. No way Gringoland or Mother Mex gets credit for this shit."

El Chamuco puts out a hand, helps him stand. "Bad-ass. I can talk to that thing?"

"*Simón.* Go for it."

The cholo leans his tattooed face toward the small iris.

"Hey, fuckers. Name's Chamuco. Yank soldiers brought a nuke into Aztlán, tried to destroy the choops, but they pussed out, got their asses killed. So now me and my clique are gonna do y'all's dirty work for you. You hear me, *pendejos*? Just us four *pachucos*."

He turns, gestures at the jeep. "Okay, climb on, homies. Let's go save the world."

An hour later the jeep rumbles off the pitted highway and Payaso smacks it into four-wheel drive. Chupacabras burrow and sleep their blood-speckled sleep when the sun is up, but the thrumming of the motor and turning tires calls to them. Black specks soon dot the dunes, moving closer, fast. Soon a sea of chittering night is flowing at the jeep from all directions. Canid faces snarl in the vanguard.

"Keep the fuckers off Einstein. I got Payaso," El Chamuco yells at la Güera above the rising din. "At all costs, *¿entiendes*?"

"My pleasure, *jefe*."

They are still ten minutes from the lip of the crater. The first wave hits. El Chamuco sprays bullets at the choops in front, clearing a path. Payaso rams and crushes the wounded. La Güera grunts and fires, kicks and stabs.

Their defense lasts three minutes before the horde swells like tsunami, choops clambering up the spiny backs of other choops, crashing upon the jeep, slashing tires, puncturing the gas tank, smashing through the engine block.

"Better hope we're close enough!" shouts el Chamuco as he slips though the shattered windshield and takes on a dozen of the beasts. "Detonate that fucker now, Einstein!"

The chupacabras have entered the back of the jeep. La Güera grapples with them, punching, kicking, biting, howling like Cihuacoatl, fierce Aztec goddess. The alien drones rip off her arm, but she keeps thrusting them away from Einstein, giving him every second she can.

"Órale, pendejo," she gurgles at last. "Now or never! *Mándalos a la verga*, and I'll see your ass in hell!"

They dismember her. The jeep drifts to a stop. Payaso is decapitated with a single, vicious blow of talons. El Chamuco is shoved back into the jeep by the squirming mass. His eyes meet Einstein's as the man makes the final connection in the firing mechanism.

"*Ahí los wacho*, fuckers," the genius mutters, smiling for the camera.

"*That's* my boy," el Chamuco manages to whisper.

The world goes white.

It doesn't take long. When the mushroom cloud expands above the Organ Mountains and every chupacabras drops dead, both the US and Mexico initially assume the military mission has been a success. But the video from Quarantined Zone goes viral, and the names of the four cholos are reported across social media and news outlets. Pirate ISPs throughout the wastelands spread the news: liberated at last.

Neither Mexico nor the US wants the responsibility of cleaning up the Quarantined Zone, so when the tens of thousands trapped within those walls insist on their right of self-determination, arguments are perfunctory, purely for show.

The flag of freedom is lifted over Aztlán.

Her saviors, whatever paradise or hell they find themselves in, flash their gang sign one final time.

CHUPACABRA VENGEANCE

1

By the time she was ten, Silvia had become the best goatherd in Zapotitlán.

Her father's eyesight had failed him. Her mother had headed north to work in America, sending money when she could. It had fallen to Silvia to care for her little brother Eliseo and to watch the family's herd.

Mateo Montiel, her father, had trained her since she could toddle, but there was something almost supernatural about the way Silvia led those two dozen goats. On her own she discovered she could abandon both walking stick and stones and just guide them by her presence. Eliseo, some five years younger than her, slipped into the quiet, ambling existence of the herd, following his sister without complaint through the foothills.

Silvia carried a machete sheathed at her waist. Wild dogs were a problem. So were other predators, including men. She understood what drove them, knew how to keep them at bay.

She was not prepared for the bloodsuckers.

It was a warm August evening. Silvia led her brother and the goats back home along the banks of a creek as the stars emerged against deepening sable. The soft chuckle of water over stones seemed to get louder, until the girl realized the sound was coming from all around her—a chittering drone, like hundreds of insects.

She saw their eyes first, bloody orbs that glowed in the gloom. Then black lips curled back to reveal yellowed dirks, and the monsters leapt upon her goats, sinking those fangs into bleating necks, spiny backs arching with pleasure as they suckled.

Shoving Eliseo behind her, Silvia drew her machete and prepared herself. Her pulse was racing, but her mind was clear.

The monster closest to her lifted its head and gave a frustrated whine like the scraping of metal upon metal. It regarded Silvia and her brother with avid greed before using powerful hind legs to launch itself toward them.

Barking a startled, feral cry, Silvia swung her machete, embedding the blade in the creature's neck as it slammed into her, pinning her down and sending Eliseo tumbling into the creek. Dark ichor squirted into her face as she jerked in a frenzy, scrabbling against reptilian skin, trying to get free. The talons of the dying bloodsucker raked against the back of her leg as she stumbled toward her brother, who had begun to keen and bleat.

Behind her, the creatures snarled as one, brandishing claws. One of their number sprang to the side of its fallen comrade. With sentient deliberation, it wrenched the machete loose, hurling it into the brush.

It glared at Silvia, all of them did, and she felt the weight of their fury in her mind. In a single, coordinated and brutal swipe, they beheaded the goats.

Then the monsters slipped silently into the deepening night.

2

More than three hundred goats were slaughtered that week in the Mexican state of Puebla, their bloodless and decapitated bodies a mystery for authorities at every level.

"Say nothing, girl," Don Mateo begged his daughter. "Those beasts were probably naguales, shape-shifters, and they'll seek revenge if they feel threatened."

Silvia loved her father, respected him. She kept silent and cared for Eliseo, whose mind had buckled beneath the weight of such bloody horror.

The weeks passed. A consensus was reached among goatherds. The slaughter was too gruesome, the lack of blood too bizarre.

Chupacabras, they whispered. Goat-sucking beings with inscrutable plans.

3

When winter had come and gone with no further attacks, Don Mateo had Silvia take their meager savings and buy another dozen goats. The daily routine continued, months and years churning round the endless cycle. Silvia taught her brother what her father had taught her. Eliseo lacked Silvia's eerie command over the herd, but he communicated with them in other subtle ways that proved nearly as effective.

Their numbers grew. Meat and milk and cheese helped keep the family alive, solvent.

Then, not long after Silvia's thirteenth birthday, a letter came from her mother. Her father blind and neither she nor Eliseo able to read much beyond their own names, Silvia walked along muddy streets to the home of her cousin Maribel. The older girl had studied up through sixth grade before getting married to a tinsmith twice her age. Four years later she was a mother of three, but she was the most literate in the family.

"Your mother says she's heading to Washington. The state. She says it may be a while before she can write again or send any money, but that this new job will help her finally scrape together enough to bring your father and you two across the border."

"Why the hell would we want to go to the US? We're fine here."

Maribel lifted a sniffling toddler, bared her breast for it. "Don't be an idiot, Silvia. You can make a lot more money over there. Maybe you can even find some rich guy to marry, if you clean yourself up. You smell like goat."

"No damn way. I'm not you. Besides, Dad can't travel. He's blind. And then there's the herd."

Her cousin shook her head and continued to lecture her, but Silvia had already stopped listening. She didn't want to hear. For hundreds of years her father's people had raised goats. She couldn't imagine any other life.

But her existence was turned on its head from that moment on. Just as the extra money from up North stopped trickling in, her father's health spiraled out of control. The diabetes that had claimed Don Mateo's sight took the toes of his right foot next, then his kidneys.

Silvia had to leave the herd penned up for longer and longer stretches while she visited the hospital. The goats and her father both began wasting away, as if they had wagered to see whether hunger or dialysis would claim a victim faster.

Don Mateo succumbed first, his body shutting down and his blind eyes glazing forever as his grip on Silvia's hand slackened. She wept, letting herself grieve in the bleak sterility of that room, shared by two other dying men, before she kissed her father and headed home.

The pen was empty. She tracked the herd to a patch of green a few kilometers north, where Eliseo sat watching them pull up grass with rickety teeth.

He buried his face in her breast when she told him, bereft and adrift. The goats lifted their heads momentarily at his sobs, but then they continued grazing.

The death of Mateo Montiel was not the end of the upheavals. Without their father to churn and process goat milk into cheese while Silvia and Eliseo pastured the herd, the siblings found themselves in dire economic straits. They lived on a small plot in a communal ejido, and greedy neighbors began to pressure the commissariat to free up the land for farming since no legal adult was using it for sustenance.

Local authorities had learned of the orphans and remanded them on paper into the custody of their uncle Beto, but the two led their herd into the foothills and disappeared for a time.

With no home or father to return to, brother and sister scraped as much sustenance as they could from the wild. By the end of the month, they had been forced to kill two rangy nannies. One cold morning they awoke to find half their remaining livestock missing, probably stolen by rival goatherds or by one of the cartels that had edged into what had been a peaceful state.

Silvia realized she had no choice. They could not survive like this much longer.

She sold the herd, packed their meager belongings, and led her brother to the train tracks.

"Where?" Eliseo asked.

"North," she told him. "To Mother."

Together, they awaited The Beast.

5

The train came rattling and snorting up from the South, having snaked its way from the Guatemalan border, through Chiapas, and along the Oaxaca-Veracruz border. Men, women and children clung to its rusted hide like remoras and lampreys or crouched atop its cars in huddled clutches.

A group of people had accreted nearby, mostly women laden with supplies, and as The Beast trundled by, they passed food, water and blankets up to outstretched hands. Silvia brought her brother right up to the edge of the tracks.

"Now!" she said as a gap between cars revealed a less occupied ladder. They leapt at the rungs; her fierce grip held, but his slipped. Before the boy could fall beneath the vicious, expectant wheels, an arm reached down from above and hauled him up. Silvia scrabbled her way to the roof, thrusting travelers aside.

"Eliseo!" she called. He was standing beside a stocky man with thinning hair. A woman and two young girls were clustered tightly beside them, and a teenaged boy perhaps two years older than Silvia was rising from a crouch.

"Thank you, sir," Silvia muttered as she approached. "Eliseo is my only family."

The man nodded. "Family is all we have, in the end. This is mine—my wife, Sabrina; our daughters, Ana and Victoria; and our son, Tomás."

The boy shot her a weary half-smile that both annoyed her and filled her with warmth.

"Nice to meet you. I'm Silvia Montiel." She gave a slight curtsy.

"And I am Salvador Castro Peña, though most just call me Don Chava. Are you headed for the US? So are we. We came out of Guatemala less than a week ago."

Gesturing for her to follow suit, Don Chava sat down in their cramped corner of the roof.

Silvia pulled their last round of goat cheese from her bag and placed it in Mrs. Castro's hands. "We don't have much, but it's yours. Thank you again."

The family seemed genuinely touched by this measure of civility, as if their journey so far had drained them of hope for reciprocated kindness. After a few more pleasantries, an agreement was reached: Eliseo and Silvia could accompany the Castro clan to the US border and beyond.

Below them The Beast bucked and shuddered and groaned.

"Your brother was lucky." It was the second day of the journey, and Tomás had clearly maneuvered his way closer to Silvia. She didn't mind. If he tried anything, she would put him in his place. If necessary, she would throw him from the train.

"What do you mean?"

"Our first day on this thing, a boy fell and got his foot sliced right off. They say it happens all the time. Blood for The Beast."

"So you've seen some bad things, huh?"

Oblivious to the traces of irony in her voice, Tomás nodded. "Yup. We're from Guatemala City, and basically you have two choices there: either you come from a rich family and hire private security or you affiliate with one of the maras, MS-13 or Barrio 18. You don't, and you become a victim. After my uncle got killed and my dad's car was firebombed during a clash between gangs and cops, we sold the family tienda and got the hell out of there."

Silvia nodded. The story was not as terrifying as a violent troop of chupacabras, but it was certainly bad. "Are there a lot of Guatemalans on The Beast?"

"Sure. And most of them are like you and Eliseo—just kids traveling alone. A bunch won't make it. They say all sorts of criminals try to take advantage of us. Cartels and stuff. Theft, kidnapping, murder … rape. People claim all that and more happens on the train." His eyes narrowed a bit as he glanced at her. "Don't worry, though. You're with us, and I … we will protect you."

She stifled a bemused chuckle. Sure you will, she thought, her hand grazing the pommel of her machete.

That night, the dream came for the first time.

She was lying in the midst of her herd, looking up at the blood-red moon.

The moon resolved into an eye. The stars were eyes.

The monsters were ranged all about her. Their alien minds twined themselves around her panicked thoughts, like thorny vines snagging cotton thread.

She felt herself unravel and snarl.

They bent their stiletto teeth to her flesh.

Silvia jerked awake under a black sky. Clouds had obscured the cosmos. All she could sense was the rattling, the constant motion of The Beast beneath her wiry flesh.

Then she felt a hand touch her hair.

"It's okay," Tomás whispered. "Just a nightmare. You're fine. Sleep."

Annoyed but a little moved, she reached up and squeezed his fingers before reluctantly easing back into dreams.

Two more days passed with a livable rhythm. The Castro girls played with Eliseo, who spoke little but smiled from time to time. Once he even laughed, and Silvia's heart ached at that unfamiliar yet lovely sound. Stories were told there atop the car, nostalgic tales of better days, tragedies recounted through tears, legends recited in hushed tones. Occasional stops at depots required some groups to abandon cars being loaded or unloaded, then to rush to board once more as The Beast staggered back to its lumbering pace. Along the way, good-hearted people passed up food and water. A child was born near the front. A couple was married between two cars by an evangelical pastor from El Salvador. Fights erupted, were quelled. It was a movable community.

As they edged into the northern state of Zacatecas, the train suddenly stopped in the midst of a wilderness.

Don Chava stood, making a warning gesture to his family and their guests. "This can't be good."

Silvia made out the sputter of motorbikes. From a distance came the sound of women screaming. She stood, looked forward. A half dozen cars away, a group of men had clambered up the side and were shouting at the passengers.

Don Chava shook his head in disgust. "Everyone, get your backpacks on. We're getting off early."

The family moved to obey. Eliseo touched Silvia's hand, gave her a questioning glance.

Predators. I know how to deal with predators.

"Wait, sir," she rasped, pulling her machete and looking around her. Raising her voice a little, she called to the other groups on their car. "They're like wolves. We can scare them off. Just make some noise. If you've got blades, do as I do."

Crouching, she started to bang her machete against the warm iron hide of The Beast. A steady rhythm, loud and clanging. Soon the others had taken up the beat. It spread from car to car.

Raging but unnerved, the thieves descended from the train, yanking a young woman from a ladder at the last moment and driving away with her.

Moments later, The Beast hissed and continued on its inexorable trek.

9

The ambush decided things for Don Chava. At the next stop, when it was time to switch from one train to the next, he drew the family together.

"We are going with Plan B. Staying on The Beast this far north is dangerous. Right now we're on the border between Durango and Coahuila, so Torreón isn't that far."

Mrs. Castro drew a sharp breath. "But, Salvador, she's going to want money."

Her husband nodded, placed a hand on her shoulder. "I know, love, but we'll figure something out. Perhaps she can at least give us advice."

Silvia looked at them both carefully. "What are you talking about?"

Tomás explained. "The money from selling the tienda? Most of it was stolen from us by some gang-bangers at the Mexican border. Dad's got the name and number of a coyote, a person who can get us into the US, but she charges a stiff fee."

Silvia looked at her brother, raising an eyebrow. He tilted his head. The little girls had been sweet to him. Mrs. Castro had treated him like a son. No words needed to be exchanged. Silvia knew he agreed.

"We have money," she said. "We'll hire the coyote for you."

10

In Torreón they quickly found the address that a friend of Don Chava's had scrawled on a scrap of letterhead back in Guatemala City. A housekeeper at a squat but expansive home led them into a make-shift office where a fifty-something woman sat doing figures with an adding machine.

"Ms. Anaya?" Don Chava muttered, doffing his broken hat.

Mariana Anaya looked up, raising a thin eyebrow at the cluster of immigrants.

"Five hundred bucks each," she grunted, glancing back down at her ledgers.

"I, uh, was hoping we could negotiate the price a little. We had a little trouble with the maras, and …"

"Yes, yes, I understand." With a sigh, the woman pushed away from her desk. She wore boots and jeans and a brightly colored blouse that clashed with the dinginess of the room. "Let's take a look at you."

She examined the children carefully, nodding to herself. Smirking at Tomás, she turned to Silvia.

"How old are you?"

"Almost fourteen."

"What do you know how to do?"

"Herd goats."

Anaya laughed. "You southern peasants, I tell you. Okay, everyone, listen up. Final price is $400 each for the four of you, plus $200 for the little ones. US dollars, mind you."

Silvia looked at Don Chava. Between them, they had just over $2000.

"What will that get us?" she asked the coyote.

"Passage from here to Piedras Negras in my SUV. Then my guys will take you across the river to Eagle Pass to a safe house there."

It seemed a good deal, the best they would get, much better than risking their lives on The Beast as it crawled through cartel-riddled Coahuila.

Money exchanged hands. They would leave first thing in the morning.

The housekeeper took them to a small room.

Exhausted, they crowded onto sagging mattresses and dropped into blissful slumber.

* * *

11

The dream again. Stars and moon that ran red, became raging eyes.

This time Eliseo was there. The Castro family as well.

The monsters buried their fangs into her loved ones' flesh.

They raised their claws in unison.

See. You. We. See. You. We. See. You.

A long, slow arc of black talons. Heads rolling away, mouths twisted in screams.

Come. Close. See. You. We. See. You. We. Remember. Come. Close.

She awoke thrashing, a hand clamped over her mouth.

"Shhhh!" It was Tomás. "You're going to wake everyone."

Her heart shuddered with painful thuds, but she nodded. He pulled his hand away, fingers brushing against his arm. He was crouched beside the mattress she shared with Eliseo.

"Bad one, huh?" he whispered.

She nodded, propping herself up on her elbows. A little starlight filtered in through a narrow window, putting glints of silver in his dark eyes. He swallowed hard, Adam's apple bobbing against the taut skin of his throat.

"Don't worry. Soon we'll be on the other …"

She leaned forward and pressed her mouth against his, almost instinctively, hungry for something she didn't quite understand. His hands slipped behind her head, pulling her into a deeper kiss. Aches arose in her, and she moved his hands, guiding them beneath her shirt and trembling at the feel of his long fingers against her breasts.

Making a pallet on the floor, they lay together for most of the night, exploring each other with hushed but earnest desire. When at last they gasped at sharp, biting pleasure, she felt his mind bleed into her own.

12

The family was awakened early, given a breakfast of beans and egg, and loaded into Mariana Ayala's dusty imported SUV. A stocky man with dark glasses and a pistol took the passenger seat, and the journey began, some seven hours along the foot of the Sierra del Carmen. Squeezed together in the very back, Silvia and Tomás alternated between surreptitiously holding hands and scouring her mother's letter for hints of a final destination in Washington State. The rest of the group talked quietly, napped or played simple games. Their coyote spent most of the trip on her cell phone, talking business of various illegal varieties. When stopped at different points by authorities or cartel members, the vehicle was readily waved through the roadblock. Clearly the woman greased a lot of palms.

They arrived in Piedras Negras around 3 p.m. Ayala pulled into the parking lot of a restaurant near the international bridge and led everyone inside. Two men in battered cowboy hats, threadbare shirts and faded denim rose from their seats at a large table, beckoning to the new arrivals. The pair was non-descript, save for the handlebar moustache that drooped down the corners of the taller fellow's mouth.

"This is the Castro family," Ayala told them as the immigrants sat down. "And their two charges. You know the drill."

The men nodded without a word. Ayala handed the shorter, clean-shaven man an envelope, then signaled to her bodyguard and turned to leave.

"Oh," she added over her shoulder, "as a favor to me, I want you to give them the special treatment. Clear?"

The man with the moustache arched an eyebrow but nodded all the same. "Okay, boss. We'll handle it."

Silvia felt an odd weight in the air as the woman left.

13

The men took them to a small ranch near the river.

"We'll wait here until nightfall," the bare-faced one explained.

Silvia sized up the pens. "Where are the goats? Grazing?"

The mustached man made a surprised sound. "Damn. How do you know there were goats here?"

"I'm a goatherd. What happened?"

He shrugged. "Beats the shit out of me. Owners say they found them dead one morning, about a month ago. Drained of blood. Decapitated."

We. See. You. We. Remember.

Silvia shuddered at the memory of that rasping chorus of alien tongues.

They were led into a barn. The girls and Eliseo clambered over bales of hay and up ladders, laughing and joking. Silvia pulled Tomás aside.

"This is going to sound stupid, but I think we might be in danger."

"What, from those two? Between you, me and my dad, I think we could …"

"No, not them."

Sighing, she told him her story, eyes downcast. When she was done, he tilted her face back up at him.

"Look, I believe you. But what are we going to do, huh? We can't go back. There's nothing for any of us south of here. Our only choice is to keeping pushing forward."

She nodded. "I agree. I just needed someone else to know. If something were to happen, I needed you to be ready to act."

Mr. and Mrs. Castro were on the other side of the barn, their backs turned. Silvia pulled Tomás closer and kissed him with the greed of starving souls unsure of when they will eat again.

14

Darkness hung about them like a shroud as they slipped into the inflatable tires and were pulled across the Río Grande by the two men, their outer garments held aloft in plastic Soriana bags.

On the far bank, the immigrants dried themselves off as best as possible before pulling clothes on over damp underwear. To the west, bluffs rose steadily over the river. A few hundred yards in front of the group stood a section of the border wall, metal slats black against the night.

"How are we getting past that?" Don Chava asked.

"Don't worry. We've got it under control, sir." The taller man gestured at them, and they walked toward a sort of gate set in the fence.

Bright lights illuminated the landscape with startling and painful clarity. Mrs. Castro pulled her daughters close.

"Oh, fuck," muttered Eliseo.

"Calm down, folks," the shorter man called out. "It's not the Border Patrol. Some ranchers got part of their property stuck on the wrong side. One of them likes to make a little extra money."

A clanging sound reverberated from the other side. Keys. A padlock. A loosened chain.

The gate swung open, and Silvia walked hand-in-hand with Tomás into the United States, right on the heels of her brother and the rest.

A large red truck had its fog lamps on. An older Anglo man stood in front of it. The mustached man exchanged some words with him in English. The Anglo grinned, nodded. He walked toward the newcomers, looked Mrs. Castro and her daughters up and down, moved on to Silvia. She could smell chewing tobacco and sweat on him. His eyes were a blue so light as to be almost white. He muttered something unintelligible but oily-sounding, then he reached out and touched her breast.

"You get the fuck away from her!" Tomás shouted, thrusting himself between them.

Silvia unsheathed her machete. "Don't worry. I'll kill him if he touches me again."

Another set of fog lights switched on nearby, and a half-dozen men in camouflage emerged from the darkness. They were carrying assault rifles, but they were not soldiers, Silvia saw. Bearded, disheveled, some bearing the flag of the old Confederacy as patches on their fatigues, the men leveled their weapons at Don Chava, Eliseo and Tomás.

"Put down your machete," one of them called in heavily accented Spanish. "Or we kill the men."

Silvia tossed the blade away without hesitation.

The Anglo with the red truck laughed and called the two coyotes to follow him. He retrieved a bag from the cab of his vehicle and handed it over. They took a look at its contents, shook his hand, and walked back toward the river.

The gate clanged shut behind them.

Silvia closed her eyes. She tried to remember the feel of the monsters' fury, pressing against her mind beside that creek nearly four years before. Dread rising within her, she called out with every fiber of her being.

Can you see me? I am here. Come closer.

The militia member who spoke Spanish lowered his rifle and approached them.

"We separate you now, okay? Girls in truck, men in jeep. No problems, understand, or we kill the men."

Eliseo snarled. "No. Fuck that. You're not taking me from my sister, you son of a bitch."

Silvia opened her eyes, but before she could silence him, the man gave a wicked laugh.

"Little guy has a big mouth, huh? Okay, you need proof. Okay."

The man turned, said something to the rancher, who shrugged. The other militia men gave shouts of approval.

Without warning, the man lifted his weapon and shot Don Chava in the head. His body tumbled lifeless in the dirt.

There was a moment of shocked silence, then Mrs. Castro screamed and threw herself on her husband's body. Tomás rushed the shooter, who simply slammed the butt of his assault rifle into the teen's face, breaking his nose and dropping him to his knees.

"Now, you stupid wetbacks, you do like I tell you, or …"

He never had time to finish. Out of the darkness they sprang, red eyes blazing, cruel teeth bared to the night, spines and talons glittering in the beams of the fog lamps. The chupacabras ripped and bit, slicing through body armor and gun barrels and flesh, sending scarlet sprays splashing thickly against ground, jeep, truck.

Silvia rushed to Tomás, tearing a piece of her t-shirt away to staunch the flood from his nostrils.

"Get up, get up, get up! We have to run, now!"

She hauled him to his feet. Eliseo had already retrieved the machete and was pulling at Mrs. Castro. Staccato gunfire and inhuman chittering and unholy screams echoed all around. The girls and their mother stumbled after Eliseo. Silvia turned to guide them back to the river.

Silence fell. The monsters barred the way. The monsters surrounded them.

Silvia felt them. Their single mind, pushing at hers. Rage with no peer on the face of this world. Rage untempered by a guiding queen. Rage at loss, any loss. An unbearable need for vengeance.

We see you. We know you. We take from you.

One of the leathery beasts flung itself through the air, snatching at Tomás, rolling him into the dewy soil.

"No!" Silvia screamed, her eyes burning, her heart breaking. "No!"

Claws hung in the air a second, glittering black. Then the monsters wreaked their revenge.

BLOODY FEATHERS

I'm a baby killer. That's the easiest way to describe what I do. I find babies, and I kill them.

Of course, they're not just any babies. I'm not a fucking serial killer or some crazy shit like that. These babies have to die. Yeah, I know that sounds nuts. If I told them, most people would think I actually am a serial killer or a goddamned loon. I'm not, though.

But I do hear voices.

This time they had led me to Star County, down in the most desert-like corner of south Texas. Just a few miles from the Rio Grande River. Westernmost part of the Rio Grande Valley, which is stupid, because it ain't a fucking valley, it's a basin or something. But yeah. There's a river running through it.

I had tracked down the mother, a Mexican girl name of Celeste Colibri, but she was all in a tizzy with a bunch of her relatives, most of them drug-runners of some sort or another. Posing as a Texas Ranger, I managed to get out of them that the baby'd been stolen by Celeste's sister Linda. You could tell some of the older ones were all sorts of upset, and not just the regular upset-because-a-baby-got-kidnapped, either. No, they knew full well what that baby was. And they were furious he'd been stolen. They wanted to be the ones raising the evil little bastard.

After an hour or so hanging out in barbershops and scouring maps online and shit, I began to recognize the signs. Assload of snake bites. Video of a huge screech owl. Stories of swarms of bats and charms of hummingbirds swooping through the sky. Sudden brush fires. I triangulated the fuck out of all this and with some help from the voices I hit on her likely hidey-hole: an abandoned shack in a remote corner of a supposedly haunted ranch, smack dab against a silty resaca. I drove my battered Dakota along caliche roads to get there, parking it beside a copse of mesquite about a half mile distant and walking the rest of the way in the dusty late-afternoon sunlight slanting from the West, shotgun in the crook of my arm, satchel slung across my chest.

The shack was weathered and bleached, its tin roof rusty and pitted. All kinds of cactus crowded close to the walls like a bunch of spiny sentinels. Weeds dotted the caliche that ran all the way to the crooked porch. Someone had hung a cross on the rotted trim. I paused for a moment, then rushed up the worn steps and kicked the door open before she had a chance to bolt. But she didn't. In fact, she had the baby in one arm and a big-ass .45 revolver in the other, a rosary twisted around that wrist, the crucifix dangling. I lifted my shotgun.

"I'll kill you both, bitch. Put that Peacemaker down."

Her hand trembled with fear and the weight of the gun. "¿Qué quieres, pendejo?"

I sized her up. Not more than five-two. Pretty brown eyes, black hair in a ponytail. Spaghetti-strap blouse revealing a teenager's body and a butterfly tattoo on her left shoulder.

She was the youngest daughter of a drug-dealer. I needed to show more respect. She'd respond to that better.

"What I want, Linda, is for you to please lower that huge freaking gun so that we can talk. I'm not here to hurt you."

Pulling her dark red lips into a thin line, she dropped her arm to her side. She couldn't hide the relief she felt. Like I say, it's a heavy gun for a sixteen-year-old girl.

"You here for little Jesse? Dad hired you, or what?"

I shook my head. "Nope. Other … people … sent me."

"Why? What the hell do you want from me?"

I set the shotgun on a rickety table, the only thing in the shack besides a moldy chair, a backpack, and pallet of blankets on the floor.

"You know what he is, yeah?"

Her eyes flitted away, down. "He's just a baby."

"He's not just a baby, Linda. Let me guess … Celeste was chosen by a bunch of older folks, including your parents. They told her she was special. Had her eat special foods and dress up in old-fashioned clothes. You were probably a little jealous, huh."

Linda stepped back a bit, dropped into the old armchair. The baby gurgled. She set the gun in her lap and adjusted his blankets.

"They … they gave her this nasty ball of white feathers. All bloody. Made her swallow it. I didn't hear till later. She always tells me everything. A few weeks later, she was pregnant. They treated her like a damn princess. Then I overheard my dad and some of his compadres … they said it was the second coming of Weets … Weetsil …"

"Huitzilopochtli," I finished for her. "Hummingbird of the South. The Bloody Stormer of Cities. Son of Chaos. Aztec god of war."

She swallowed heavy. "Yeah. Then a few days ago all these birds started showing up. The house was covered with them. The sun seemed closer, you know? All big and blood red in the sky. And when the partera helped little Jesse be born … he didn't cry. Just looked around at everybody with his big green eyes …"

Looking down at her nephew, Linda stroked his cheek. A little wrinkled fist reached up, tinged slightly blue, and grabbed her finger.

"So you understand what they want, right?" She nodded without lifting her gaze. It wasn't enough. "Say it."

Her eyes were red-rimmed. "They want him to end the world. Bring the darkness. Open the doors to all the bad things."

"So you stole him." I took a few steps in her direction and crouched to look her right in the eyes. "And you figure if you raise him different, if you teach him to be good, to love his fellow man, to worship God, all that shit, you can turn the incarnation of war into a benevolent man."

She winced to hear it stated so plainly. Then her pretty face tightened with anger. "Fuck you. I just want him to have a choice, okay?"

I shook my head. "No. He can't be allowed to have a choice, Linda. We can't risk it. What if he chooses to fulfill his destiny? Can you imagine the weight of that responsibility on you? Being the one who could've stopped him?"

"Stopped him?" she said, only now understanding. I didn't wait another second. My hand darted forward, grabbing the gun off her lap. I snapped it open, let the bullets clatter to the planking of the floor. Standing, I tossed the pistol out the door onto the caliche path.

Eyes wild, she hunched over the baby, holding out the crucifix.

"You stay the hell away from him, you son of a bitch!"

I unslung the leather satchel I was wearing across my chest. Setting it on the rickety table, I withdrew an oilcloth. Inside were the tools of my trade.

Before I could unwrap them, however, there came a sound like the wind blowing through clothes hung out to dry. A large form dropped from the sky, landing on the warped steps. It was a little taller than me, maybe six foot two, with a wingspan of some five yards. It folded those wings to its body and cocked its owl head at me. Its golden brown feathers were lit almost red by the setting sun. Legs that ended in vicious talons took one step. Another.

"What the fuck is that?" screamed Linda.

Tlacatecolotl, the voices muttered. Shotgun. Now.

I swept the weapon off the table and fired, blasting the owl demon with a mixture of salt, silver, garlic, wood shavings and iron pellets. A little bit of everything, just in case. It gave a harrowing shriek as the impact drove it back.

Obsidian.

I reached into my satchel with my left and pulled out a jade sheath. Yanking the black blade free, gripping its silver handle tight, I rushed after the beast. Out on the caliche path it had regained its balance and was spreading its wings. As I lifted the shotgun again, it launched itself at me, beating at the air and screeching. I emptied the other barrel into the bastard, but even bloodied and spinning it kept coming. Its beak tore into my shoulder savagely. With a grunt, I brought up the obsidian knife and slammed it into the thing's chest. It dropped to the ground, writhing and hissing. Pressing a boot against its abdomen, I reloaded the shotgun and reduced its head to a bloody mass of feathers and bone.

Inside the shack, Linda had gotten up and was laying Jesse on the armchair, wedging him in with her backpack. She saw me, and though her eyes were all hollowed out by fear, her skin white, her hands shaking, she came toward me slowly. Pointing at my shoulder, she muttered, "You're hurt."

"I'll live."

The teen swallowed heavily and closed the rest of the distance between us. "You … you saved us."

"For a little while, yeah. But they know where you are now. They'll be coming for you, and it ain't going to be just one owl demon."

She reached up one of her hands, small, with slender fingers. Laying it against my chest, she drew even closer. Her scent filled my nostrils: youth, innocence, promise. Her head didn't quite reach my chin. She was half my age. Something dead inside me may've stirred slightly.

"But," she whispered, looking up at me, trying desperately to be seductive, "you could protect us, couldn't you? You know how to fight them."

"I've fought lots worse, yeah."

Her hand slipped down my chest, along my stomach. "We couldn't just leave here? You, me, Jesse? I could raise him, make sure he takes the right path. You could protect us. And you and me …" Her voice went raspy as she ran her hand down the front of my jeans. "I could be yours."

I allowed myself a moment. The voices were growling at me, but I deserved that much. Just a moment. I put my arms around her, pressed all that vitality against me, let it counter the death that hung on me like holy vestments.

"What's your name?" she murmured, her eyes closed.

I don't remember, I didn't say. "They call me Peck."

"Thank you, Peck. Thank you."

It was too much. I pressed my lips against her forehead and gave her one last gentle squeeze.

"I'm sorry, Linda," I whispered in her ear. "There is only one way to keep you safe."

She struggled, vainly. It was all too easy, clamping my big hand around her neck till she'd passed out. I laid her down gently beside the armchair. Then I picked Jesse up, unwrapping his blankets and draping them over his aunt. He stared at me with preternatural understanding, blinking his big green eyes.

"Okay, Jesse, time to wrap this shit up."

I put him on his back on the rickety table and unrolled the oil cloth. Inside were two copper blades, etched with ancient symbols that time and polishing had near rubbed away. I picked them up by their yellowed bone handles.

"One for the heart, one for the head," I explained to the baby. "Only way to send you abominations back to the darkness."

I lifted my right hand. The knife was a tool. So was I. An instrument of death that kept the monsters at bay. An unknown savior, unsung, obscure. Hated by the few who crossed my path. Like Linda, who would awaken alone.

"Ah, lucky ignorant bastards," I spat at the universe. "Time to save your asses one more time."

Outside a gale of fluttering wings grew louder and louder. As the knife dropped, Jesse finally began to cry.

SPIRITUAL PROTECTORS

(from *The Secret Diary of Donna Hooks*)

April 25, 1908

It has finally happened, after years of persistence: My father has given me a slice of wild land north of town, a rambling stretch of brushy thicket, one hundred acres of promise. Here I can be actively adventurous, though my folks, for the longest time, have been dead set against such total independence. I had a hard time overcoming their opposition, certainly. They would not abandon the notion that I might renounce the wicked ways of a divorcee and return to Clyde Fletcher's side. But our marriage, I made them understand, is irrevocably broken. What I need now is to erase all visible memories of that shattered covenant by rescuing this tract of arable land from the hungry grip of the south Texas desert.

May 17, 1908

Having no liquid money of my own, I have arranged to borrow funds for the development of my land as well as the construction of an office building in town on the west side of 6th Street which will house my father's La Blanca Land Company. The bank had no compunction about issuing me the money given my status and history of entrepreneurship with the boarding house. I've hired a foreman, Roberto Blas, who will be putting together a team of workers to clear the land and carpenters to build a small house. My excitement has my nerves a-jitter: I can hardly focus or sleep.

June 17, 1908

I've not written a word for nearly three weeks, so exhausted has each evening found me. Astride my pony, I have gone forth daily with a gang of Mexican laborers into that wilderness with its varied wildlife population of deer, quail, and turkey, its habitats of mountain lion and *jabalí* or wild hog. We commenced from the first day to chopping through mesquite, cactus, *huisache*, cat claw, etc. and after a while had hewed out a clearing large enough for a garden, flower beds, and the site for my little cabin. That home, where I have lived alone now for three whole days, is in reality a tiny, primitive shack hardly the size of a woodshed, bare of all modern conveniences, but it is my very own. I am immensely proud of it.

June 24, 1908

Today has been extraordinary. I look at the three nestling forms on my quilt, and I still have trouble believing what they are.

This morning I went out early upon my pony to greet Roberto and discuss plans for the day. Converting a brushy wilderness into a model farm is grueling, exacting work, and neither of us wanted to waste even a moment of the laborers' time. Once we had marked out the area to be cleared, the team began their steady sweep across the *monte*, as they call it, machetes glinting in the slanting light of dawn.

Yapping voices came to my ears, and I dismounted to greet my four rat terriers: Trixy, Oke, Teddy and Nkakwu. They had rushed into the scrub the minute I opened the door, off hunting field mice as was their custom. I petted them and kissed their noses, praising their bravery and skill at tracking.

Ah, I shall never be lonely on my farm so long as I have the companionship of animals, so long as the Green World surrounds me—tree and flower, herb and grain.

A hue and cry went up in the distance then, and I heard the retort of a rifle, firing once and falling silent. Mounting my pony, the dogs barking madly at its heels, I rode toward the commotion. The men were standing over some dying creature. Roberto dismounted from his gelding; I did the same and motioned for the workers to move aside. There, sprawled in the sandy earth, lay a very large wildcat of the sort the locals call *jaguarundi*. It had been shot through the chest, and its breathing slowed as it looked on me with eyes that seemed to plead. Then they glazed with death, and before our very eyes the beast transformed, twitching and stretching, pelt falling away to reveal a young Mexican woman, naked and dead.

"Look away!" I cried at once, wanting to preserve the deceased's dignity. Roberto translated with a harsh bark, and the men complied, many of them crossing themselves and muttering *bruja* and a word I had never hear before: *nagual.*

As I stood, contemplating the body and wondering what to do, a plaintive mewling came from nearby. Striding into the brush, I found a hollowed-out den in a bramble of wolfberry and within it three newborn cubs, blind and helpless. I knelt, whispered a prayer to Ala, protectoress of living things. Then I saw it: the magical glow of *chi* that Aunty Hester had taught me to perceive when I was a little girl. These were not normal animals.

I felt Roberto standing nearby. "Ms. Hooks, this is deep witchcraft, ma'am. Please don't go running off to tell your people. They don't know nothing about this. Let me get Doña Gabriela. She is a *curandera*, a shaman. She can tell us what should we do with this woman and her babies."

"Yes," I said. Long had I yearned to speak with an illuminated soul from the local culture, and now a horrible tragedy would grant me that desire. "And send one of the men into town for bottles and milk. The cubs are hungry."

When Roberto returned, I was sitting on the dusty ground, my skirt spread round me, the three squirming kits clambering over each other to get at the nipple of the bottle. I gave preference to the russet-furred one above his grey siblings, feeding him first. As he started suckling, I looked up at the old woman descending from a burro beside my foreman. She wore a simple white *huipil* blouse and blue skirt. Her head was covered by a purple-and-gold *rebozo* or shawl, and she went barefoot. Across her chest was slung a worn leather bag.

"Ms. Hooks, this is Doña Gabriela Rivera," Roberto began, but the shaman first walked over to the body, which I had covered with a saddle blanket. Drawing it back, Doña Gabriela regarded the dead woman's face, muttering quietly. Then she nodded and turned to me.

"So, you are the *gringa* that she claims ownership of this land, yes? Let me see." She stepped close and crouched. Her eyes widened slightly, and then a smile cracked her lips. "*Dios mío, una gringa santera.* Never knew your folk had magic. But I can see the *teotl* all over you, girl."

"What's *teotl*?" I asked, ignoring her presumptuousness.

"Divine spark. Flows from heaven to earth. It's in everything, a little. But in you there's more. And it's focused."

I nodded. "So it's *chi.* That's what Hester called it. She was a practitioner of Obeah … a *santera*, I think you would say. She was first a slave and then a servant for my family. But she was more than that. She was a holy woman and my teacher."

"*Bien.* You have some knowledge and skill. That makes this easier." Doña Gabriela gestured at the corpse. "That was a *nagual*, a shapeshifting witch. But she did a very stupid thing. She gave birth in *jaguarundi* form. Maybe she got pregnant and realized she had triplets inside. Hard birth. She decided to shift to make it easier. Or maybe there's some other explanation. No matter. Her babies were born *mitzon*, shifted. They are trapped. Better we kill them."

"What?" I was appalled. "If they are human children, we certainly cannot kill them, Doña Gabriela."

She sighed. "Problem is they don't know they are human.

Right now their *tonal*, their animal soul, it's in charge. How you're going to get them to understand, *gringa* witch? How you're going to awaken the human soul and get it to take charge? The older they get, the harder it's going to be to put them down. Can't release them: their personhood would twist inside them, make them mankillers. So what's the solution, Miss Donna?"

I had no answer, but I refused to see the little things killed. I bundled them up and mounted my pony. Leaving Roberto and his shaman to give the *nagual* woman a decent burial, I returned to my humble home. Now here I sit, staring at the chubby little cubs.

I realize that Doña Gabriela was right. I have no idea how to awaken their humanity. But I must try.

July 6, 1908

I've taken to calling the grey female cubs *Smoke* and *Ash*. They are inseparable, waddling around on rickety legs, jumping at each other in play. Trixy has adopted the russet male, who struts around like he is a dog as well, so I have named him *Nkita,* which in Igbo means "dog." Of course, I must nickname him Kitty and laugh at my own foolish little joke.

My experiments in dressing the young shifted babes availed me nothing. Nor did speaking to them as one would a child. Ill-equipped for casting glamours that would alter their form, I attempted repeatedly to structure a spell out of existing formulae, but I succeeded only in turning Smoke black for a day and a half.

I was thumbing through the Bible one afternoon, searching for inspiration, when I began to read a psalm aloud for my own edification. The *jaguarundi* cubs purred and chirped excitedly at the sing-song cadence of my voice, crowding round me the better to hear. The Pauline epistles and the prophets send them scuttling off to play, but any verse-like passage draws them like the pied piper.

This attraction got me to thinking, and so today I spent hours crooning lullabies and hymns, folksongs and spirituals. The three sat utterly enrapt, and when I had exhausted my repertoire, Ash clawed her way up my blouse and thrust her little weaselly head at me, nuzzling my lips and mewling.

Their behavior is so startlingly human. I am convinced that music is the key to undoing their *mitzon* state.

July 23, 1908

For the last two weeks I have used every free moment to envelop the kits in a womb of melodic sound. Roberto has the work of clearing well in hand: we are very nearly ready to begin planting. So I have had my gramophone brought here from my parents' home in the town they named for me, and I crank the handle over and over, slipping on a new ten- or twelve-inch of popular and classical work. They are mad for the machine. I can see in their eyes both remarkable joy and the human need to understand, much deeper and meaningful than mere feline curiosity.

However, until today I felt my efforts would prove ultimately fruitless. Then Doña Gabriela paid me a visit.

"They tell me you have been singing to the *gatitos*, the kitties. That is well. For just having a month of life, they are very awake."

"Yes, they are very alert and inquisitive for a trio of young wildcats, but they've shown no sign of transforming into human babies."

"I figured as much," she said, unslinging her leather bag. "The music reaches them, but there's not much there to reach, yes? Must expand that intelligence. I bring the ingredients that can maybe help."

She spread across my narrow table a variety of spices and herbs: cocoa beans, almonds, Spanish sage, sunflower seeds, myrtle grass. Next to them she set a stone mortar and pestle.

"Got to grind them down in in *molcajete,* capture oil in phial. Three drops a night, then the singing and gramophone discs. Then, maybe, perhaps, one or two shifts into human form. If the Virgin smiles on us."

She showed me the right measures for each element of the potion and then set me to twisting the pestle, commenting on my technique, correcting my stance. It was a little like having Hester back, God rest her soul.

We gave the cubs three drops each and then I sang my mother's favorite songs to them, hugging them close. Doña Gabriela seemed moved, and she kissed the crown of my head before leaving.

"Your love is strong. I think you are maybe the final ingredient, Miss Donna. Find a way to mix yourself in."

August 20, 1908

We sowed the alfalfa today, broadcasting my magicked seeds into well-ploughed furrows, a dozen of us working in harmonic tandem. If only it were as easy to mix myself in to the transformative magic I have been weaving for my little *nagual* friends.

When I got back to the house, I was overwhelmed by excitement: a group of men were unloading from a wagon my new upright piano, just delivered from Goggan's in Galveston. It scarcely fit through the door, and Smoke, Ash and Kitty all immediately commenced to scaling its heights.

Before I could get on with the experiment of live music, however, Father trotted up on his mare, a look of genuine irritation upon his face.

"Donna, dear," he began as he slid off his mount. "It's bad enough that you insist on going into these fields with the Mexicans, standing shoulder-to-shoulder and working with them as if you were a man—but now tongues are wagging about gramophone music blaring through the wee hours, and you have dragged a blasted piano out here. I can only imagine the gossip: 'The divorcee has started up a honky-tonk … she's putting on hurdy-gurdy shows!' Can't you think of the reputation of this family for once, child?"

Twenty-nine years old, and he still calls me child. Had he even an inkling of the green magic I wield, that for two decades I have studied and honed, his silly moralistic concerns would evaporate in a firestorm of righteous ire.

"Father, that's hardly fair. I've done all I can to build up the reputation of this family. First postmaster in town, first notary public, founder of the Women's Club at First Baptist, owner of the first boarding house … We are almost done with the construction of the first office building in Donna, which will house *your* business. Have I chosen a life unencumbered by the yoke of defective marriage? Certainly. But that doesn't make me some Jezebel. Look."

I gestured at the wildcat cubs, who had crowded at the threshold to my house and were staring at us with the quizzical looks of toddlers. "That's whom the music is for.

My wildcats. We killed their mother by mistake a month ago, and I am nursing them till they can be set free. Songs calm them, Father."

This news appeased him to some degree, being a lover of animals himself. Warning me against all manner of iniquity and danger, he left before sunset. I pulled out sheet music for Bach's inventions, and soon the trio of kits was purring loudly, mesmerized by the dance of my fingers and the melodies they drew forth.

September 9, 1908

At last. What peace I feel. What joy.

Between my caring for the sprouting crops and weaving potion and song into a transformative woof of *chi*, the weeks have gone by fast. I have seen the music working its way into their souls, pushing past *tonal* to get at the human core. But they didn't know what to do. Gabriela told me that I was the final piece in this complex quilt of magic, yet I couldn't see how to make myself fit.

But this morning, as the irrigation ditches spilled their precious moisture onto the seedlings, I thought back to my spiritual naming. We were sitting in the pine woods of East Texas, there near my childhood home. I was just eleven, and Aunty Hester revealed my Igbo name: "*Akachi*. 'Hand of the divine within.' You will use your inner spark to help and heal, child."

I understood in an instant that I had been holding back, so used was I to the delicate craft required to tweak seed and soil so plants reached their greatest potential. The babies needed more than that. They needed to be flooded with love, with *chi*, with—with *me*.

Rushing back to my house without a word of explanation to the men, I drew the napping cubs to my breast there on my bed and began to croon a lullaby that Hester had sung to me in the cradle. And as the words tumbled from my lips, I called up my reservoirs of love, love that had been dammed by an aloof husband, love that I had denied the children I refused to conceive, love that had trickled out of me in meager rivulets to nurture flowers and strangers, love that Hester and mother and siblings had poured into my heart but that I quailed before releasing. I channeled that flood of rushing compassion through my words, my fingers, my chest, and I felt it *unfold* within me, revealing even greater wells of untrammeled love that had no bottom for they tapped the very cosmos and drew up its power.

And the cubs—oh, they began to quiver and stretch and mewl and finally cry, wailing like babies bereft for that is what they are.

I was holding two very human baby girls, a few months old, with beautiful black hair and deep brown eyes that ran with human tears.

But Kitty, ah, Kitty is unchanged. Hissing, he has leapt atop the piano and glares at his sisters with naked ire. I am spent. I can barely stand. I'll call to Roberto, have him bring Gabriela. The shaman will know what to do, whom to give the girls to, a good family that will love and guide them.

Kitty, I'll try again when I can. For now, let me revel in this peace. Your sisters are free.

October 1, 1908

Today we began harvesting my alfalfa, that gorgeous sea of green stretching to the north of my humble home. Kitty crept along behind me, leaping at lizards and bugs with a ragged little snarl. Earlier in the week Doña Gabriela visited to keep me abreast of the girls' progress. The family has baptized them Neblina and Ceniza (something like Smoke and Ash, I gather). They will grow up in a community that respects the old ways and reveres the magic of the earth, and when they are old enough, their true origin will be revealed to them.

This one, though, seems impenetrable. Twice more I have outpoured my soul into music, opening floodgates of power I never dreamed accessible, but the cub clings, stubborn, to his feline form. Thus have all the males in my life shown their obstinacy, refusing to be reshaped.

December 24, 1908

In the week that I have been back from my trip to Falfurrias to purchase Jersey cattle from the Lasater Ranch, Nkita has not let me out of his sight. Given that I treat him as protector and friend, this is not unexpected. My absence apparently caused him considerable grief. None of my workers could get near him—everyone is afraid of Kitty, and sensibly so, as he has grown to the size of a small cougar and uses his deadly claws at a moment's notice. My return brought on such a spell of his rubbing against my legs that I could scarcely walk three feet without tripping.

Pampered beyond the dream of many a regular house cat, at night he usually curls up at the foot of my bed. The little lamb that went everywhere with Mary has nothing on Kitty, for he follows me all over the place, like a toddler clinging to his nanny's apron. He plays outdoors with Trixy and the other rat terriers, but music still has such charms for Kitty that the moment I touch a key on the piano, he insists on coming inside and staying as long as there is music. He lays stretched across the top of the instrument, and his contented purr can be heard all over the house, made much bigger and prone to echoes since last month's expansion. When I finally get a telephone installed, I wonder how he will react to its ringing?

Yet for all my yuletide carols, magic oils and spiritual outpourings, Kitty grows more feline, more feral, with every passing day. I fear that in his case Gabriela's warning was well placed. I have no idea what I will do if he becomes too vicious. I love him so, you see.

It's Christmas Eve, so I have treated him to blissful herbs and a few hand-made toys with bells and strings. I hope they will keep him occupied while I spend the night with my parents and siblings. Strange. I am quite reluctant to step out the door and head for town. My family feels so alien, so distant: this farm, these workers, this wildcat—they dominate my heart and mind now.

March 4, 1909

For the last six weeks, Nkita has become a veritable terror to my little farm, stalking and harrowing the livestock to the point that Roberto demands I do something to curb him. My once adorable overgrown jaguarundi loves to eat chicken off the roost, though it isn't hunger that sends him foraging. Looking at him with shaman eyes, I feel certain that, as Gabriela warned, his animal soul is twisting his humanity, making him eager for the kill.

At the start one fowl was enough to take the edge off his appetite. But as the weeks wore on, I believe he got a taste for blood. I have tried locking him indoors with me at night, but he is extraordinarily clever and light of foot. He always manages to prise open the shutters and escape.

I then sketched wardings into the earth, spells to contain him within a reasonable area, but he is magic to the core in his *mitzon* state, and he easily erases my runes. Driven by the killer urge, he keeps feasting on my geese, turkeys and ducks at intervals whenever he gets out. Not only is my livelihood being impacted, but I fear what will happen once he's slaughtered them all. Will my terriers be next? Will he attack the cows? Will he slink into town on the prowl?

I hold him in my arms, grappling with his wiry strength, humming to him, pleading with him. "Nkita, my child, my sweet little boy. Be calm. Sleep. Listen to my song. Momma wants to sing to you."

But he cannot answer me.

September 13, 1909

Oh, God, what have I done?

All spring and half the summer, Nkita's restlessness and hunger grew. I no longer could keep him indoors unless I played records over and over, an exhausting task, changing the discs or resetting the needle every four minutes. So I took to locking the dogs up with me and letting the wildcat roam, hoping to heaven for a change.

Doña Gabriela visited me in July, and her words gave me no comfort. "You started down this path when you let him live. I know you saved them girls. That was some mighty magic. But the male, he's another story, and now you got to deal with it. He is past transformation, Miss Donna. He can't be human. But he ain't *jaguarundi,* neither. Between worlds. No hope, because he can't have freedom."

I could imagine no solution, however, so I did nothing.

In mid-August, I was roused from my slumbers by a neighbor living a mile away, excitingly shouting into the telephone that my wildcat was rushing after and catching her chickens. I had to rush over and bring him home, a lariat round his neck like a noose, Kitty snarling and hissing the entire way.

For two nights I kept him tied up though he made a piteous racket until each dawn. But on the third night he got free.

That morning my father arrived in a wagon with several other men, all with rifles or shotguns draped over their arms. They had lassoed and lashed Nkita down, muzzled him. My hand went to my mouth as I rushed to his side.

"Donna," my father said, "this can't go on. Your pet slaughtered three good horses last night and nearly clawed Mr. Turner's leg off!"

I wept, inconsolable, but I nodded my understanding.

"Listen, darling, my friend Archibald Palmer has started a zoo in Brownsville. I think a specimen this fine would make a great addition. He'll be well fed—and contained. You can visit him whenever you like. But we can't let him stay here any longer, dear. It's either the zoo, or we put him down."

And so I let them take my baby away, struggling uselessly in his bonds. As they trundled off, I called out in desperation:

"He loves music, Father! Tell them to play music for him!"

A month later I took a river barge down to see Kitty's new home. Mr. Palmer walked me through the lovely gardens, and for a second I felt some relief. But then I saw that all the animals were caged. Enveloped by the Green World, but unable ever to touch it. It was torturous.

Finally we reached the iron-rod box that held my Nkita. He stood listless, eying the world with cautious hate. I covered my face with my bonnet: I couldn't bear for him to see me. The thought of recognition playing across that defeated face was almost as bad as the possibility that he might not know me at all.

Seeing me so distraught, Mr. Palmer leaned closer and muttered, "We play him music, just as you asked."

He gestured at an employee, who wound a hurdy-gurdy and let the carnival tune explode with undue gaiety. Kitty's head snapped around, and he flung himself at the bars, scrabbling toward the wood-slat roof, yowling and gibbering, sounding a rough bark over and over and over again. I ran as far away from that voice as I could, boarding the barge and sailing back up the Rio Grande, trying to drown his call with the noise of water, birds, engines, the shouts of industrious river men.

At home, surrounded by the beautiful works of my hand, I hoped to find surcease. But I am haunted by that cry, night after night. Amidst a pitch black dreamscape, the wildcat climbs the walls of his cage, howling miserably. In my nightmares the call is quite distinct: two heart-wrenching syllables that reverberate with the pain of betrayal:

Momma.

October 19, 1909

I did not believe I would have the strength. I imagined my mind would shiver and splinter with grief and shame. But I have done what needed doing, and somehow I will live with the memory.

I returned to Brownsville three days ago, telling no one of my business. Then, in the still of the night, I took up my bible and shotgun and made my way to the zoological gardens.

A whisper of magic loosened lock and chains upon the gate. I pushed my way in and walked slowly through the darkness, feeling the entrapped life snuffling hoarsely all around. The moon was but a sliver that faintly glinted off wakeful, mistrusting eyes.

At last I stood before Nkita's cage. I called to him softly, and he surged with panic to press himself against the bars. His plaintive mewling was nearly more than I could bear.

I opened the scriptures to the twenty-third Psalm and began to recite in the sing-song whisper that had so often stilled the boy's anxiety: "The Lord is my shepherd; I shall not want."

Kitty eased down the bars as I read by starlight and memory. Purring hitched like sobs in his chest. His kneading claws grated against the wooden planks beneath him.

"Surely goodness and mercy shall follow me all the days of my life," I concluded, my voice thick with emotion, "and I will dwell in the house of the Lord forever."

Setting down the bible, I sketched a gesture in the air. The door of the cage swung open. Nkita hesitated for a moment, testing the air with his muzzle, before leaping onto the gravel and shaking himself as if shrugging captivity from his back. His eyes met mine.

"Go, son. You are free. Go."

He twitched his tail once, blinked, and then turned away, looking into the deep shadows which only vision like his could penetrate.

Biting back the cry rising in my breast, I lifted the shotgun to my shoulder. He waited a second more, a moment that stretched eternally in my aching heart, and then he burst into a run.

I aimed carefully despite my shaking hands. I fired. Without a sound, he sprawled in the inky pools upon the path. When I reached him, he was already transforming, his familiar pelt dissolving to reveal a lovely boy with thick black hair and wiry limbs.

As I knelt, weeping, to wrap his body in my coat, I saw his dark eyes were wide even in death, and a wild smile of freedom hollowed dimples in both his perfect cheeks.

THE BONES OF RÍO RICO

(from *The Secret Diary of Donna Hooks*)

February 2, 1928

Ah, how banal yet humbling to watch one's business fade. Despite my reputation as an imaginative merchandiser, despite my owning and operating the finest department store in the Rio Grande Valley, a decade of effort is slowly ebbing into nothing. Only eight years ago the local broadsheet praised the variety nestled within these walls: elegant little general store, high-fashioned specialty shop, millinery and beauty salon. The best merchandise and bargains were always found here. Now the community's economic woes have forced me to close all but the dry goods and grocery departments.

Nonetheless, I ride here each morning from Alameda Ranch—the last of my profitable enterprises—and attend my sporadic customers. I suppose as I near my fiftieth decade on this earth, I simply crave human warmth. So many of those I loved have passed beyond—father, Beatrice, my sweet Roberto. Though I feel great affection for my nephews and nieces, we have never been particularly close. And, of course, Mother's failing mind remembers less and less, so our conversations are one-sided at best. It seems, then, that fleeting contact with strangers and acquaintances must sustain me.

Today brought Hattie McLellan, sister-in-law of my late sibling Beatrice. Unaware of the recent attrition in my business, she had come hoping to have her hair styled in a bob, signaling to my mind the end of that fashion's novelty.

"I'm truly sorry," I told her. "But Daisy's still cutting hair out of her own front parlor. If you drop in, she'll be happy to oblige."

Hattie pulled at her curls with a bemused expression. "Yes, but that would mean driving into Weslaco. I'm not entirely sure I feel safe in that town, what with the rumors and all."

It was an invitation to gossip, so of course I played along. "And what, my dear, might those rumors be?"

"Haven't you heard, Miss Donna? Al Capone is here in south Texas. They say he wants to open a greyhound racing track just across the border. It seems he's residing in Weslaco and tipping big wherever he goes."

I shook my head in disbelief. "I guess I shouldn't be surprised, given the man who runs things on the Mexican side of the river."

Everyone knows Don Ernesto Arrendondo by reputation. The now Mexican town of Rio Rico, all 413 acres of it, used to sit north of the Rio Grande. But in 1906 the Rio Grande Land and Irrigation Company redirected the flow of the river without authorization, placing that tract of US soil in a sort of international limbo. For the past twenty-two years, Arrendondo has reaped the benefits of this confusion, offering dog races, dance halls, cantinas and entertainment not available in Texas, especially since Prohibition became the law of the land.

"With this new bridge being built between Weslaco and Río Rico, I'd bet the mob's curiosity is piqued," Hattie mused.

"Sure," I agreed. "And it's easy to imagine that Arrendondo might ally himself with Chicago crime syndicates."

She nodded. "Horrifying, isn't it, the thought of all that northern violence and vice piled atop our own local problems? More so with the disappearances."

"Of the children, you mean." This story I have been following closely. A child a month has gone missing from working-class Mexican families in the area. Officers of the law have done little to track down those responsible. Sheriff Baker swears his men are investigating, but I suspect this is mere hand-waving to ensure Mexican votes. The Texas Rangers, spread thin in order to quell violence in oil boomtowns, are abstaining from the case.

"Yes. Poor things." So she declared before seguing into the ins and outs of her own family conflicts. I struggled not to berate her for such fleeting concern. Were the children Anglo, I'm certain both she and the authorities would make a much greater fuss. But we are products of our upbringing, are we not? I thank heaven that my childhood was spent under the care and guidance of "Auntie" Hester, whose compassion and Igbo sorcery are the keystones of my soul.

I closed the store early, the children weighing on my mind. After changing into trousers and a loose blouse, I went to stand amidst my alfalfa fields as the setting sun streamed pink-tinged gold upon my head. Brushing my fingers against the purple flowers of my unusually tall crop, I closed my eyes and sent my heart questing, using green magic to feel along soil and root. The droning of bees filled my ears as they swarmed about me, drawn by the gentle power.

I thrummed through the Green World, exploring the natural fabric that undergirds my community, grazing human spirits, attuned to the accustomed patterns, hoping to be jolted by any sense of wrong, any disturbance that might hint at the whereabouts of the missing boys and girls. Armed with this knowledge, I would go to the *tenanches,* let those old women take the necessary action. But the magic frayed at the very edges of my reach and once again I found no trace.

My heart heavy, I have retired to my humble home. I cannot help thinking of all the terrible things that might have befallen the little ones. Craving easy and dreamless sleep, I have drunk some chamomile tea infused with lime flower.

The dogs have leapt into bed with me. I pull them close and blow out the candle.

February 4, 1928

Though I swore seven years ago nevermore to get involved in such potentially violent matters, I find myself drawn against my will toward a new maelstrom. I can only pray that this time I can rise to the task. Another failure, another *death,* will surely break me.

I had not quite left my home this morning when a tentative knock stirred my dogs to a frenzy of barking. I shooed them aside and opened the door to find a young Mexican woman standing on my porch, flanked by three shy children.

"¿Señora *Hooks?*" she assayed in Spanish.

"Please, just call me Donna," I replied in the same language.

A little flustered by the intimacy, she hesitated before continuing. "My name is Isabel Quiñones, ma'am. I know I'm a stranger, but please believe that I come from a respectable family. My husband Arturo and I run a little fruit stand in Weslaco, down by the railroad tracks. We attend mass each Sunday."

She seemed desperate for me to acknowledge her as a decent woman. Whatever she sought, it was difficult for her to come all this way and look me in the eye.

"Without a doubt, your standing in the community is blameless," I assured her, and she visibly relaxed.

"I'm terribly sorry to bother you at such an early hour, but I'm desperate for help. It's my son, you see. Jorge."

My stomach lurched with foresight. I lifted a hand as if to ward off her words, but she spoke nonetheless.

"He's been taken, ma'am. Like the others."

Sighing, I stared past her at the sun, glowing white on a horizon swathed in winter fog. "I am not the right person, Mrs. Quiñones. You need to speak to the *tenanches*. They'll know what to do."

Her fingers plucked at the dark rosary around her neck. "You don't understand, Mrs. Hooks … *Donna*. The old women have already seen me. They told me to come to you. '*La güera santera*,' they said. 'She will be your champion.'"

The Pale Witch. One of the many epithets I have collected down the years, most of them deserved. But I made it clear to the council after Roberto's death what my role would be in the welfare of this community, and it is frustrating that they have simply ignored my wishes in sending this poor woman my way.

Of course, I had no intention of dashing her hopes there on my doorstep. I would get her the help she needed, somehow. My heart ached to think of their suffering, their fear, their possible demise …

"Very well. Can you describe Jorge to me? Do you have something of his that you can lend me for a time?"

Handing me a wooden top and some marbles, she managed to give me details, her voice hitching constantly. Her oldest son is ten years old, nearly five feet tall, with striking hazel eyes and lanky black hair, a scar at the right corner of his mouth from a childhood accident. He was wearing black trousers and a blue shirt when he left his house yesterday morning. He never arrived at the schoolhouse for Friday classes. He never came home.

Of all the folk along the river's edge, I am the last woman who ought to make such promises, but her expression of anguish so moved me that I seized one of her hands and whispered with hoarse fierceness:

"We will get your son back, I swear."

Weeping, she kissed my cold fingers and swept her children off into the fog.

There was little point in going to confront the *tenanches.* They had decided to thrust this responsibility on me, so I would have to find an ally, a real champion for young Jorge Quiñones.

Getting in my Nash sedan, I headed south along rutted roads to the lushly wooded land on which Gabriela Rivera had established the retreat where she lived and practiced her shamanistic healing.

I found her in her garden, teaching an apprentice how to

recognize and select herbs. Though approaching eighty years of age, Doña Gabriela seemed as sturdy as ever, barefoot among her luxurious plants, silver hair in a long braid that reached the hem of her orange skirt, a worn leather bag strapped across her immaculate white blouse.

Her impassive face was illuminated briefly by a smile as she crooked a rheumatoid finger at me.

"Come, Miss Donna," she called. "Anita here was just collecting ingredients for a poultice."

The younger woman curtsied and averted her eyes. My reputation, I suppose, preceded me.

"*Ya métete. Ahorita voy,*" the shaman muttered, shooing her apprentice away. Turning back to me, she nodded. "So. A long time, no?"

"Yes, Doña Gabriela. And that's entirely my fault."

The shaman scoffed. "Course it is, silly woman. All caught up in making money. Bah. Who ever heard of a rich *santera*? Waste of your damn time."

I didn't disagree. Experience has taught me that arguing with Gabriela is pointless: she is stubborn as a mule and almost always right.

"I've come about the missing children," I explained, ignoring her long-standing criticisms of my lifestyle. "The *tenanches* sent a woman to me. Her son disappeared yesterday."

"And then? You already know how to track folk down. The hell you want from me?"

"It's not enough to find the children, Doña. They must be rescued."

The old woman reached out and grabbed her walking stick, which she had left leaning against a mesquite. She took a few hobbling steps toward me.

"Well, rescue them!"

I shook my head. "I can't. I need help. Don't you know someone? Some younger woman or man with enough power to confront the kidnappers?"

A look of dismay spread across her wizened face. "Whatever happened to that tough young witch I met twenty years ago, eh? Divorced, living alone in the *monte*, overseeing a passel of men workers with a shotgun in her hands? Trying to tell me you're *afraid* now?"

Grief squeezed my chest like a vice. "I'm not afraid of whoever or whatever has taken the children, Doña. I'm afraid of *myself*, don't you understand? I'm afraid of *failing*. Again. And the cost of that failure. People I love lost their lives because … because I wasn't *adequate*."

My eyes were blurred by tears, so I didn't realize the shaman had moved until I felt her warm, calloused palm on my face.

"Hush, Miss Donna," she whispered kindly, her breath smelling of eucalyptus and sage. "We ain't none of us 'adequate.' But the Virgin smiles down upon us with love all the same. Ain't no one can say if we will win or lose. Don't matter, in the end. What matters is we fought for order, for goodness, for innocence. We may suffer, but we suffer in the name of the Light, my daughter. You hear me?"

Her words loosened the knot in my heart. I laid my cheek atop her head, bending into her embrace. "I hear you, wise one. I have been selfish, not wanting to risk pain. But … very well. I accept the charge placed upon me. If the boy is still alive, I will be his champion. However, I will not seek revenge if he is dead. Others will have to enact justice."

Gabriela pulled away and nodded. "Fair enough, *santera*."

We conferred a while longer in that magical garden,

speculating as to the identity of the child-snatchers and their possible weaknesses. Gabriela replenished my supply of rare but potent herbs, and I set out for my store.

It was well past 10 a.m. when I arrived. Several women were waiting impatiently on the sidewalk, unnerved by my tardiness on a normally lucrative Saturday. I attended them as quickly as I could, and then I drew up a sign to post in the window:

Closed until further notice—Management.

Now I am home. I have the afternoon to ready and equip myself. Tomorrow, come hell or high water, I will find young Jorge Quiñones.

February 5, 1928

It seems clear who is behind the disappearances. I will set out to confront them at first light. If I do not return, today's entry will be the last in my secret diary. Since anyone capable of reading it in my absence will perforce possess some degree of sorcery, I can only hope you will seek out and destroy the monsters responsible.

This morning, after I was certain the first mass at Saint Joan of Arc had ended, I drove into Weslaco's "Mexican Town," just north of the railroad tracks. *Frutería Quiñones* stands close to that cultural dividing line, so I had no trouble locating it. A small but well-tended shack of wood and tin, the store boasts an entrance lovingly paved with rustic flagstones, and the family had set boxes of seasonal fruit just outside the door.

Isabel saw me first as I emerged from my car, and she hurried to me, beaming with expectation. I took great care to both curb her excitement and give her hope.

"Mrs. Quiñones, we have not yet found your son, but I have conferred with specialists, preparing myself. There are a few questions, however."

Somewhat crestfallen, she nodded and led me into the shack. Her husband was unpacking fruit from crates. Short but sturdy in build, Arturo Quiñones turned and regarded me with forced calm that belied the anguish I sensed within him.

"Good morning, sir. My name is ..."

"I know who you are," he said gruffly. "My wife told me she approached you about our son."

"I must ask," I continued, ignoring his rudeness, "whether anyone has threatened you. Whether you have angered anyone. Especially ... someone powerful."

Arturo swallowed heavily, but after a moment's hesitation, shook his head. "No, ma'am."

"Are you certain?" I prodded, convinced that he was not being honest.

At that moment, a woman thrust herself in our midst, hands clenched in anger. She was about Isabel's age, Mexican but light-skinned with green eyes. She wore a demure Sunday bonnet pinned to hair that had been drawn back into a severe bun at the nape of her neck. A high-collared grey dress completed her church-going ensemble.

"He's lying to you," she said in English before looking pointedly at Quiñones and repeating for his benefit, "*Le está mintiendo.*"

The fruit-seller's eyes narrowed. "I warned you, Miss Leticia, to stay away from my family."

"I am trying to *help*, Mr. Quiñones! Even after you rudely rebuffed me at church this morning, I might add. I care very deeply for Jorge, and you need to tell the police the truth!"

Clearing my throat to catch her attention, I addressed the newcomer. "I'm sorry, Miss … Leticia, was it?"

"Yes, ma'am. Leticia Franco. I'm the school teacher at the Mexican elementary school. Jorge was one of my pupils."

"A pleasure. My name is Donna Hooks. I am … assisting the family in finding young Jorge."

Nodding, she glowered at the silent couple. "Well, that will be nearly impossible as long as they hide key information from you. Ask him, Mrs. Hooks. Ask him about the extortion."

It was my turn to glare at the man, but instead of putting the question to him, I turned to his wife. She knew what I was. "Tell me. Now."

Tears quivering in her eyes, she confessed. "It's Don Ernesto, from across the river. He demands protection money from us, sends his hoodlums to collect. Last year, the percentage increased. Many have refused to pay."

She shot a pregnant glance at her husband.

Leticia touched my arm. In a quiet but determined voice, she confirmed the suspicions welling within me.

"All the boys and girls who have gone missing are the children of merchants north of the tracks. Even more have been taken, but their parents paid the demanded ransom right away."

"And they were returned? What did they report?"

"They will not speak of what happened. I suspect they have suppressed some sort of trauma. Or perhaps fear has overwhelmed them. Arredondo refuses to return any child whose parents delayed in meeting his terms."

A sob escaped the lips of Arturo Quiñones. "Like *I* did! Oh, forgive me, God. I have failed my son!"

Leticia moved closer to him. "And still you will not talk to the police? Are you as frightened as the rest of the sheep who just turn their backs on their own children?"

I took hold of her arm and forcibly drew her into the sunlight. "That's enough," I said in English. "Let them be. They're terrified of what Arredondo will do to their other little ones if they denounce him to the authorities. Instead of railing indignantly, help me."

The school teacher arched a dubious eyebrow. "Help you? How?"

"Show me the path Jorge takes to school each day."

She scoffed. "To what end?"

"Someone or something took the boy. There may be clues to its identity."

"Ah, yes. You said you were assisting the family. Do you fancy yourself some sort of female gumshoe, Mrs. Hook? What can you possibly do that the police cannot?"

"Quite a bit," I snapped back. "I'm the Pale Witch, you see."

Her eyes wide, she crossed herself instinctively.

As we walked the few blocks to the shanty in which the Quiñones lived, Leticia shared her theories with me. A few weeks ago—visiting *el pueblo americano* on one of those Saturdays when Mexican women were patronizingly permitted to shop in the Anglo part of town—she had overheard socialite Deanna Board chatting with a friend. Mrs. Board claimed to have just sold her second house to a man named Rhea, apparently a representative of Alphonse Capone.

Leticia was convinced that the Chicago gangster had been wooed by Don Ernesto. She had been distraught for weeks about the missing children, and the impending arrival of

Capone acted as a catalyst, leading to her discovery of the links among the cases. From there, the conclusion seemed obvious. Such a criminal alliance meant a greater capital outlay, hence the hike in the cost of "protection" and the brutal extortion of those unwilling to pay.

"A fine piece of detecting," I offered. "Female gumshoe, indeed."

The schoolmarm smirked and gestured at an irrigation ditch running behind a row of meager homes. "Jorge walked along that canal to school from this brightly painted house. I'm not wearing the most appropriate shoes for such a hike, but I'm willing to accompany you."

We trudged up the clayey banks in silence, our eyes scanning the surroundings as we went. Eventually the canal curved away, and I could make out the barn-like structure of the Mexican elementary school on a low rise just ahead. A well-worn footpath took us past a copse of mesquite, and there I found what I most dreaded.

Owl feathers. Large, black-fringed plumes, much longer than possible even for the biggest screeching predator on record.

"Oh, Dear Lord," I breathed, kneeling to pick up one of the feathers.

"What is it? You look utterly mortified, Mrs. Hooks!"

I stood, running my finger along the vanes, wincing at the dark energies they contained.

"*Lechuzas*," I managed to say at last. "Witch owls."

After leaving the teacher at her school, I made my way back to my car. I would have to make one more visit, I knew, before honing in on Jorge Quiñones. If, as it appeared, shape-shifting witches were assuming the form of giant barn owls and snatching children away, I required the most current information on the parliament's numbers and its possible location.

That meant going to *La Hierbería Guadalupana* and facing Roberto's mother, a woman who rightly despises me, blaming me for the death of her only son.

My chest aching at the thought of the encounter, I nonetheless stood by my promise. I am the boy's champion. I will face what I must.

I entered the cool gloom of Doña Élida's store. She was hanging *ristras* of garlic, and turned her head slightly to look at the entrance. Grunting, she made her laborious way back down her step ladder and stood to face me, her steel-gray hair clamped down by a net. Behind her, candles flickered weirdly near the dark passage into the less wholesome area of her apothecary. Since Roberto's death Élida Ramírez has irrevocably changed. She will sell anything to anyone, even the darker sorcerers of these parts.

Squat and toad-like in her black shift, she seemed the very antithesis of Doña Gabriela.

"I told you to stay away," she said after a moment.

"Yes, and I would not bother you were it not important."

Her rheumy eyes narrowed. "Speak, then."

Pulling the feather from my bag, I thrust it at her. "The missing children. A witch owl took at least one of them. I need to know if there is a parliament of witches nearby."

Doña Élida coughed wetly, drawing a handkerchief from somewhere on her person and spitting into it with a grimace. "And what will you do with such information, *gringa maldita*?"

Cursed white woman. My cheeks were burning, but I choked back tears and harsh words. "The *tenanches* have chosen me to rescue a boy."

Her laughter was low and horrible, a mirthless moan. "Rescue a boy. Like you rescued my Roberto, you pallid bitch? The *tenanches* are more senile than I had imagined."

Stoic, I returned her burning gaze. "I won't bother apologizing again. But Roberto's loss nearly destroyed me as well, you know."

"Would that it had," she growled. "You have no business interfering with powerful men and women armed only with that weak African magic you learned at your nurse's knee, not even adding the piddling potions and spells you got from Gabriela."

I waited, seething with grief. After a moment, she jerked the feather from my hands.

"Yes. There is a coven nearby, in Río Rico. A group of young witches, hired by Arredondo to safeguard his operations. Between the thirteen of them and the hard men they work with, they are going to rip you apart. Go now, Hooks. Go and be damned."

So now I lie in the darkling upon my bed. My equipment sits waiting for dawn. I think of my encounter with the Luminous seven years ago, how those blood-sucking sorcerers batted my magic aside, laughing. I remember Roberto, calloused hands clutching the air as his life was drained away, my limbs locked by a spell I could not counter. But it is time to set aside the failures of the past. Tomorrow I either prove myself worthy of the old women's trust, or I join my beloved there Beyond.

February 6, 1928

Allies arise where one least expects them, even on the very plains of Hell.

I drove to the river this morning and took the ferry across. In the foggy twilight, the pilot mistook me for a man, all decked out as I was in boots, trousers, mackintosh and slouch hat, a shotgun in the crook of my arm. I did not bother to correct him. To the east loomed the pylons of the nascent bridge, like the bones of some antediluvian dragon.

On the far bank I stood among the reeds. Clutching Jorge's toys in my free hand, I sent my green magic threading outward, feeling for the soul whose essence lingered on his prized possessions. Without warning, my senses slammed into a vast area of *wrong*, of *sick*, of *evil.* Staggered by the intensity of the magical recoil, I dropped to one knee in the mud.

In the midst of that malignity, Jorge Quiñones trembled, still alive against all hope.

I stowed the toys in my pocket and broke into a run, pulling *chi* from the Green World around me to sustain my middle-aged flesh. About a mile from the river, a mansion sat among a pecan grove, a fleet of black Model A sedans flanking its ample verandah. Arredondo's home. Giving it a wide berth, I slowed, the cold touch of evil a nauseous wave.

Behind the mansion loomed a wooden barn, weathered and ominous. Beyond it, a field of bones stretched away south.

Human bones. Children's bones. Dozens. Hundreds. The Green World squirmed with their restless souls, trapped by vicious and murderous and lonely deaths. Oh, how they clutched at me! Oh, how they cried for release! But I steeled myself, ignored their pleas. My first duty was to the living.

Shuddering, I lifted the shotgun and rounded the barn until, standing in the midst of all that wreckage, that death, those plaintive lost souls, I faced the open door.

"Jorge!" I called. "Jorge Quiñones!"

With a startled sob, a boy-shaped silhouette appeared in the entrance.

"That's it, son. It's okay. Your parents sent me to get you. Just come on out of there. Come to me."

Jorge assayed a few cautious steps. His clothes were in tatters, smeared with blood. His eyes were wide with fear and hope.

"My parents?" he asked, emerging fully into the slanting light of dawn.

And then the witch burst from the barn—an enormous screech owl with lifeless black eyes, a vicious curving beak and talon-tipped wings that gripped the shoulders of the terrified child before he could take another step.

"*Step back!*" it shrieked in a harrowing voice. "*Step back or I claw out his throat!*"

Training the shotgun on the shifted witch, I complied, searching for an opening.

"All I want is the boy!" I called. "Turn him over, and I will leave in peace."

The monstrosity cackled madly. "*You stupid bitch! My sisters are already on their way! We felt you coming! There will be no peace!*"

Someone came running from the house, but it was not another witch. I spared a glimpse at the hefty young man in the expensive suit as he pulled up short, regarding the human-sized owl with incredulity—I had seen his scarred face in enough newspapers to recognize the infamous Alphonse Capone.

Behind him there *did* come a black-clad witch in human form, along with an elegant fellow I assumed was Ernesto Arredondo. They were flanked by men with tommy guns, both from Río Rico and Chicago to judge by their appearance.

"What in the hell?" Capone began, just as a tall young Mexican criminal raised his machine gun.

His bullets would wound or kill the boy. Instinctively, I thrust my left hand into the air, sketching a glyph that wrenched the weapon from the mobster's hands.

On the edge of my perception, I felt the witches gathering, drawing closer. They would all converge at once, I knew. Too many. Too powerful. I would be overwhelmed. Despair edged into my mind. I was going to fail, again. People were going to die.

Then I took another sidelong glance at the newcomers, their weapons. A glimmer of hope. The ghost of a plan.

"You men stop right there," I said. "I'm here for the boy. And to stop this coven from ever hurting another child."

Capone ran his hand down his face, trying to regain his composure. "Coven? Who are you?"

As if in answer, the witch beside him stepped forward as her sisters emerged from the morning mist. Now there were twelve in a ring around the field of bones. "It's her," one of them hissed. "*La pinche güera santera.*"

Ignoring them, I turned my head slightly. "You're Capone, aren't you? I heard a rumor you were staying in Weslaco. Let me put it this way: I don't interfere with the crimes of men. If you and this other gentleman want to smuggle alcohol across the border, that's none of my concern. But your partner has been employing shape-shifting witches, *lechuzas*, to collect protection money from business owners in Weslaco. When they don't pay, the creatures kidnap a child for extortion. If the money isn't ready soon enough, these witch owls kill the child."

Keeping the shotgun steady, I sent green magic down into the corrupt field. *Listen*, I whispered to the children's squirming souls. *Listen. Let me show you the way.* They clung to my power with eager hope.

"What?" Capone turned to Arredondo. "Is this true, you son of a bitch?"

I guided the spirits, twined them with the stunted roots that lay beneath their bones.

Arredondo shrugged and said nothing.

"Believe me, Mr. Capone. This boy's mother came to me yesterday, begging for help. I'm here to end this atrocity. You can either side with them and be damned, or you can help me."

"This broad," Capone muttered, turning back to me. "Help you *how*?"

Now. Now, children.

"Kill them. Kill them all."

The earth burst open at the foot of each witch, green tendrils of spirit and plant winding around their legs as they struggled and screamed.

Capone appeared to quickly appraise the situation. Don Ernesto had fled. The young criminal I had disarmed was trying to unjam the weapon he had retrieved. And the women in black were transforming. Their clothing morphed into feathers, their faces twisted into beaks, their arms widened into vast, cruel wings.

Facing his men, Scarface shouted. "Fill those goddamn monsters with lead, boys!"

His team fired upon the witch owls. The one holding Jorge pulled its beak and talons just far enough away from the boy's throat—I squeezed the trigger, wending magic around the pellets to keep them from scattering. The *lechuza*'s head exploded in a profusion of gore, and I rushed to Jorge's side, wrapping my arms around him.

Several of the fiends, though wounded, broke free of the tendrils and hurled themselves into the air. They plunged toward the boy and me, wailing and gibbering

"*Amen*!" I shouted, lifting a hand and twisting my fingers in a ward. "*Aeternam vitam*! *Resurrectionem carnis*!"

The Latin words, an inversion of the Apostles' Creed, repelled them for a moment, but the witch owls screeched in fury and redoubled their attack. Capone snatched the tommy gun away from the young Mexican mobster and took aim, unleashing a barrage of bullets against the winged monsters above my head. In moments, the bodies of the women sprawled lifeless among the bones.

I pulled Jorge away from my embrace and began to look him over. His eyes flitted over the dead witches, spilling tears of relief when he realized his ordeal was over.

"Are you okay?" I asked. "Were you seriously wounded?"

He shook his head and stood a little taller, wiping his nose on a tattered sleeve. Sustained by a stiff pride that reminded me of his parents, he spoke in a hoarse whisper.

"They were going to eat me. That's what they said. Eat me while I watched."

Hollow eyes. Shell shock. Pulling the top and marbles from my pocket, I placed them in his hand.

"Come on. Let's get you home." I took his hand and began to lead him away, using my boots gingerly to move aside the bones. They were silent and still now.

To my right, Capone's men hurried to his side, checking to see if he'd been wounded.

At his gesture, they seized the young Mexican who had remained though Don Ernesto had fled. They forced him to his knees. Scarface spat on the ground.

"What was your name again, gunsel?"

"*Me llamo Juan Nepomuceno Guerra Cárdenas.*"

"All right, Johnny. You find your boss," Capone said, "and you take him out. In a few years I'll come looking for you. You got a good operation going, maybe you and me can do business. But no black magic or witches, *capisce*? And *no goddamn kids*, fer crissakes."

He tossed the machine gun at the youth and approached us. I kept walking.

"Lady," he said, "I don't know who you are, but you are one gutsy dame."

I smiled despite myself. "Thank you, I guess."

"Do you need anything? A ride? Money?"

Pulling Jorge closer, I stopped and turned to regard Capone.

"Just one thing, please."

He doffed his hat in an awkward gesture of respect. "Name it."

"Burn the witches, and bury these bones."

Scarface gave a sober nod and put his men to work.

As black smoke filled the morning air behind me, I guided the boy North, toward hearth and home and happy embraces for us both.

At last, a victory. Life has taught me that such joy is fleeting, that darkness will creep back into the world and challenge me afresh. But for now the dead are still, and my heart is light. I have left my fear and grief upon that field of bones, fading into the Green World like the souls of stolen children.

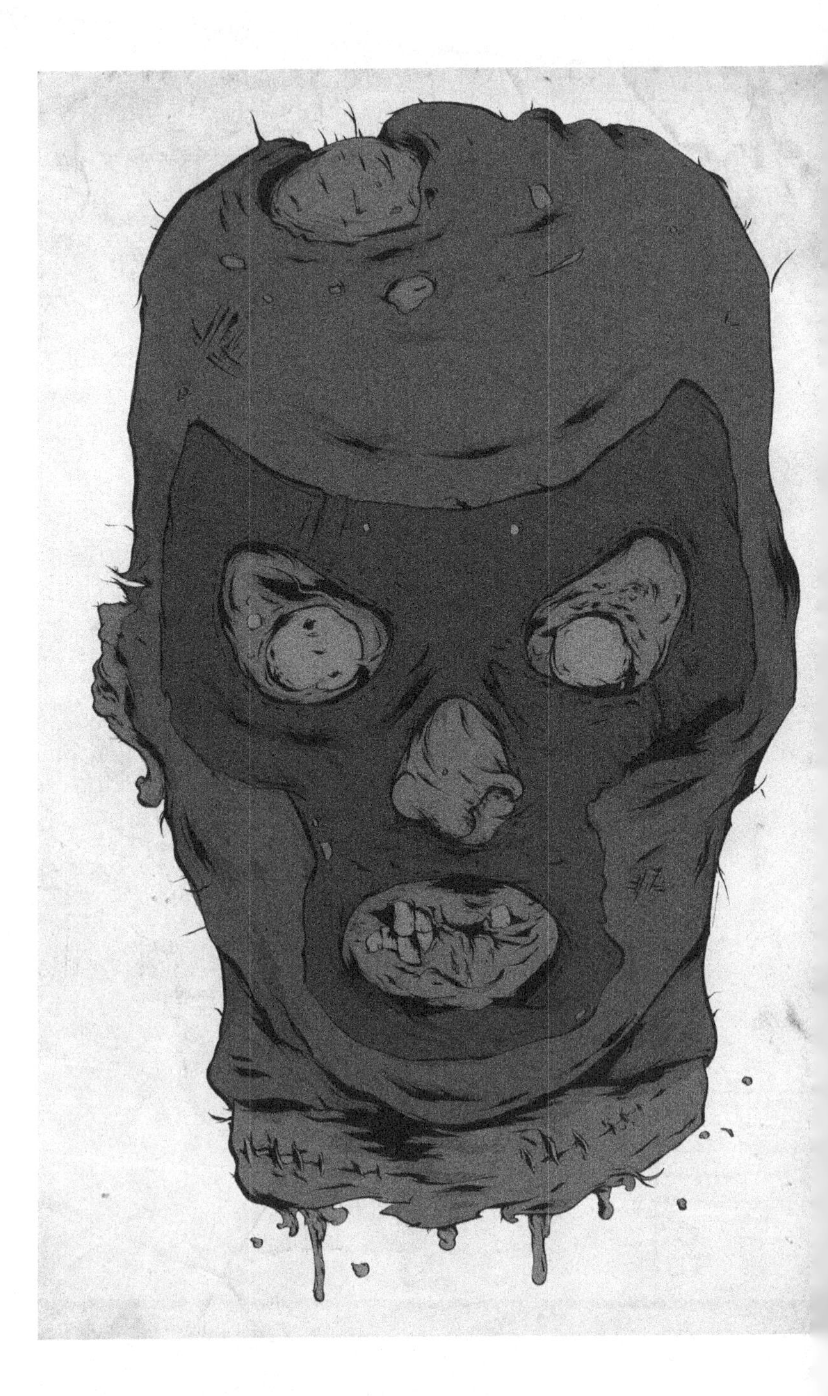

BARBIE VERSUS EL PUMA NEGRO

The second time I saw *el Puma Negro* was outside the American Legion Hall. He'd been dead for nine years, but he still looked the same as the day my dad took me to the *luchas* in Reynosa in 1975. I had wasted most of the matches watching my three-year-old brother Jesse, which sucked: for a teenage girl I was a *major* wrestling fan. I got to see *el Puma Negro* rip the mask off *el Divino*, though. Gnarly.

So you'd think I'd be excited, walking from Rivas Grocery to my parents' and bumping into my childhood idol.

The problem was that *el Puma Negro* had just spent the better part of a decade in the grave. He had suffered a fatal embolism a few months after beating *el Divino*. Half of Mexico had gone into mourning. I'd cried for days.

Which meant that the massive, masked *luchador* standing in the moonlight was either an impostor or a zombie. This being Donna, Texas, and me being Barbie de los Ángeles, elementary teacher and *cihuatzin*—spiritual protector of the Rio Grande Valley—he was *totally* a freaking zombie.

Easing the groceries onto the sidewalk, I called out to the sweat-suit-wearing hulk.

"Hey, *Pumita*, aren't you supposed to be six feet under?"

He grunted and turned away, heading back inside the American Legion Hall. I hurried after him, shouting "Hang on! Where do you think you're going, dead dude?"

As I entered, I noticed several things: a wrestling ring had been set up in the center of the hall, in preparation for some amateur matches I'd seen flyers for; *el Puma Negro* was climbing into the ring, pulling off his windbreaker and jogging pants to reveal his black and silver spandex; and in the far southeast corner of the hall, beside a stack of folding chairs, two men stood watching me. One of them I recognized right away: our mayor Tom Gómez, one of the most corrupt politicians in the Valley. The other was a tall, thin old man gripping a strange stone scepter in his gnarled hands. Whenever he would gesture with it and mutter, the undead wrestler would move differently.

If I take that away, he loses control. I rushed the old sorcerer, my Reeboks pounding against the slick concrete floor. With a snaggle-toothed grin, he lifted a trembling hand and made a weird gesture in the air. A dim silence suddenly cocooned me, filtering sound and light. *Cehualli*, I thought. *This damn* brujo *is trying to use shadow magic on me. Doesn't he know who I am?*

My hand curled around the jade medallion hanging from a silver chain around my neck. It was a very old piece of jewelry, an image of *Tonantzin*, the Great Mother. It's like an amulet for me, helping me to focus all the *teotl* or spiritual energy that the wise women of my town infused me with four years ago, when I agreed to protect my people from the dark forces that had robbed me of the man I loved.

Energy surged within me, and I pushed it outward, sweeping my left hand to counter the attack. But the sorcerer had merely been distracting me. No sooner was my vision clear than I felt thick cold fingers bury themselves in my hair, slamming my head against the lip of the raised platform and then yanking me up over the ropes and into the ring.

After he smashed me against the matting, I crabbed away, my breath knocked out of me. Scrabbling to my feet, I crouched low, rubbing my head and trying to ignore the throbbing pain.

"Do you realize how long it takes me to get my bangs perfect, you creep? Now I really have to kick your ass!"

He shambled toward me, growling. I crouched and leapt, ancient power allowing me to rise high in the air, hurtling toward the zombie in a *tope suicida*. I slammed into his cold flesh, knocking him over and rolling away. His thick fingers twitched, seeking some purchase and finding none; I jumped again, slamming down onto his thick chest with both feet then dropping to my knees, pinning his arms. Looking up, I saw that the old man and the mayor were gone. With a sigh, I regarded *el Puma Negro*.

"I don't know who you are, *pendejo,*" I muttered into those dead eyes, addressing the *brujo* that was controlling him, "but you don't come into *my* town with your grody living dead and stir up trouble."

I reached down the back of my blouse and unsheathed the knife that rested snugly in my special behind-the-back rig. The obsidian glinted in the moonlight. The silver handle seemed to merge with my right hand, an extension of me.

"*Adios, Puma Negro.*" With a sharp slash, I severed his head from his shoulders. There was no blood: the man was dead already. But a fetid stench washed over me, and I retched a bit as I vaulted over the ropes and headed for the back exit. I burst through the door in time to see a Mercury Bobcat speeding away. I memorized the license plate, for all the good it would do me. If crooked politicians were enlisting the help of black magic, the police wouldn't be of much help.

Sighing resignedly, I went back in the building. There lay my hero, broken like a lot of things I had cherished as a child. Climbing back into the ring, I stared at the grey flesh and silvered-piped spandex for a long while. Then I picked up the head. The black mask felt slick in my hands. I was tempted to unmask him, to look on the face of my childhood idol. But he had already been desecrated enough, so I just closed his eyes.

It took me a while to lug his body out back and hide it under the bushes that grew close to the wall. Then I collected my groceries and walked the rest of the way home, trying to understand this new threat. The *brujo* obviously didn't have enough power to attack me directly. But he could apparently animate the dead, so I figured I'd have more zombies to deal with soon enough.

I had no idea *why*, however. Obviously the mayor was involved, but what did he need a sorcerer for? Didn't he already have the whole town eating out of his hand?

I got home long after I'd told my parents to expect me. My mother had figured I was still planning my lesson for the next day, so she'd prepared something different for dinner. My twelve-year-old brother was watching *Family Ties* with my dad, snatching the last thirty minutes before mom's *telenovela* started. In quiet tones, as we put the groceries away, I explained what had happened and my confusion as to the motives of that creep Tom Gómez.

"*Ah, cómo serás niña,*" she muttered, shaking her head at my ignorance. "It's an election year, *m'ija.* And just like Reagan, Tom wants to get re-elected. Problem is, Dr. César Flores just signed up to run against him, and the people really like the doc. They're tired of all the *tranzas* and corruption of Gómez. So I guess he wants to use black magic to influence the outcome. There's just one obstacle."

"Me."

"You. And since you're too strong, *pues*, he goes out and raises your idol from the grave. That way you are affected psychologically and it's easier for him to beat you."

"What a jerk."

She simply nodded, taking off her apron and draping it from the oven handle. "You called Chava?"

I slapped my forehead. "Oh, crap. I forgot."

Grabbing the receiver of the avocado-colored phone hanging beside the refrigerator, I dialed the number.

"Good evening. This is the answering service of Doctor Andrew Rodrigues."

"Hi. I need to leave him a message. My dog is really sick and won't come out from under the bushes behind the American Legion Hall. I need him to help me get … uh … *Bandit* out from there and do something for him."

"Your name?"

"Magdalena Márez," I replied, giving my secret handle. Salvador "Chava" Cervantes had worked out this system with the council of wise women when they'd hired him to dispose of the evidence of supernatural attacks. We only had a few each year, but it was really nice for someone else to clean up the mess I left every time I fought some nasty ghoul or *cucuy*. I hung up and showered. By the time I padded back into the kitchen wearing warm-ups and an oversized sweatshirt, the phone was ringing. It was Salvador.

"Ain't nothing there, Barbie."

"Huh? I left a decapitated zombie for you, Chava. A big dude, in spandex."

"Well, either someone else carted him off, or your zombie got up and walked off. Sorry."

The line went dead and I scratched my scalp through my wet hair. I'd never fought a zombie before, though they were on the list of creatures previous women in my position had faced. I couldn't remember whether beheading was enough. My head swam.

"I called them when you were in the shower." My mom walked in and pulled a plate of *carne guisada* from the oven, setting it on the table for me. "They want you to meet with them tomorrow evening."

I knew she meant the local *cofradía de tenanches,* the council of wise old women. "At Doña Licha's house?"

"Yes. They said not to eat dinner."

Ironically I sat down and began forking chunks of stewed beef into a flour tortilla. "Really? Are they going to bring tamales or something?"

My mother frowned at me. "No. I'm sure it's a ritual thing. They need you pure, maybe."

Bummer. Doña Licha's tamales are, like, totally. Yeah.

The next morning my curling iron was on the fritz and I just could *not* get my bangs teased right, no matter how much hairspray I used. *Oh, well. It's not like fifth-graders are going to care,* I thought, though some of the girls would probably have better 'dos than me. *And really, since Johnny died, who have I been doing this for?* Depressed at the thought, I applied more base to hide the bruise on my temple.

I walked to Stainke Elementary, arriving in my classroom at 7:30 a.m. The day was like any other. We did reading, social studies and music in the morning (I always left the boring stuff for the afternoon, like math and science), and then we had lunch. Once my group had eaten, I took them outside for recess, happy to have a little breather from the kids. I leaned against a mesquite and watched a group of girls skip rope, chanting in Spanish. Not far away, some boys went swinging their way across a jungle gym. And there, beyond them, standing on the sidewalk of Hester Avenue …

It was him. *El Puma Negro.* Someone had sewn his head back on, and the ragged black stitching around his neck made him resemble a masked Frankenstein's monster. He took a shambling step toward the children.

"No." My voice was rough with terror and rage. I came off the mesquite trunk with a start. "*No.* Boys and girls!" I shouted. Several of my colleagues turned toward me. "Everyone inside. *Now*! Move it!"

The other teachers blinked in confusion for a second until they saw me start running toward the hulking figure. Then they, too, began to shout, herding the kids indoors. I slammed into the zombie wrestler with all my force, spinning him around. I kept running, glancing over my shoulder to make sure he was in pursuit. His shambling jog would have been laughable were I not so freaking pissed. *How dare they? A damn* school*! Children!*

El Puma Negro was going down. So was his *pinche brujo* master.

An abandoned cannery sprawled near the train tracks just two blocks away—a relic of my town's former economic heyday. I ducked inside, kicking through the rusted chain that held corroded doors shut. I quickly looked around in the dusty gloom and saw what I wanted: a large, round disk of spotted tin, its edge jagged and deadly. When el Puma Negro stumbled in, I swung it with all my magic-enhanced might and sliced right through his sewn-up, grody neck.

"Bag your face, *cabrón*," I snarled as his masked head tumbled to the ground and I kicked it into a vat of some nasty-smelling black liquid. The dead wrestler's body collapsed heavily, and I dragged him into a moldy office. *Got to get back. No time for this. Can't afford a bunch of questions.*

I returned to Stainke Elementary and spun a totally Oscar-winning story about wanting to keep the kids safe and drawing the weird hobo toward the train tracks just beyond the old cannery. The police officers who had arrived in response to the principal's frantic call hurried in that direction to investigate. It took a while to get the kids sorted, but after a couple of cookies, they were more or less manageable.

I, on the other hand, had a hard time being a cheerful dispenser of bitchin' education. But most of my life is about pretending. I pretend to be a well-adjusted single twenty-four-year-old who chooses not to date, when in reality I can't bear the thought of loving anyone other than Johnny. I pretend to be a mild-mannered, righteously cool teacher, when in reality I'm a violent, knife-wielding kicker of supernatural ass.

Sometimes that two-facedness really worries me. But my people need me to be fake, so I am. It's the price I'm willing to pay for their peace.

School wrapped up. I tutored some of the recent immigrant kids, helping them to hone their English skills. I made sure my emergency lesson plans were ready to go in case the loser *brujo* got the drop on me and I needed a sub tomorrow. Then I went home, showered, didn't eat, and walked down Silver Avenue to the fuchsia and blue house where Doña Licha lived at the center of a half-acre lot. It was late autumn, so the sun had already begun to set, highlighting the modest home in dying, golden light.

Right across the street sprawled our city cemetery, resting place of hundreds of deceased Donneños. Including Johnny, God rest his soul.

Clearly this is the perfect place for this meeting, I thought snarkily, trying to distract myself from the empty loss yawning open like a chasm within me. *The old ladies can be so weird sometimes.*

The door opened before I could knock. Sister Consuelo Cruz, a wizened old nun with vast knowledge of supernatural beasts, smiled at me and led me to the living room, where the other thirteen women had spread themselves out as best they could in the cramped space. I nodded with respect at the wisdom around me, from the owner of the hierbería to a retired high school counselor, teachers and grandmothers and healers, all of them over fifty, all of them loving, strong-willed and tireless.

Doña Licha, her hair severe, her hazel eyes kind, smoothed her flower-pattern shift and spoke. "Daughter, *cihuatzín*, protector … welcome. Your mother Lupita has told us of the *brujo* and his undead servant. Sister Consuelo and I consulted the lore and realized that this man is wielding a *k'awiil* scepter, a powerful tool used by some ancient Mayan kings. Though the scepter is meant to promote the health and happiness of a kingdom, it can be bent by dark minds to more sinister purposes."

"Like raising the dead and controlling them," I said, swallowing hard.

"*Así es.* The only way to stop this *brujo* is either to take the scepter from him or to shatter it. But it will be difficult to approach him. He cannot control you directly, but he can control people and animals around you, and he can bombard you with the silent darkness of *cehualli* to keep you off balance."

I tightened my hands into fists. "I get it. So how am I supposed to snatch his little stone stick from him?"

Sister Consuelo reached behind the sofa and pulled out a strange, curved sword, rusted except for the edge, which I could see had been recently sharpened. The weapon was obviously very old.

"This is a *falcata,*" the nun explained, "an iron sword made by the ancient Iberians long before Rome conquered the peninsula." She lifted it toward me, and I accepted it. The hilt was strange, carved like a feathered dragon that curled in on itself, protecting the wielder's fingers. "The 'zombie' you've been facing is a *micqui*, a sort of animated corpse that once plagued southern Mexico. While a sorcerer controls them, they are very difficult to destroy. One of the surest ways is with an iron blade, as some lucky Spaniards discovered centuries ago."

"Thanks," I said, making a few tentative thrusts and parries.

Doña Blanca Alba, the *santera* who owned the *hierbería*, stood and approached me, her eyes lowered in a respect that I could never get used to. In her hands was a *molcajete* full of thick, black goo that smelled slightly like mildew. She extended the basalt mortar to me, and I took it with my left hand, thinking briefly about pleasant times in Mom's kitchen, making salsas in just such a stone bowl.

"This is *teotlacualli*, spirit food. It'll make you temporarily much more powerful. The *teotl* magic you wield can increase like ten times with that small amount."

I sniffed at it again. "I've got to eat this stuff? Really? What's in it? Smells pretty gross."

Even if Doña Blanca had been willing to share her secrets with me, she didn't get a chance. A sound of shattering glass made my head snap around. A figure had leapt through the living room window: it was the goddamn wrestler again, his head sewn back on and covered with oil.

"Fantastic. You are so *totally* not on my top ten list anymore, dude." Pinching my nose closed, I brought the *molcajete* to my lips and slurped up the spirit food. "Oh, my God," I gasped after forcing it down. "Gag me with a freaking spoon!"

In seconds, though, my whole body was thrumming with power. The *tenanches* had slowly backed away into the kitchen and bedrooms, warding off the zombie with crosses and spells and such. Dropping the stone mortar and sword, I stepped up to *el Puma Negro* eagerly, grabbing him by the thigh and shoulder and lifting him over my head with very little effort. I hurled him back out the window. Scooping up the *falcata*, I followed, leaping over the jagged shards. He struggled to his knees, but I ran and drop-kicked him in the chest with all the magical force I could muster.

He exploded. Body parts went flying everywhere. Bits of spandex floated down to the ground as I twitched like a junky, scanning the street for signs of the *brujo*. I tightened my grip on the iron sword. It felt oddly warm, as if eager to slay the undead once more.

From behind me came the shuffling sounds of an approaching zombie.

"Hey … babe." Though the voice was grating and muffled, I recognized it immediately.

Oh, that son of a bitch wizard is going to pay for this with his life.

I slowly turned. Standing before me, dressed in the tuxedo he was supposed to have worn to our wedding, his head dented and misshapen despite the mortician's best efforts, stood my dead boyfriend, Johnny Garza.

"I … miss … you," the zombie drawled. Its face twisted into a horrible smile.

I can't … I can't face this. A demon-possessed psychopath had murdered my fiancé on the very day he was supposed to pick up our marriage license. The madman had gutted him and chopped off his head. He had nearly killed me, too. I had learned a lot about myself that horrible night. I was stronger than I could ever have imagined.

But I wasn't strong enough to do this. I faltered. The *micqui* took a staggering step toward me. Then another. I felt all desire to live slipping away. Darkness enfolded me: still, eternal black. Rest. I could rest forever. Let them defend themselves. I was sick with loss and regret.

But as Johnny's arms went about me and the world went dim, I saw him. The *brujo*. Standing just a few yards away, near the stop sign. He was gripping his white stone scepter and mumbling, his eyes half closed.

No, you bastard. I clenched my heart against the onslaught. I sought out the coursing warmth of the *teotlacualli*, thrumming through my soul. My left hand clutched at the jade medallion. And the *tenanches'* voices, harmonizing with an even older whisper, echoed through every fiber of my being.

Rise, daughter, woman among women, cihuatzin *who protects her people. Because of you the children sleep in peace. Because of you mothers do not weep. Rise, angel and guardian. Rise!*

With a shuddering sob that became a shout, I swept aside the darkness and swung the iron blade through the air, beheading my poor Johnny once again. His body crumbled into dust, and I rushed though the powdery cloud to pursue the sorcerer, who jerked into movement as he saw me coming at him. Stumbling with fear, he hurried across the street into the cemetery. The sun was nearly gone from the sky, and the shadows of the tombstones stretched east into the encroaching night.

The *brujo* gestured with the scepter and graves burst open. I barreled through the onslaught of undead with single-minded fury, hacking *micqui* after *micqui* into ribbons of dust that twisted in the wind. In moments I had reached him. He turned to make a stand, slashing at me with the axe-shaped scepter. I ducked under his inexpert blow and rammed the sword into his abdomen, angling the curved blade up to pierce his black heart.

"That's for Johnny, *hijo de la chingada.*"

He dropped to his knees, blood bubbling from his lips. I reached my hand behind me and down my shirt to unsheathe the obsidian blade. He lifted his scepter weakly, like a bug that twitches in the moments before it dies.

"And this is for *el Puma Negro.*" With a *teotl*-powered slash, I shattered the ancient device into thousands of stone shards. The light faltered in the sorcerer's eyes.

"Guess your boy isn't winning the election this year, huh?" I spat.

He gasped his last and dropped dead to the ground.

The wise old women were waiting for me when I crossed the street back to Doña Licha's house. They gave me *té de tila*, and the linden flower tea settled my stomach to the point that I could eat some of Licha's famous tamales. The *falcata* was put away, the window was covered with plastic, and the *tenanches* hovered over me, muttering kind words and prayers, anointing me with herbs and oils. After a while, I felt more or less myself again.

"What about the mayor? What about the election?"

They *tsk*ed my questions away. Those were matters for the men, who foolishly thought that politics and money controlled the world. We had kept the community safe from the darkness. Let the children and men play their games safely, unknowingly.

It fell to me to call Chava and enlist his help in the clean up. His reaction to the shattered coffins and ejected dirt was classic. He just shrugged and started shoveling.

We worked far into the night. I helped clean Doña Licha's front yard, scooping up bone fragments and dropping them into a bag. It seemed I was done when by chance I looked up at the branches of the mesquite tree that shades Licha's home. Caught on a limb was the mask of *el Puma Negro*, somehow intact despite everything. I clambered up and retrieved it, leaning against the bough as I examined it in the moonlight.

"Goodbye," I whispered. The tears came then, and I rocked myself silently beneath the glittering stars that stand out so beautifully against the deep velvet robe of the Goddess, who protects the protectors throughout the long night.

DARK GRIMOIRE

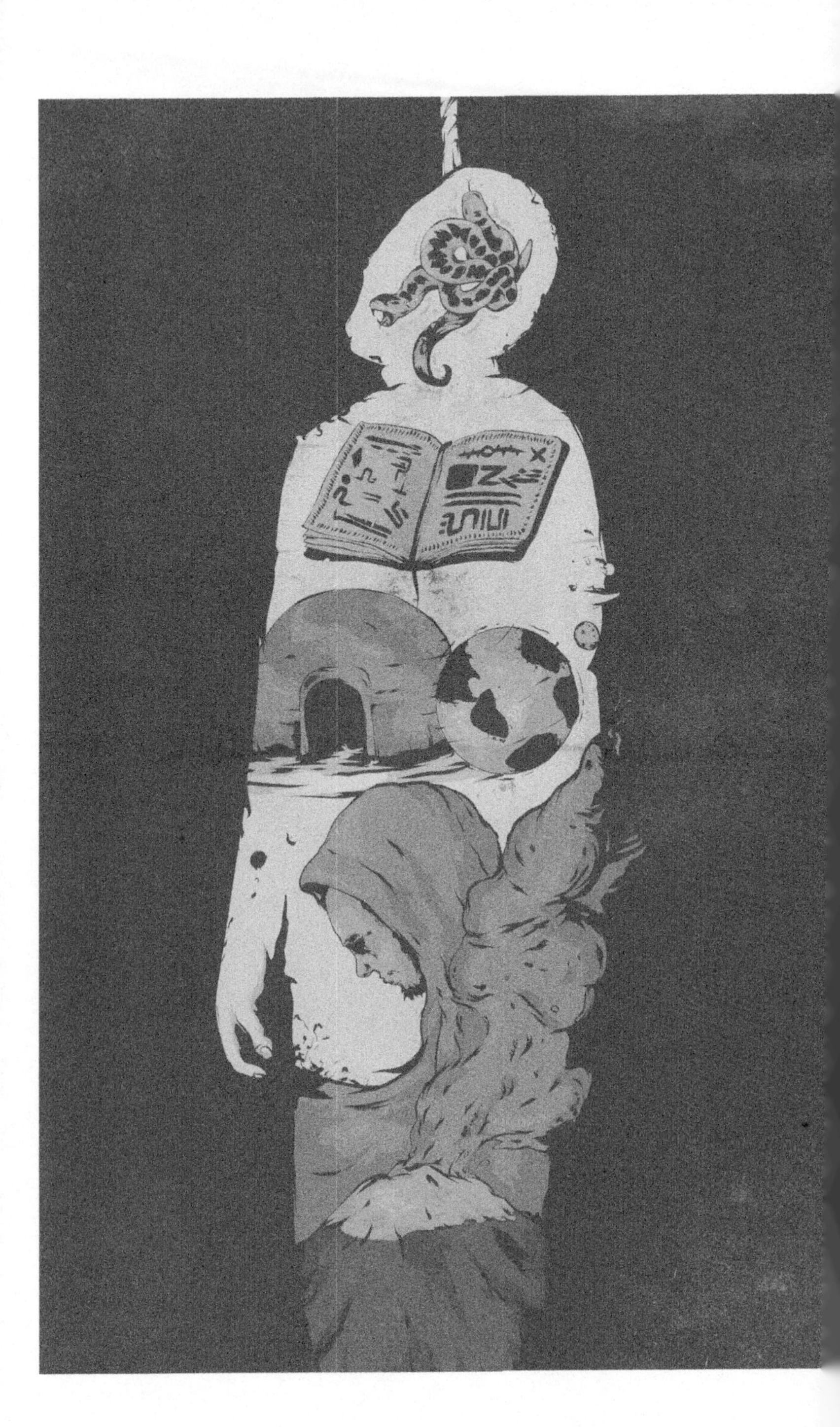

THE OBSIDIAN CODEX

1

The package arrived two weeks after I had laid the last of my loved ones to rest in the stony soil of the Mexican Plateau.

The burial was a small affair. "May her soul and the souls of all the faithful departed through the mercy of God rest in peace," the parish priest murmured in Spanish, concluding the mass that had been intoned solemnly in the San José Chapel, suspended for the night-long wake, and then continued when our meager procession made its way to the cemetery, a trio of altar boys singing "In Paradisum" in Latin.

As the coffin was lowered into freshly spaded earth, I looked around at the handful of friends, mourners and family members present. Martha Ochoa de Kerr had been something of a recluse in her later years: as the young girl who had married an older archaeologist from America and gone gallivanting across Mexico with him, my paternal grandmother had long been ostracized by her family, despite having become a reputable cardiologist. The decade she had spent back in her native Tepoztlán since her husband's passing had done nothing to seal that rift, nor had the old woman made attempts to connect with anyone beyond a scattering of cherished friends.

I accepted with a perfunctory and bereft smile the final condolences of those in attendance, eager for them all to leave. There were just two days before my flight, and I longed to explore what I could of the town, fabled birthplace of divine Quetzalcoatl's human incarnation. As much as I had loved the old woman, my heart had been wrung dry of grief for years, and I had learned it best to keep my mind busy with research and discovery, the most effective weapons for staving off despair.

Soon I had picked my way through the tombstones, crypts and mausoleums that gleamed ghastly white in the morning sun, like the partially disinterred bones of some antediluvian beast. I took a bus to the broad square of the zócalo, wandered through the gorgeous colonial arches of the former Convent of Our Lady of the Nativity, explored the four stone chapels standing at each corner of the parish courtyard, and struggled to converse with older indigenes whose modern Nahuatl was markedly different from the classical language of the Aztecs, the source of my academic reputation among fellow linguists.

The real delight came the following day, September eighth, when a procession set out from the town toward the nearby hill of Tepozteco, site of a pyramid erected by the Aztec Triple Alliance sometime in the late fifteenth century CE in honor of Tepoztecatl, god of drink and wind and fertility, beloved son of Quetzalcoatl. Once arrived at the site, locals put on a mystery play in Nahuatl that recounted how the human ruler of the town at the time of the Conquest, an avatar of Tepoztecatl himself, had overcome monstrous and monomythic obstacles to lead his people to Catholicism, which he had proclaimed perfectly compatible with their mores and traditions.

Intrigued by this syncretic ceremony, I relished the more archaic dialect, recording the entire performance for later transcription and translation. Then I spent some time exploring the ruins so beloved of my late grandfather before taking the bus to Mexico City in time to catch my flight back to Texas.

Two weeks later I was grading a stack of egregiously documented graduate research papers in my Austin home when a knock came at the door. I glimpsed a brown truck parked in the street as I went to answer. The uniformed delivery man on my porch gave a slight nod, his rugged, handsome features crinkling a bit.

"Dr. Robert Kerr?"

"Yes, that's me."

"Delivery from Morelos, Mexico. Can you sign here?"

I took his battered electronic device and scrawled my name with the dangling stylus. As I handed it back, he turned over a small package bound in brown paper and twine. Its dimensions and heft suggested two or three small books. Thanking the man, I went back inside, closing the door with my foot and heading to my office.

Dropping into my leather chair, I regarded the package. The return address was in Cuernavaca, the capital city of Morelos, not far from Tepoztlán. There was no name, so I quickly searched online and found that this was the site of the Monasterio de Nuestra Señora de los Ángeles, founded some fifty years ago in the Ajusco Mountains on the outskirts of the city proper.

Setting aside the mystery of its sender, I proceeded to open the package. Inside were two leather-bound volumes in which notes in a flowing cursive script were broken here and there by ink sketches or watercolor renderings of ancient structures, artwork and glyphs.

I recognized the handwriting. I knew it well.

These were my grandfather's missing journals.

2

Nelson Kerr was one of the most respected archaeologists of the twentieth century, a man whose groundbreaking work alongside colleagues Dibble and Anderson would define the study of Mesoamerica for more than five decades. In 1925, after graduating with degrees in history and Romance languages from the University of Texas in Austin, he traveled to Mexico for a time, investigating the roots of his own grandmother's *criollo* family. He was soon drawn to the rich indigenous culture, submerged though it was in European dross, so he remained, enrolling at the Universidad Nacional Autónoma de México in Mexico City and receiving a Master's degree in archaeology in 1928.

Grandfather came home to Austin to teach at his alma mater for a time, but he soon returned to Mexico to pursue a doctorate, which he completed in 1934. Ten years later, he shocked academics everywhere by marrying a girl of eighteen summers from a small town in Morelos. Their son Gregorio was born within eleven months, and he would go on to study Nahuatl under the great Ángel María Garibay Kintana, passing on a love for that language to his son Robert.

Me.

We were a tight-knit family, with ups and downs, certainly, but sharing a passion for history and language that kept us all engaged and excited at each other's company.

Shuttling back and forth over the decades between Austin and Mexico City, we were bicultural and binational, but more than anything, we belonged to the intellectual world of academic pursuits, largely unconcerned with the rapid twists and turns of modern life, preferring the steady ebb and flow of historical and linguistic investigation.

Grandfather was nearly a hundred years old when he died, but he was remarkably spry puttering about in the garden with his wife and keeping up on the latest work by Mesoamericanists. When the strokes came, one after another, I rushed to the hospital to be by his side, gripping a gnarly old hand and searching for the light in his dimming eyes.

"Secret journals," he rasped to me as the dark swirled his mind shut at last. "Find them. Keep them safe."

After his funeral, I asked my grandmother about his papers, but she swore most of them had been turned over to the university and gave me full access to what remained in their home. I found little that he hadn't already published during his long and stellar career, and certainly nothing that needed safekeeping.

Once that search had fizzled out, his death finally hit me, hard. Yet I would have probably been fine had it not been for the accident that claimed the life of my mother and father just six weeks after his passing. I was an only child like my mother, and my father's sister had succumbed to polio before adolescence. Beyond the estranged members of my grandmother's clan in Tepoztlán and my two sons, I was essentially bereft of family.

Perhaps in answer to the pain that gnawed at my heart, I plunged into a massive project: a new translation of the Florentine Codex, with a normative transcription of the

Nahuatl and an ample concordance. The work devoured every moment of my free time, one of many reasons my wife cited when she left me, taking the boys and moving to Maine, the land of her pedigreed ancestors.

Devastated at the distance between my sons and me, I immersed myself even more deeply in my work. Yet, though teaching and translating consumed me, there were other hungers that surfaced from time to time. A need for companionship. The urge to feel another's warm flesh against mine.

So had begun a string of affairs, mostly with research assistants. I discovered to my astonishment that I was attracted both to males and females, and I encouraged the attentions of gruff young men as often as those of the fairer sex.

But my heart I kept sealed away. Summers were for my sons, a lovely season in which I tried to recapture the bliss of my own youth, the joy of moments spent at the side of my father and grandfather. My boys, however, withdrew from me emotionally as they entered adolescence, following the lead of their new stepfather, a typical sports-loving, conservative man of some means who married my ex-wife not long after our divorce was final.

So it was that my grandmother's passing had left me nearly unmoored from family connections of any real weight, adrift in sargassoes of souring solitude.

To hold my grandfather's most hidden, private thoughts in my hands filled me with a sense of profound happiness tempered only slightly by intrigue and wonder.

What were his secrets? Who had hidden them? Why had they turned them over to me now, precisely?

I began to read.

3

The first entry was dated some seventy years previous. Nelson Kerr, deep in research for his dissertation, found himself poring over a treasure trove of new documents from the sixteenth century discovered in an abandoned monastery. He became intrigued by a passage in a letter to an abbot from Bernardino de Sahagún in which the Franciscan priest mentioned what he called *El libro de obsidiana* or *The Book of Obsidian*, insisting that this indigenous text was dangerous and must be burned, despite his own desire to preserve as much of the history and language of the Aztecs as possible.

My grandfather started scouring every scrap of Conquest-era writing for additional mentions of this mysterious codex. For seven years his normal work was punctuated by his new obsession. Finally, he managed to track down the diary of Father Rodrigo Alcina, who had drawn reproductions of some of the pages in the codex, including one showing the destruction of earth, a man standing at the center of this apocalypse with a speech curl twisting from his mouth. The priest noted the name of act performed: *in tlālpoloa xōxtli*, which he glossed "rito de aniquilación." Rite of Annihilation. Alcina affirmed that the codex had been destroyed by Juan de Torquemada, who had discovered it during his wide-ranging research into the details of the Conquest and the history of the conquered.

Devastated by the dead end, Nelson Kerr was nonetheless determined to discover the source of the codex. At the very least, he hoped to learn more details concerning its contents. If luck were on his side, he might even unearth another copy of the pre-Colombian pictorial text.

Three more years of study yielded a clue: a marginal Latin gloss in an obscure collection of Indochristian hymns in Nahuatl that warned darkly against "librum nefandum ex urbe Tepuçtlan." The abominable book from the city of Tepoztlán.

Needless to say, my grandfather wasted no time in catching a bus.

4

May 25, 1944—I had always assumed that Redfield was glossing over the darker aspects of Tepoztlán in his 1930 study, but I have been quite honestly taken aback at the hostility and suspicion with which my questions and entreaties have been met in this town.

I have spent most of the past week fruitlessly inquiring of various elders, church leaders and municipal functionaries whether any knowledge has been preserved locally concerning the Obsidian Codex, *its origin, its authorship, and the possibility of its continued existence.*

Most of the time, I have been left gawking in confused silence as my interlocutors simply stand and leave. Occasionally, threats or summary dismissals have been my reward.

Today, however, I have experienced a breakthrough. Oscar Lewis, who teaches anthropology at Brooklyn College, has just arrived in town. He apparently spent some time here last year, laying the groundwork for an in-depth study of the community that will more fully round the profile Redfield produced a decade and a half ago.

Fascinated by the general thrust of my own research, Lewis has kindly introduced me to certain contacts of his. My credentials thus being confirmed by someone in whom they trust, these individuals promised to aid me, affirming their knowledge of a man who likely has information of value to my investigation.

May 29, 1944—Yesterday, I was taken to an aging shaman named Don Félix. In halting Nahuatl (for the man knows little Spanish), I explained my quest.

"Ah, yes. I imagined that someday an outsider would come searching for just such a thing. And even in this small town we hear of the hunger for destruction that gnaws at the bellies of Europeans and Americans. There is little I can tell you, stranger. But know this: the ancient stories say that when Quetzalcoatl was preparing to leave this world, he entrusted his most dangerous lore to a secret society. Though this knowledge was to be passed orally from adept to acolyte down the years, the cabal painted a pictographic folding book to serve as a memory aid, a document that they knew must be kept from prying eyes. As a result, they became known as in ītēpixcāuh itzāmoxtli*—the Keepers of the Obsidian Codex."*

"Does this cabal still exist?" I pressed.

"Perhaps," he muttered, exhaustion visibly pulling on his ancient flesh. "I know not, stranger. The scant words I have shared with you were spoken to me when I was very young. I have never pursued the knowledge you seek, and I urge you to turn away from this path. The Keepers, if they are still among us, have kept their lore locked away for more than a thousand years. I can only assume that it is destructive enough to warrant such secrecy."

He dismissed me with an innervated wave of the hand.

The next day, I learned he had died in his sleep.

June 3, 1944—I have met the most incredible, loveliest girl. I went to the fountain just after dawn to retrieve some of the delicious, stone-cooled water. I drew up short at the foot of the steps, however, when I saw her: an elegant ichpōcatl *or maiden of some eighteen years, lifting her clay jar to her shoulder. Ah, what lustrous black hair, honey wheat eyes that glittered with intelligence, a wide mouth accustomed to laughter and conversation, soft curves that seemed to call out to my hands.*

Respectfully, but with confidence, I introduced myself to her and learned from her guarded responses that her name is Martha Ochoa Ortiz, daughter of one of the eight ayudantes *or representatives of municipal districts that serve in the* ayuntamiento *or city government. A few more questions revealed that I had guessed her age correctly and that she just finished her schooling, one of the few females in the town to continue her studies beyond the age of fifteen. She was well spoken and remarkably poised.*

Understanding the treacherous waters I was dipping into, but driven nonetheless by emotions I had almost despaired of ever feeling, I asked whether I might write her. After a long pause that nearly stopped my heart, Martha agreed, naming an older shopkeeper who could serve as an intermediary for the time being so as not to enrage her parents.

Though nearing my fourth decade of life, I find myself grinning and humming romantic songs like a love-struck adolescent boy.

She changes everything.

5

Of course, I knew the rest of that story well. My grandfather had told it and retold it to me on countless occasions, how their courtship had grown more and more passionate, how Martha's father had learned of his daughter's love for a foreign professor twice her age, how the town had turned on the couple, forcing them to finally elope, as many men and women had done in Tepoztlán down the centuries.

But they had never returned. The following year my father was born, but Nelson Kerr vowed not to force his wife into a traditional female role. He encouraged her to continue her studies as soon as the child could be cared for by a nanny, and Martha Ochoa de Kerr embarked on her medical career just after her twenty-first birthday.

There was a lapse of nearly a decade in the journal, during which my grandfather was slavishly dedicated to his wife, son and chairmanship of his department.

Then, as if destiny itself were warping the world to draw him closer to its darkest secrets, Nelson Kerr stumbled across a letter dated February 21, 1812, sent from priest and revolutionary general José María Morelos to Miguel Hidalgo y Costilla, leader of the Mexican insurgency against Spain. In the midst of his discussion of the siege of the city of Cuautla, Morelos warned he had discovered "possible infiltration of one or more monastic orders on the slopes of Popocatepetl by an order of pagan priests known as *los Guardianes*."

The Keepers.

The journal then went on to document the sporadic visits by my grandfather to the fourteen monasteries built by Franciscan, Dominican and Augustinian orders just after the Conquest, sprawling masterpieces of architecture whose broad open-air atria were designed to make indigenous converts more comfortable with the imposing symbols of the new religion. With the pretext of archaeological study, he scoured their archives and interviewed the monks, finding little other than the most tenuous of hints.

A breakthrough came when Nelson learned that four monks were leaving one of the Franciscan monasteries at the urging of Father Alcuin Heibel, an American priest who had been petitioning Rome for decades to establish a Benedictine priory in Mexico. Now, with the support of the Mount Angel Abbey in Oregon, Heibel's dream of outreach would become a reality, and the order-switching monks had already moved to Cuernavaca to help navigate the initial bureaucratic red-tape.

Each of the four monks was from Tepoztlán. A little digging revealed they were all related. More promising was the fact members of that family had served in the same monastery for a hundred and fifty years.

Cornering the youngest of the group, Nelson Kerr laid out his evidence and insisted he be told the truth before he went to Church leaders and revealed the cabal's existence.

The monk agreed to recite the *Obsidian Codex.*

6

There the first volume ended. Though eager to delve into the second, I stood, rubbed my eyes, and went to the kitchen to prepare myself a meal and a pot of coffee. I suspected I would be working well into the small hours of the night, and I needed to keep myself energized and sharp.

The eaves of my home creaked as an unseasonably chilly front worked its way into the Hill Country of Texas. From my dining table I watched the sun set in a strange purple and yellow miasma, like a festering bruise on the western horizon. A sense of unease frittered along my nerves as I sipped my coffee. If the Keepers had become part of the priory in Cuernavaca that meant the cabal itself had sent me my grandfather's journals. But why? And how had they gotten their hands on the two volumes? Had he turned his notes over to the Keepers? Had they acquired them through other means?

I shrugged off those questions, buoyed by the excitement of exploring unknown nooks and crannies of Mesoamerican lore. Returning to my study, I cracked open the second book. The first entry was dated June 6, 1964, and Nelson reported meeting with Brother Fausto Quevedo, whose recitation of the ancient learning he recorded using a portable reel-to-reel.

Setting aside the question of where those tapes might now be, I perused the transcription, presumably made at some later date when my grandfather could take his time listening to and pausing the recording.

There were five sections: *tētlachīhuiliztli* (incantations), īmmōtzalōca (invocations), *teōcuīcatl* (hymns), *tlateōmatiliztli* (rites) and īntlahtōl *in tlaciuhqueh* (words of the prophets). At first blush, it seemed clear that all the material concerned, invoked or drew upon the power of the darkest elements of Aztec religion. Songs of dark import praised the *Huēhuehtēteoh* or Great Old Ones, godlike beings from the dawn of time, the females of which ancient race were named Tzitzimimeh—those who devour stars. The mightiest of the Great Old Ones was Tezcatlipoca, a creature of chaos who held humanity in utter contempt. His worshippers begged him for the destruction of this age, using epithets like Enemy of Both Sides, Our Enslaver, Night Wind, Lord of the Near and the Nigh.

Some ten thousand words were dedicated to glorifying the cyclopean, indifferent puissance of the Great Old Ones, gods whose names were both familiar—Cihuacoatl, Coatlicue, Itzpapalotl—and some altogether unknown to me: Quetzollo, Aztol, Catanotoa. There were weird spells for drawing on their slumbering power, unholy rituals to keep them dreaming deep, and prophecies about their final, apocalyptic awakening.

The ancient words—fraught with existential bleakness, heavy with hellish lore not meant for the eyes of men—wormed deep into the bereft passageways of my soul. I could not believe the cosmic truths they revealed: my rational, methodical mind refused even to consider the possibility. Yet at a fundamental level, my being responded with horrified, transformative fascination. I read on and on, transfixed not only as a linguist, but almost as a willing acolyte.

The gist of the codex was that an adept of chaos would at some point in the future speak aloud the terrible incantation of which Father Rodrigo Alcina had made mention: *in tlālpoloa xōxtli*, the Rite of Annihilation, more accurately translated "the magic that destroys the earth." At that point, the Tzitzimimeh would rip open the heavens, and the Great Old Ones would awaken to devour everything.

My palms ached with unaccountable dread as I turned to the page my grandfather had labeled *compolōz tlālticpactli*: "this will put an end to the things of this world." But my anxiety crumbled into confusion when I ran my eyes across Nelson Kerr's angular script.

It was gibberish.

The following afternoon I called Santiago Taboada, a graduate student who had worked as my research assistant for nearly a year.

"Hey, Chano, can you come over?"

There was a moment of silence, then he cleared his throat softly. "I thought you said we were going to start keeping it professional, Robert."

"We are, trust me. But I have a linguistic puzzle I need help on, something unpublished that you'll be excited to see."

Another pregnant pause ensued. Even over the phone, however, I could feel his characteristic curiosity quickening.

"All right, color me intrigued. Be over in a bit."

In less than an hour he stood over my desk, adjusting the lamp to better read the small-lettered, careful script. As he bent his face closer, I could not help but admire the clean lines of his form, a swimmer's broad shoulders and long torso moving smoothly beneath his non-descript t-shirt, narrowing with maddening precision to that slender waist. The loose, tattered jeans he had thrown on did not obscure his physical perfection; instead, they hung on his flesh in ways that made my chest ache.

Taking a deep breath, I forced my focus back on the codex.

"Well? Your thoughts?"

Santiago tapped a finger on the Rite of Annihilation. "First off, Robert, unless you find the tapes, you're going to have a hard time convincing people this isn't a hoax. I mean, there's plenty of overlap with the established canon of religious texts and songs, but some of this stuff is flat-out nuts and unprecedented."

"I understand that, of course. A cabal purportedly protecting secret knowledge for the better part of a millennium is not going to be in-line with the state-sponsored religion, Chano. But what about the *in tlālpoloa xōxtli*? What do you make of it?"

"It's pretty clearly encoded. I see in the margins and at the end of the text that your grandfather made some initial attempts at deciphering the thing, but he gave up pretty easily. I'm guessing you don't want to take this to a cryptographer, huh?"

"No, definitely not. We're going to publish at some point, Chano, but I don't want anyone else getting wind of this before we fact-check and find the tapes. Let's try to break the cipher ourselves first before asking people to help."

Santiago looked at me with careful deliberation, dark brow impassive over eyes that glittered like volcanic glass. "You're going to give me co-author credit on this publication?"

"Of course I am. If this text is genuine, if we can establish its authenticity with the tools of archaeology and linguistics, it will be a game-changer for the study of Mesoamerica. So I need you to scan the pages in question and get to work."

I knew him well, understood the hunger for excellence and renown that drove him. He was hooked. In minutes he had used my printer to send himself images from the journals, and after an awkward, lingering handshake, he was out the door.

Two days later I was preparing a PowerPoint for an undergraduate class when my phone started vibrating. It was Santiago. He got right to the point.

"Figured it out. You at home?"

"Yeah."

"In my car. Be there in a couple."

He pushed past me through the door when he arrived, restless with exhilaration and nervous energy, his mahogany curls unruly on his head as he nodded with excitement.

"It was all that background stuff on the Keepers that clued me in," he said between breaths as we walked back to my study. "Your grandfather said that they claimed to have received their lore directly from the god Quetzalcoatl before he left the physical plane."

"And they committed his words to memory, using a pictographic codex to aid in transmission of the dangerous knowledge."

"Got it. So, according to legend, the human incarnation of Quetzalcoatl, the Toltec prince Ce Acatl, was born on the day 1 Reed—hence his name—which also happened to be the first day of the year according to the solar calendar. And it of course has 365 days that are named using the 260-day ritual calendar, with its twenty 'months' of thirteen days. Its *trecenas*. Every fifty-two years the two calendars line up again."

"Right. That's how long it would take for Ce Acatl's birthday to fall on the first day of the year again—and don't the legends say he died on his fifty-second birthday?"

"Yes, by self-immolation. And that's what got me really thinking. If he had lived one more year, the days of his last year would all line up with his first. But he didn't, and the Keepers know that."

Santiago's excitement was palpable and contagious, like an electrical current flowing between us, the very same hungry energy that had brought us crashing passionately into each other six months ago.

"You mean they used that to encode the incantation?"

"Yes. Twenty *trecenas*, each corresponding to a different Nahuatl sound."

I could see the answer beginning to unfold before me, like the glacial wheels of time whose cogs slip together ponderous and slow to keep the engine of existence in motion. "But there are twenty-four sounds."

"Set aside vowel lengthening. Twenty sounds. Now

transpose them to the fifty-first year of the cycle, shifting the sounds completely. Of course, the problem is knowing what sounds were assigned to what *trecena.* It's a substitution cipher—88-bit key, simple stuff—but it's in Nahuatl, so existing tools for breaking it don't really work. If the words were separated out, we could start guessing based on the two- and one-letter combination. But since everything's all run together, I used my mad computer skills—wrote a quick script and ran the first line of text through different options till a string of Nahuatl words was generated."

His grin lit his whole face up, and I had to fight back an urge to seize the back of his head and kiss him hard. "Well? Jesus, don't keep me in suspense, Chano."

"I had to clean up a sound or two, but it's definitely the beginning of the rite. Here goes."

Taking a few steps back, Santiago straightened his back, closed his eyes, and began to recite.

"in tepētl īhtic mihcuiloa,
īpan tlālli īomiyo mocuihcui,
moxihxīma in tlahtōlli
īca īmātzin ahtlācacemēleh."

A rush of wind howled outside, as if feral with rage, and my attic creaked and groaned with theatrical solemnity. My stomach squirmed with something like excitement or dread as I mouthed the words over and over to myself, translating.

"In the heart of the mountain was written, upon the bones of the earth was carved, was engraved this incantation by inhuman hands."

Santiago nodded as he took a seat. "Yup. Sweet. And freaky as shit."

We looked at each other, intoxicated by the breakthrough, giddy with discovery and conquest. But there was something else, a need—latent for weeks, but suddenly acute—tinged with madness I find it hard to describe, the touch of some dark talon on secret places of our souls, awakening nameless hungers of which sexual desire was a pale but immediate shadow.

A few steps and I was in his arms. As we kissed, my hands scoured his body, slipped along its firm angles, found him hardening eagerly in response. Blind with lust and unearned knowledge we came together, stripping free of occluding clothes, his breath hot and quick on my neck as he plunged into me, and amidst the ecstasy that followed I would have gladly let the world be torn asunder by cold cyclopean forces if only they would stretch those torrid moments of delicious release into an eternity …

9

I awoke alone in the darkness.

Momentarily panicked, I flailed about for several seconds before finding the switch to the lamp on my bedside bureau. Santiago was gone, along with his clothes. He had left a note taped to the door.

Robert—too pumped to sleep. Going back to my apartment to work. Check your email.

Now drained of the evening's excitement, I stood for a long time under the showerhead, letting steaming water pelt my numb flesh. I felt submerged, apathetic. I fantasized about standing on misty tropical shores, staring out upon vast black depths beneath a glassy surface. As the steam built thicker in the bathroom, a realization came over me: in the midst of my fancy, something terrible awaited. Dread curled cold fingers around my guts. At any moment a shapeless bulk would arise from the enshrouded pitch of my mind …

With a disgusted grunt at my own foolishness, I shut off the water and toweled myself dry, wrapping a bathrobe around me and heading for my study.

My inbox contained three emails from Santiago. I opened the first one.

Here's the next one hundred words. Manos a la obra. *Send you more in a bit.*

I printed the deciphered Nahuatl text he had pasted and went to prepare coffee. Soon I was immersed in the work of translation, several dictionaries and grammar books open in front of me as I rendered in English for the first time these ancient, guarded words.

For an hour the arcane pronouncements became my universe. A sort of preface, sketching history. The Rite, preserved in antediluvian tongues by inhuman hands scrawling alien glyphs in ancient bedrock. Its use, four times, to wipe life from the earth. Musings on agony. Warnings and promises.

Pouring more coffee to combat the encroaching cold, I opened the next email. Here the incantation itself began, calling on lurid and recondite beings—*Huēhuehtēteoh* dormant in dire demesnes—sharing words wrought in the cooling fires of a young universe that would awaken those colossal gods and open the cosmos to their lumbering and frigid insouciance.

As my lips moved soundlessly and my pen scratched with fanatical jerks across a blank page, I became aware of a sort of thinning of the darkness around me, not in response to any illumination—it was only 4 a.m., the sunrise a few hours distant—but as if reality were being pulled tauter and tauter. Strange sounds, distant and muffled and unaccountably bleak, bled into the biting air.

Shrugging off these developments as tricks of an overtasked mind, I opened Santiago's third email.

Robert—Something's wrong. I've just finished the bulk of it, just a small chunk left to go. I'll paste the next part, but ... I'm not feeling well, Robert. I keep thinking about us. You told me the dean had found out, that he directed you to stop fraternizing with students, but that's bullshit, isn't it? I know I'm not the first. People notice, Robert. They notice, and they talk, quietly. How many assistants have you gone through? Five? How do you end it? I'm pretty sure you trot out the old "the dean busted us" story every time you start to feel something. Because you don't want to feel, do you? You want pleasure, sure. But beyond that, you have more in common with the monsters in your precious fucking codex.

I keep feeling like someone's here in the apartment with me, Robert. Whispering to me. Telling me you already have your eye on another poor bastard. René? It's fucking René Cordero, isn't it? You son of a bitch. Keep it professional.

See, I hear it again. Low. Dark. Pitiless. It sees into me. Past me. I'm nothing. But you know that, don't you? I'm deciphering this shit for you, but I'm betting you'll figure out a way to fuck me over, to cut me out. I'll be a goddamn footnote in a peer-reviewed article. You're the mighty Dr. Robert Kerr, no?

Here's your magic that destroys the earth, Robert. Enjoy it. You're good at destruction.

As the printer hummed to life again, I picked up my phone and called Santiago. The line rang and rang until his voicemail answered. My concern growing, I sent text message after text message in between attempts at calling. There was no response. My worry became annoyance.

I went back to translating feverishly, forgetting Santiago until my inbox dinged.

Another message. A single word.

10

Goodbye. I still had the key to Santiago's dilapidated East-Austin apartment, and in the predawn dark I very quietly let myself in. Part of me already knew what I would find. Hadn't death visited me often enough for me to recognize her approaching footsteps, like the sound of familiar feet coming down the hallway of one's own home?

Santiago had hanged himself from a ratty ceiling fan using an orange extension cord. The worn rolling chair from his desk was on the other side of the room, where he had presumably kicked it before asphyxiating or snapping his neck.

It is cowardly to admit, but I could not look at him. Choking down a few shreds of grief, I walked to his computer, still open to his email account. I deleted the last four sent messages. No doubt they could be retrieved somehow, but I had no intention of letting my work fall into other hands that easily. I found the last section of deciphered text in a strange little minimized window. After figuring out how to print the Nahuatl, I hunted up any scrap of paper on which Santiago might have attempted translations, and I stuffed all this into my coat pocket.

Taking up his phone, I deleted my texts and phone calls. I thought about wiping everything down, but figured I would simply tell the police right off that we had been lovers, as they were bound to discover that fact anyway.

I had broken things off with him. He was devastated, kept trying to change my mind. Finally he threatened to kill himself. I should have believed him, Detective. Why didn't I listen?

Another man would not have been capable of such cold calculation. But the darkness was wearing thinner around me, fraying in spots, and I had been uniquely prepared by tragedy and solitude to set aside my humanity in order to move ever onward.

The sun was struggling to rise as I slipped back into my car, scant rays of washed-out light that scratched feebly at the emboldened, starless sable. Needing to be seen, I pulled into a diner for breakfast and then drove to the university, greeting with a gentle smile everyone whose bad luck drew them to class so early.

In my office I pulled the sheaf of paper from my coat with shaking hands and began to translate what remained of the Rite. Appalling epithets, grotesque turns of phrase, ungodly acts perpetuated without smile or sneer. The lights of the university flickered whenever I mouthed the age-old words, so I gritted my teeth and hissed like a madman.

Atom-ripping powers invoked. Destruction sworn upon mothers and children and generations of souls, ready to be damned. The speaker a conduit, begging for the might to rend the universe itself so that the impassive horrors might roam free.

Then, in mid-sentence, right at the climactic declaration, the rite ended.

"No!" I snarled, slamming my fists against the desk, transported by alien rage that roiled and seethed. "That's not all of it! The last line! Chano, you stupid fuck!"

Snatching up my keys, I rushed to the car. The sky was black with storm clouds that swallowed the sun and blew strange squalls across the city. Traffic on the highway was at a piteous crawl, and I hurled vile insults at the other drivers, foaming rabidly, beating my hands on the steering wheel.

Finally I broke my car free from the jam and hurtled home, running to my desk and yanking open the journal. Blinking my eyes, I calmed myself enough to focus on the encoded words, comparing them to what Santiago had deciphered just before his suicide.

He hadn't left anything out. The transcription was simply incomplete. Either the Keeper had refrained from speaking the final words of the rite, or my grandfather had failed to transcribe them.

Numbed, I slumped into my leather desk chair. The winds keened like a chorus of demons outside my window.

He can't have died for nothing. I have to know it all. Need every word. Have to publish.

The lamplight wavered. Once. Twice. I leaned forward to yank the chain.

There it was, the brown paper in which the journals had been wrapped and mailed.

And upon it, the return address.

11

There were no law enforcement complications as I boarded the flight from Houston to General Mariano Matamoros Airport in Cuernavaca. I knew it would be at least three days before anyone noticed that Santiago was missing, and likely another twenty-four hours would go by before anyone from the police decided to question me. I had time to accomplish this task unimpeded.

For the greater part of the trip, I slept fretfully, my dreams full of half-glimpsed behemoths that crushed nations with slow, ineluctable steps. When the plane touched down, I grabbed my carry-on—containing two changes of clothes and my grandfather's journals—and hurried through the terminal.

A taxi took me from the airport to the monastery, a relatively quick trip north along the Cuernavaca-Tepoztlán Highway to Ahuatepec, a suburb nestled in a fold of the Ajusco Mountains. The monastic complex was a very modern yet subdued affair with lush greenery and buildings for retreats and guests. I paid the driver and entered the priory proper.

A young novice approached me politely.

"I am looking for Brother Fausto Quevedo," I told him.

His eyes widening slightly, he asked me to wait and then slipped off through an arched passageway. A few moments later an older monk arrived, a man about my age, gray beginning to rime his temples.

"Good afternoon," he said. "I have been told you are looking for Brother Fausto. I am afraid he passed on to greater glory several years ago. I am his nephew, Brother Marco Quevedo. And you, I presume, are Dr. Robert Kerr."

Taken momentarily aback, I could only mutter, "How?"

"Because I am the one who sent you the journals, of course. But bear with me a moment." He gestured at the novice. "Take Dr. Kerr's bag to the available room at the hostel. He will be staying with us for a time."

The monk placed a hand on my elbow. "Let us walk for a while in the gardens. Our conversation is not meant for other ears."

Once we were outside in the greenery, I swallowed heavily and asked the question that had been weighing on my mind. "But why? Why send them to me?"

Brother Marco smiled. "It was necessary that you have them, for they are yours, Dr. Kerr. Not only because your grandfather's hand committed words to those pages, but also because you can make use of them as none other dares to do."

"You mean … say the Rite of Annihilation aloud. Why would the Keepers want me to do that? You believe the world would be destroyed as a result, do you not?"

The monk nodded. "Indeed we do. But you have clearly misunderstood the reasons that we kept this lore secret for such long millennia. Indeed, for as long as man has had a mind capable of learning language, there have been Keepers. For the most part, the knowledge has been kept from other eyes, beyond a few phrases and prayers sold by traitors that found their way into esoteric texts like the *al-Azif, Las reglas de ruina,* or the *Liber Ivonis*.

"Yet it was not to avoid the destruction of the earth that the Rite of Annihilation was hidden. I of course understand your confusion, as most of the Keepers themselves believed that to be our purpose, including the great compiler Ce Acatl Topiltzin. But a core cabal within our group knew the truth—we have merely postponed the prophesied end until the time was ripe, until mankind had proven himself wholly unworthy of either salvation or damnation, an insignificant and execrable blight deserving only eradication. And we awaited one uniquely molded to be the speaker of such bleak and puissant words. You."

We had traveled far from the compound, deep into shadow-dappled woods where the path gradually faded into untrodden verge. I stopped, glanced about me with a sense of disorientation.

"Me? Why me? Who molded me?"

"Ah, you misunderstand. No one deliberately prepared you for this. Blind, sluggish historical processes down thousands and thousands of years have brought us to this moment. Therein lies the greatest and most despair-riddled mystery: there is no reason. The knowledge simply exists, and you are uniquely equipped to use it."

"Nonsense. I believe none of this."

Brother Marco smiled. "Yes, precisely. No man who believed it could say the words."

Frustration and rage curled my fingers into fists. "All I want from you is the final line. Your uncle kept it from my grandfather, and its absence from the codex is unacceptable. There was an agreement made. I have all the same evidence. Give me the words, or I will reveal the Keepers to the Benedictine Order."

"I cannot give you the words. You must take them from me."

"What?"

"Come, walk with me a little farther. We are almost there, Dr. Kerr."

Fuming, I nonetheless followed him to a small clearing through which a stream flashed bright in the afternoon sun. On its banks, half-hidden by reeds, was a temazcal, a stone sweat lodge of the sort used in pre-Colombian religious rituals.

Brother Marco began pulling his robes over his head. "If you want the missing line, you will have to come inside with me."

Wearing only his smallclothes, he ducked inside. I stripped down to my boxers and followed.

I find it difficult to explain what happened next. The monk ladled stream water onto volcanic rock heated somehow from below, perhaps by desultory fires glowing unseen in the pit of the mountain. Into the steam he released strange powders, ground herbs of clearly psychedelic properties, chanting obscure hymns from the codex. Soon my sweating pores seemed to absorb profane mysteries annealed with the very fabric of nature. I was in the rock, in the stream, in the reeds. I was Robert Kerr, but I was also Marco Quevedo, feeling with his flesh, seeing with his eyes, thinking with his mind.

And within the blasted recesses of his soul, I found the words, coiling like adders.

12

Now here I sit in my room beside the priory, watching the thunderheads gather around the distant peak of Popocateptl, which has been belching smoke and fire for more than an hour. The Keepers stand outside on the lawn, robed in black, hair smeared with blood, deaf to the frightened entreaties of the Benedictines as they chant their apocalyptic dirges.

I have written out the deciphered Rite of Annihilation in my grandfather's journal, all except for the harrowing final syllables, awful sounds from an inhuman tongue that can only be approximated with human alphabets or syllabaries. For this reason I was lured here—to perceive the vile vocables first-hand.

Upon the very last page of the journal I have discovered an unsettling final entry. There is no date, but my grandfather's normally careful script is scrawling and shaky. Three inexplicable words in Nahuatl—*nitlācatlachiye huel ahnitlācatl*: "I seem to be a man, but I am truly inhuman."

And though I have no inkling of what drove the most caring soul in my life to judge himself thus, I get to my feet, poised between humanity and monstrosity as the merciless winds scream along the mountains like frenzied harbingers, spiraling down toward Tepoztlán and beyond. Toward the rest of the fleeting and meaningless earth.

I should catch the next flight back to Texas. I should face the truth of Santiago's death. It will complicate my career, no doubt, but others have rebounded from such scandals. And I have the codex, complete. I will join the ranks of the greatest minds in history.

The problem is that now I believe. I hear the cataclysmic rumble of awakening gods through the tearing tissue of reality, and I admit the truth at last.

I hold your lives in my hands. All I have to do is utter the words.

THE CHILDREN IN THE TREES

1

Dr. Nelson Kerr knew that some unspeakable horror had drawn near, though he could not explain the peril or how he perceived it.

A sense of unease had been building in him for weeks, an existential dread that prised at his mind, slow and unrelenting. It was not political angst: his home in this quiet borough of Mexico City lay at a great distance from the nuclear posturing of Reagan and Gorbachev. It was not a crisis of faith: Kerr had long ago abandoned his parents' religion for the steady agnosticism of the sciences.

Martha, his wife and physician, intuited his struggle. She had an easy explanation.

"You've just turned eighty, my love. Mortality looms large."

Then her wistful smile glowed as lovely as it had four decades before, when first they'd met in the little town of Tepoztlán, so the aging archaeologist had set aside his strange anxiety and tried to be happy once more at her side.

But in late May strange tremors thrummed throughout Central Mexico, their epicenter roughly two hundred miles off the coast of Michoacán. Something about the news nagged at Kerr and wouldn't let him be; for days he scanned every article in *El Universal* and hung on each word broadcast by Televisa.

Michoacán. Tremors. Shuddering earth all the way to Mexico City. To the site of old Tenochtitlan. Where Lake Texcoco once spread jade green beneath the sun.

When the connection clicked in his mind, Kerr hurried to his study and spun open the safe. Inside sat two worn leather journals, packed with dense writing in his careful hand and sketches of his most important finds.

He did not need to search to find the relevant section: these were the most read and bookmarked pages in the second volume, transcribed twenty years ago, letters shaky with tremulous excitement.

Early in his career, Kerr had stumbled across the diary of a Franciscan monk in which were reproduced images from that pictographic pre-Colombian document, burned during the Conquest by Jesuit priests terrified at its implications. But though the archaeologist had made faithful copies of these few illustrations from the codex, he had never discovered a written record of the lore it represented. In preliterate Aztec society, such knowledge was passed mind to mind down the long years.

Then, after decades of intermittent and frustrated search, Kerr had finally tracked down in 1964 a member of the esoteric sect known in Nahuatl, the Aztec tongue, as *in ītēpixcāuh itzāmoxtli*—the Keepers of the *Obsidian Codex*. The man, one of the last disciples of that millennial cult, had agreed to recite their obscure scriptures, some ten thousand words in Classical Nahuatl.

This secret journal contained Dr. Kerr's transcription of that text.

2

For the first time in a decade, the archaeologist pored over the yellowed pages, skimming past weird incantations and eldritch hexes, black-hearted hymns and ciphered rites, until he found the passage that chilled his very soul.

The rambling verses foretold the awakening of Cihuacoatl, one of the *Huēhuehtēteoh* or Great Old Ones, godlike beings from the dawn of time, the females of which were named *Tzitzimimeh* by the Aztecs—*those who devour stars.* Still as death beneath the waters of great Lake Texcoco, Cihuacoatl has lain dreaming, the text explained, for tens of thousands of years, attended by the *Centlancah* or Deep Ones, whom the Aztecs also called *Tlācamichin*, ageless beings of the oceans who await the awakening of the Huēhuehtēteoh.

Kerr turned to his other journal, flipping to the page upon which he had sketched one of the few existing images from the codex: a massive creature with skeletal visage, black-plumed wings, and a torso that ended in squirming, serpentine tentacles. This was Cihuacoatl, and she had been depicted bursting through the lake, flooding all of Cemānāhuac, "the sea-ringed earth," as she sought for her brethren beneath the rising water.

Returning to the apocalyptic poem, Kerr read a prophecy: unrest would arise among the Centlancah that abided in depths not far from Michhuahcān, the lands of the Tarascan Empire that had since become the Mexican state of Michoacán. Those gilled and scaly servants of the Great Old Ones would seek to rouse their queen from her tenebrous dreams, shaking the earth so as to reopen antediluvian tunnels that once bored through the foundations of the earth to join lake to sea, now blocked by mankind's insect swarming.

If awakened, the codex warned, Cihuacoatl would stir to life the others, leviathans not mentioned in any other surviving record, queer names that hardly seemed to fit the Aztec tongue: Quetzollo, Aztol, Catanotoa

The final strophe ended with a cryptic line: only *in pillōtl quitlatzihui tlācatl*—"someone indifferent to youth"—could lull Cihuacoatl back into her unsoundable dreams.

Dr. Kerr could only guess at the meaning of this obscure phrase.

3

For a time, it seemed he had solved the mystery: events in the real world had stirred his unconscious mind, dredging up connections to a bizarre quest that had eaten up so much of his early career. In the end, however, he was left with the same sinking realization as twenty years before. Even if he broke his old promise to the Keepers that he would never reveal their secrets, his transcription of scriptures of an obscure Mesoamerican cult would likely be dismissed as a bizarre fraud by the academic world. His rational mind would, of course, never admit the possibility that the contents of the *Obsidian Codex* had any relevance beyond the halls of academe.

Yet as a mild summer crept into the Valley of Mexico, bringing slate skies and a seemingly endless cycle of drizzle, rain and hail, a pall settled upon the archaeologist's heart. It was as if the world had been draped in grave clothes, gray cerements that wound themselves around the vast syncretic metropolis. Every hollow horn of every dingy automobile seemed a plaintive dirge. Pedestrians, their heads down against the rain, struck Kerr as little more than mourners filing away from a massive tomb in silence or ants scurrying before a swirling storm.

Try as he might, Kerr could not rid himself of the despair that grew with each bleak day that passed, filling his mind with squirming blackness. Though he was a principal consultant on the project, his weekly trips to the Templo Mayor, the massive excavation in the former religious quarter of Tenochtitlan, no longer presented wonder and joy to his eyes. Instead, the ruins of the massive pyramid, erected to honor the gods of war and rain, engendered fear, a gnawing at his innards, a tightness in his aging chest. When he stood on the disk at the foot of those ancient steps, its ten foot diameter displaying the dismembered moon goddess Coyolxauhqui in bas-relief, he thought on the hundreds of thousands of men and women and children whose broken, bleeding bodies had tumbled from on high to rest on that very spot. He could not even weep for them: instead, he feared for all the other lives that awaited unwitting their own indifferent shattering.

Overwhelmed again and again, he would hobble away from the dig only to find himself in the Zócalo, surrounded by colonial structures built with the rubble of the razed Aztec capital. Staring unseeingly at the Metropolitan Cathedral, Kerr thought he sensed the cobblestones vibrating beneath the soles of his shoes, pictured that ageless and cyclopean bulk buried deep beneath the rock and silt, imagined tentacles curled dormant around the foundations of the Mexican highlands. Shrouded peaks in the distance lost their majesty and permanence, seemed paltry boulders silhouetted against the vast, blank grayness of the sky.

Hoping to efface his enervating desolation, Kerr took his wife for a stroll through Chapultepec Park on a Saturday in September when the clouds parted and the sun promised to melt all gloom to gaiety. But despite the feel of his beloved's hand on his arm, the colossal redwoods and cypress trees loomed like hoodoos, their roosting flocks still and silent as sentinels. The zoo echoed with raucous screeches and moans of animals driven to frenzy by unseen prods, and their keepers considered closing the gates to the public.

The couple climbed the great hill, crowned by its castle, once home to the Colegio Militar and Emperor Maximilian, now housing the Museo Nacional de Historia. As Kerr stood at the foot of the stairs, looking up at the mural of the heroic teens who had died protecting the hill from US forces 138 years before, he buckled for a moment under the weight of all the deaths wrought upon that rocky promontory down the millennia, most vividly those killed there by the mercenary Mexica or the Mexica that neighboring tribes ambushed and slaughtered in return.

Corpse upon corpse, nameless, forgotten. Not even sneered at or despised. Simply irrelevant to the never-ending turn of the cosmic gears. Small. Insignificant. Meaningless.

Martha drew him away from his dejected ambling, and he realized as they emerged into the aloof sunlight that he had walked the entire museum without truly seeing a single thing. His wife wanted to take a boat ride on the lake; there were threats implicit in the glistening water, but he sighed and agreed. They rented a small, bright blue boat paddled efficiently by a father and son team that took the couple out into the very center of the Lago Menor. Kerr watched the reflections of nearby skyscrapers twisted in and out of the shadows upon the green surface while Martha made small talk with the rowers.

He saw, in a panic, something was watching him as well, a pair of black eyes looking up through the water. Heart pounding, the archaeologist leaned forward, squinting. He made out a form there, amidst the waving fronds: a humanoid of mottled ochre flesh, gills gaping at its throat. It bared white, predatory teeth at him and jerked away into the depths with a pistoning movement of webbed feet that sent unmistakable bubbles to the surface.

Fishman, he thought, gasping and gripping the gunwale. *A* tlācamichin. *One of the* Centlancah. *The Deep Ones.*

It was all he could do to not scream.

In the cool of that evening, recovering from the massive shock of the sighting, Dr. Kerr sat at his desk, surrounded by dozens of open books, reviewing all he knew from his research of the Aztec pantheon. He gritted his teeth, discouraged by the paucity of information: the lid had been ripped off of the world, and he was left staring into its writhing black bowels with only secondary sources and the accounts of conquerors to aid him.

He stood and went to the kitchen, where Martha was preparing their meal. Hugging her from behind till she giggled like a schoolgirl, he soaked in her vitality and warmth. Then he took a seat at their rough-hewn wooden table and sighed.

"Feeling better, I take it," she quipped, glancing at him.

"Somewhat. Certain … doubts I had have been … clarified to a degree."

Dishes clanked as she worked. "The knotty problem that's been bugging you, yes?"

"Just so. That is to say, it's still a problem, but I understand the scope better. I'm no longer confused. Now I need to do a little research before I … decide what must be done."

She made a soft noise of vague understanding, turning to set a glass of lemonade before him. "Drink up. I think your blood sugar must be low. You look so pale today."

He sipped and regarded her narrow back. She was twenty-seven years his junior, gray only now beginning to rime the edges of her long, black hair. As she moved through the kitchen, he was reminded of the intricate steps of native dances. His heart ached with love for her.

She will be okay even when I'm gone, if it should come to that. She's still young enough to find another. She can live with our son in Austin. There are so many possibilities for her.

Setting a steaming plate of food before him, she settled in at his side, eyes bright with the contentment that had bound them for decades.

"Do you mind if I ask you something? In Tepoztlán when you were growing up, did you hear stories of the goddess Cihuacoatl?"

Martha finished chewing and nodded thoughtfully. "Sure. Legends and so forth."

"Tell me some of them."

She raised an eyebrow. "Nelson, dear, I'm a cardiologist, not an anthropologist. You know more about all that than I ever will. I'm sure you've studied all the old gods again and again."

"I learned Nahuatl among your people, Martha. I know there's lore passed teacher to student, generation after generation, that only small communities retain."

"Perhaps. But why would you want to listen to my half-remembered and probably skewed versions of those tales?"

"Humor me, beautiful. I want to hear you."

Kerr took one of her hands in his and kissed those nimble fingers, gifted in surgery and cuisine and so much more. She ruffled his silver hair playfully.

"In that case, okay. Let's see. The old folks used to say that Cihuacoatl was the mother of mankind, that at the beginning of the present age she took the bones of giants and sirens and dwarves and ground them down to a fine powder, like cornmeal. Then she made her brothers and sisters bleed into her mortar, mixing divine blood with the old bones to fashion men and women.

"But, the wise ones always added, Cihuacoatl went mad one day, killing Mixcoatl and others of the first humans. Her own children. Quetzalcoatl, the god who had brought her the bones, plunged Cihuacoatl into the waters of the ancient lakes of the Valley of Mexico. He could not kill her, but he sank her deep into sleep.

"Of course sleep means dreams, and the dreams of a goddess are more powerful than reality. Nightmare apparitions terrified all the Nahua tribes living in the area, wailing like some insane woman, calling out from the depths of the lake for the children she herself had slain. Kind of like *la Llorona*. She entered the thoughts of women who had lost their own children, driving them mad. She twisted the souls of mothers who died giving birth, turning them into *cihuateteoh:* avenging demons who haunt crossroads, searching for kids to steal away. Cihuacoatl became known as a devourer, a horrifying force that brought nothing but death and destruction. The only way to calm her deadly dreams was through sacrifice. The old folks told us that more people were slain to appease her than any other goddess: usually young women. Virgins."

Martha ate a few bites, drank half of her lemonade.

"That's about all I remember. Pretty scary stuff, isn't it?"

Trying to hide the shaking of his hands as he continued eating, Kerr nodded. "Yes. Much more vivid the way you retell it."

"Yes, well, the stories were great deterrents. None of us children dared go out at night, and even less to lakes or rivers or crossroads."

Kerr sketched a smiled to hide his dismay "No, I suppose you didn't. Thanks, my dear. This helps. A lot."

"Happy to oblige, love."

Later, as they sat on the verandah and watched the stars struggle valiantly against the encroaching clouds, Kerr told his wife he would be visiting the borough of Xochimilco the following week.

"Is that why you were asking about Cihuacoatl? Have they discovered something important down there in what's left of the old lakes?"

"Something like that, yes. I've been asked to … consult … again. Shouldn't be more than a day or two. But it's a bit far to drive, so I thought I'd stay overnight in a hostel."

Martha, accustomed to her husband's sporadic trips across Mexico, simply nodded and touched his spotted hand. Then, shivering at the wind, a foretaste of impending autumn, she slipped inside to grab a sweater, leaving Dr. Kerr alone in the gathering night.

On September 18, 1985, Dr. Nelson Kerr travelled to the borough of Xochimilco on the south side of Mexico City.

He had the taxi take him to a humble inn at the edges of the neighborhood known as La Asunción, where he slept uneasily after a light supper. In his dreams serpents or tentacles writhed amid scales and feathers and vast red eyes that opened to look upon him with vacant insouciance.

By 5 a.m. he had slept all he could. An early-morning cab dropped him at the canals, where he wandered aimlessly along the empty dock, staring at the mist-wreathed water. Finally, as the sun thrust its pale, arthritic fingers above the horizon, a small chalupa pulled up alongside him. Manning its oars were a boy and girl of between ten and twelve years of age, the similarities in their features suggesting close kinship.

"Are you looking to hire a boat, sir?" the boy asked, pushing his lanky black hair from his eyes.

"Yes, please." He stepped into the chalupa, sitting on a wooden bench at about its midpoint.

"My name is Carlos. This is my sister, Azucena. Where to, sir?"

"For right now, just give me a tour of the canals."

"As you wish, boss. It's a little foggy, but that should burn off by seven or so."

They set off along the waterways, the mist gradually thinning to reveal little islands called *chinampas*, farming plots built up over the years from artificial mangroves of juniper and soil. The former lake was now a labyrinth of these gardens, the passages between them transformed into the canals for which this area was famous. Azucena softly revealed she and Carlos lived on just such an isle with their elderly grandmother, their parents having left more than a year ago to find work in the US before sending for the siblings.

As they made their way toward the northeast, a new sensation joined the constant dread curling in Kerr's gut: a tangible oppression, as if invisible hands were pushing against him. Out of the corner of his eye, he caught strange movements in the water.

"Is there a … *scary* place nearby, kids? Maybe with bones or something really weird like that?"

Carlos lifted his oar from the water and turned to him with a thoughtful expression. "Maybe. There's the Isle of Dolls a little farther ahead. It's definitely weird."

Azucena nodded in agreement. "Really scary."

"Good. Take me there."

The rhythmic splash of rowing was the only sound for another fifteen minutes or so. Kerr checked the water for signs of the Deep Ones, then glanced at his watch. It was nearly 7 a.m.

The moment he looked up, the mists parted ahead of the boat, revealing a startling scene. Hanging from a dozen trees upon a broad chinampa were what at first glance appeared to be children. Adrenaline kicked at the archaeologist's heart for a moment, but then he remembered the name of the place. Isle of the Dolls.

Carlos leapt out onto the bare roots of the mangrove and pulled the chalupa up out of the water, signaling for Kerr to disembark as well. He did, eyes flitting over the broken and moldy forms of dolls with which the branches had been festooned.

After walking a few yards, he turned around, eyes narrowing.

"Who lives here?" he asked the children.

Carlos jerked his head at something behind him. "Here he comes now."

A middle-aged man was approaching, machete in hand. His clothes were threadbare and dirty. Even in the morning chill, his shirt was stained with sweat, as if he had been working in his tangled fields since before sun-up.

"What do you folks want?" he asked, swinging his machete and burying its blade in a nearby tree.

"Good morning. I'm Dr. Kerr."

The farmer stepped closer, accepted the archaeologist's proffered hand.

"Julián Santana Barrera, at your service."

"A pleasure. I wanted to ask you about these dolls."

Santana Barrera looked up, confused, as if noticing the bizarre display for the first time. "Oh, them. It's, you know, a tradition. Keeps evil spirits away. Helps at harvest time. Like having an *alux* around. A garden gnome, I mean."

"A tradition, huh?"

"Yes, sir."

"I don't see other chinampas with dolls hanging from the trees, Julián."

Rubbing his stubbly cheeks, the farmer shrugged. "It's not the dolls, so much."

A sound reached Kerr then, a strange bubbling from the water. Fear gripped his chest like a taloned fist. Struggling for air, he cut to the chase.

"Are they for Cihuacoatl, Julián? Is that why you do it?"

The man's eyes went wide. "How? How could you know?"

"I just know. Tell me."

Spreading his hands wide in an almost plaintive gesture, the farmer explained. "No one makes the sacrifices anymore. Her sleep is uneasy. Crops spoil, folks get crazy. Weird specters roam the canals at night. One day I found a doll floating near the dock. I don't know how it occurred to me, but I brought the thing back and stuck it in a tree, saying some of the old words. It helped. My crops were better. No more nightmares, for a time.

"But it didn't last. We could all feel her twisting and turning down below. So I started trolling the dumps and canals, looking for these lost companions of children who have grown too old to care, who turned their back on innocence and tossed aside their toys.

"I hang them from the trees as the ancients did to the maidens they offered up to her. It's a poor substitute, but it's worked so far."

The faint outlines of a plan began to form as Kerr studied the trees. Some sort of foundation that would collect unwanted dolls. A network that would transport them here. Chinampa farmers paid to hang the child-like forms, all innocence lost, from broad branches. Perhaps there was a way to stave off oblivion …

Azucena gave a startled screech and rushed toward Julián. Dr. Kerr turned to see sleek green heads emerging from the water, obsidian eyes glaring unblinkingly. Then webbed claws gripped the dangling roots, and the Deep Ones dragged themselves into the autumnal air.

"Holy Mother of God!" cried Carlos, backing away.

At that moment, the entire world seemed to shudder in horror. The dolls danced grotesquely at the end of their makeshift nooses as the trees quivered and the ground shook like a palsied leviathan.

"They're waking her!" screamed Dr. Kerr, despair tearing at his mind. "The green bastards are waking Cihuacoatl!"

Without warning, Julián slammed his fist into the back of Carlos's head, tumbling the youth unconscious to the quaking soil. Then he grabbed Azucena, pinning her arms to her sides as she struggled, howling, to be free.

"My machete, Doctor!" shouted Julián as a half-dozen Deep Ones slunk closer and the island shuddered, pounded by waves of rising water. "Pull it from the tree and slit her throat!"

"What? Are you insane?"

"Do it now! The dolls are not enough. A child's blood must be spilled today!"

Quailing at the sight of the blubbering girl, the mad-eyed farmer, the encroaching beasts, Dr. Kerr recalled the words of the *Obsidian Codex* and finally understood. "*Indifferent to youth." Able to destroy it without a second thought.*

"No!" he wailed. "I can't!"

"You old fool! Why did you come here then? You must kill her, or be damned and damn the rest of us with you. I can't do it alone, Doctor. Even now, she's slipping from my arms!"

Martha, their home crumbling around her, trapped or dead beneath some structural beam. The city in ruins, burning, millions of lives snuffed. A dozen Great Old Ones, rising from their slumber to join their sister. The world consumed by cyclopean forces for which mankind was but an insect to swat aside unthinkingly.

No. Not now. As whistling breath in slimy gills blew cold upon his neck, Nelson Kerr stumbled to the twisted bole, yanked the blade free, and drew it quick across the girl's bare neck. Blood burbled and flowed in streams down her blouse.

Julián dropped her, ripped a doll from its noose, looped the rope under the girl's arms and hoisted her with a savage grunt into the branches. Arterial spray arced over Kerr's head, spattering the Deep Ones and the water beyond them.

The earthquake slowly stilled.

The silent creatures of the depths seized the body of the unconscious boy and dragged it along as they slipped back into the canal and disappeared.

Nelson Kerr dropped to his knees, staring at the blood smeared on the machete, on his hands, on his clothes.

The dread he had felt for months was gone. So was every other feeling. He was left empty and dark, like the black void between dying stars.

6

Nearly ten thousand people died in the event. Large sections of Mexico City were virtually flattened. Public services could not be restored for weeks in some areas. The metro was shut down. The authorities prohibited any automobile circulation into the most impacted boroughs.

Kerr spent several agonizing days trying to find Martha. Rumors reached him that Hospital Juárez, where his wife worked, had collapsed and trapped hundreds. A thirteen-second aftershock nearly broke what was left of his mind, but then the tremors ceased altogether.

After many ordeals and bureaucratic maneuvering, the couple reunited. Martha was fine, if shaken and distraught at her husband's absence. She had worked a night shift and was asleep in bed when the earthquake hit. Their house remained standing, one of the few not damaged in their neighborhood.

When Kerr at last rushed up the steps to their verandah, he embraced his wife, weeping, and she held him like a disconsolate child.

Autumn deepened over the broken city, and Nelson Kerr recognized in its chill the same frigid winds that scoured the desolate landscapes of his soul. Taking up his secret journals, he added a final line before locking them away—*nitlăcatlachiye huel ahnitlăcatl*: I seem to be a man, but I am truly inhuman.

The worst part was that he had tossed aside his humanity for a fleeting reprieve.

He and Martha moved to Austin to be near family. For short spans of time, usually spent in the company of his grandson or his wife, he could forget, allow the illusion of purpose and place to settle lightly on the world.

But it never lasted. Kerr would live another twenty years, but he would never again know joy. Joy was for the blind. His eyes were open. At any moment, the world might crack open and swallow everything he loved down its cold, amoral maw.

The knowledge annihilated his soul by relentless, insidious stages. Reality had turned on him. He could get no purchase on the universe. It moved onward, pitiless, caring not a whit.

In his dreams, white figures swayed against the green—

The children in the trees.

THE LUMINOUS

1

On the second day of spring, Achitomal finally spotted the jade serpentine of Hueyitepol Atoyatl, the Great River, which marked the northernmost edge of the Chichimec wastelands. Fifty-two days had passed since he had left Tenochtitlan under the Emperor's orders, and despite several stops and lucrative trades during his trek over mountains, along the coast and through dusty brush land, provisions were running low. He had left his caravan of porters, bathers and apprentices camped with the remaining supplies near the sea some two thousand rods to the southeast under the command of his eldest son.

Sun glinted off surging currents in the distance, and Achitomal smiled, a thrill thrumming along his nerves.

Now, if I can just cross the gods-damned thing, I shall reach my destination and perhaps wring a profit out of this reconnaissance.

He covered the remaining three hundred rods or so at a loping run. Once he had reached the silty, reed-thick southern bank, he slipped the carrying frame from his back, stripping himself of breechclout, sandals and cape and stowing them in his bags. Then, using his pack as a flotation device, he waded into the broad expanse of water and began to make his way across. The rush and eddy of the mighty river proved challenging, but Achitomal was an accomplished swimmer: his wiry muscles and sturdy sinews bore him to the far edge some fifty rods downstream.

The sun was low in the sky, the spirits of bereft mothers guiding it toward the Underworld, plunging the earth by degrees into darkness. Achitomal decided to wait until morning for the final leg of his journey; he spotted rabbit sign and soon had killed a rangy hare with an obsidian-tipped arrow. Skinned and gutted, it was roasting in short order above a campfire of fallen mesquite limbs.

Later, licking grease and chili juice from his fingers, the merchant observed the emerging stars, orienting himself for the morrow. Then he banked the fire, wrapped himself in a blanket, and slipped effortlessly into sleep, his hand lightly clutching a stone blade.

He arose before dawn and followed the river course toward the northwest. The sun was dragging itself from the netherworld with rosy orange fingers when at last he came to an oxbow lake cut off by a high ridge of silt. Ascending the loamy dune, he looked down at the ramshackle collection of wickiups and poorly tended fields that sprawled at the center of the stagnant semicircle. Nothing stirred beyond a few ragged canines that seemed more coyote than dog. As he watched, the mangy beasts began to fight over a carcass of some sort, snarling and snapping.

Squinting, Achitomal realized the hounds were rending the flesh of a human baby.

"Fuck," he spat, pulling his bow free from his pack and sending arrows plunging into their hides until all had tumbled dead.

Dragging the carrying frame behind him like a travois, he descended into the settlement to get a better look. He leaned his pack against a stunted acacia and began to examine each wickiup, an arrow notched on his bow. Most of the dwellings were empty, but in several the corpses of the very old or very young had begun to bloat.

Not long. Maybe two days. But where are the rest of the savages?

As he exited the largest structure, likely the quarters of the tribal chief, he was confronted by a group of children who had crept up on him out of nowhere, making not a sound.

Only they were not children, Achitomal realized. They stood no taller than a boy of eight summers or so, perhaps three cubits high, but they were most assuredly not children.

Small and pale, with shocks of black hair and wide-set eyes of sea-dark jade, the man-like beings were adorned with bracelets and necklaces that sported bangles of feather, bone, metal and jewels. Their breeches and tunics were of roughspun linen, and their long toes gripped the soil as if hungry for bedrock. In their hands they yielded, not weapons, but stones that glowed with inexplicable power.

One of their number, female by the slight swell beneath her vest, stepped forward. Achitomal bent his bow in answer, but she gestured with spindly fingers and his muscles locked against his will, making it impossible for the merchant to move.

"Tenochcatl," she said simply, her voice clear and bright. "When I release you, lower your weapon. I sense your outrage, but we are not responsible for what has happened to these humans."

With another twist of her fingers, the creature freed him. Achitomal pointed his arrow at the ground.

"Who are you? How did you know I hail from Tenochtitlan? How is it you speak my people's tongue?"

"We are the Hidden, the Little Folk. Your kind call us the *Tzapatoton.*"

Achitomal narrowed his eyes. As a child he had been told stories of mankind's elder brethren, who had burrowed deep into earth and forest at the beginning of the Fifth Age. He himself had entertained his own sons and daughters with such whimsy. Yet here they stood, a coterie of the magical beings. The merchant was never one to doubt his own eyes, which had beheld many wonders during his wide-ranging travels.

"I am the leader of this group," the female *tzapatzin* continued. "For your ears, my name is Chapotetini. My people know your tongue because we have watched your tribes for hundreds of years, ever since they emerged from ancient Aztlán and began their long and wending journey south.

"As for your city of origin, there are many clues. The curve of your bow. The shade of your fletchings. The weave of your breechclout. The cut of your hair. Lingering scents on your flesh. The structure of your carrying frame."

Achitomal smirked. "Very well. As hard as it may be to credit, you are without doubt magical beings with keen powers of observation. So tell me, Chapotetini, what has happened here? I arrive, hoping to establish trade with the Atenhuahqueh only to find one of their villages deserted and wild dogs feasting on a few abandoned dead."

She blinked at him impassively for a moment. Glancing about her, she rasped a few words in a language like gems against a grindstone. Her fellows turned at once and with fluid movements began to collect fallen wood and convey the corpses to the center of the village.

With a slight nod, Chapotetini focused again on Achitomal. "Before we begin, let us dispense with falsehood. You have come, I am certain, with a dual purpose—to discover the fate of the vanguard merchants who crossed the river six moons ago but never returned and to take as many as possible of these underfed humans captive to sell as slaves in the markets of Tlatelolco."

There was no anger in her voice, just dispassion and a hint of disapproval.

"Shit." With a shrug, the merchant slung his bow across his shoulder and dropped into a crouch. "Forgive me. Surely you realize I am a *nahualoztomecatl*, a merchant spy, trained to use wiles and subterfuge in the service of the Triple Alliance. I insinuate myself into the cultures of our enemies, live among them as a native, learn their weaknesses and their resources. Having reported this information, I return as myself to make a profit at their expense. I am, shall we say, unaccustomed to speaking the truth with complete strangers. But I must admit: your deductions are again accurate.

"My name is Achitomal. My family controls the most influential merchant guild on Lake Texcoco, and, yes, slaves are one of our primary imports. They fetch a handsome price and help me sidle up even closer to the aristocrats, ensuring greater success for my family and brighter prospects for my children. Three moons ago my father, the Merchant Arbiter of Tenochtitlan, called me before him.

Emperor Ahuizotl, hearing reports from our tributaries in the Chichimec wastelands of the tribes along the banks of the Great River, had sent a vanguard of our very best scouts to weigh the merits of trade or conquest. They, as you said, never returned."

"So your father sent you to discover their fate?"

Achitomal nodded. "At the behest of the Emperor, yes. My experience with danger, my stint in the Flower Wars, my considerable linguistic and cultural knowledge—all these talents made me the best candidate for the mission. So I spent a few weeks gleaning what knowledge I could concerning these Northerners, and then I set out with my retinue. For the sake of stealth, I have approached alone. And here you have me."

The elfin woman arched an eyebrow. "Indeed we do. You have come at a most opportune moment. The humans of this village, along with the inhabitants of a dozen more such settlements, have been abducted by the *Tlahuillohqueh*, the Luminous."

"The 'Luminous'? Who are they?"

"A group of corrupt creatures that worship the Great Old Ones, godlike beings from the dawn of time whom your people name *Tzitzimimeh—those who devour stars.* Enemies of the natural world, the Luminous work the blackest magic and sup on the blood of the innocent. They are led by a puissant sorceress, Ezmeya, beautiful and brutal."

A low chanting drew Achitomal's bewildered attention away for a moment. The other Hidden were ranged in a circle around the dead, whom they had piled upon the gathered tender. As their murmured incantation continued, they lifted their stones into the air and the branches erupted with a golden fire that quickly consumed the bodies.

Achitomal noticed with a start that the wood itself was whole, unmarked by scorches.

"But, how?"

"The Little Folk learned from the Feathered God how to draw the divine spark, *teotl*, from wood and rock and wave. Though we possess dire lore, we do not destroy nature to meet our needs; rather, we seek to more utterly wed ourselves to the bounty that awaits in every nook of the cosmos.

"The Luminous, however, hunger for annihilation. Ezmeya has sought for centuries to steal the knowledge that would permit her to awaken the Great Old Ones, who slumber down the ages, dreaming evil into the souls of men and women alike. Once roused, they would tear the world apart."

Achitomal understood in a rush. "So she has abducted these poor bastards for some sort of bloody ritual, is that not so?"

"Yes. Some weeks ago, in a bold and devastating stratagem, the Luminous ambushed a group of Hidden and managed to seize one of our revered elders, whom they then tortured endlessly. We believe he has been broken."

"Broken? Do you mean forced to reveal something that would help the bitch destroy the world? By the gods! Why in fuck would you even preserve such knowledge?"

Chapotetini stiffened, her fingers twitching upon her stone. "Do not presume to judge us, you treacherous slaver and spy. Thus were we charged by the Feathered God before your kind were formed by the Mother's hands. The lore of the First Age had already been carved into the bones of the earth; we were to keep it secret."

The merchant unbent his knees, standing and lifting a hand. "Hold. I have myself witnessed the might of the

Hidden. Why do you not stop her? Why do you waste your breath explaining this shit to me instead of rounding up the rest of the Little Folk and flaying the very skin from the witch?"

Achitomal saw that the others had returned and were glaring at him. Their leader's eyes glinted with shame and frustration.

"Because we *cannot*," she hissed through clenched teeth. "It is forbidden us. We cannot attack. We cannot hurt. We cannot kill. To do so is to forfeit our power forever."

She stepped closer to him, raising her long, slender fingers to gesture pointedly.

"But *you*, Achitomal, merchant of the Triple Alliance—you are under no such interdiction."

2

Having taken a long piss in the sickly maize field and gathered up his pack, Achitomal stood at the base of the silt dune a few minutes later, gesturing at the Hidden to stand aside.

"I have said *no*, gods damn you! By all the doomed fucking shades of Mictlan, I refuse! I do not fear danger, but why should I risk my life when you are unwilling to sacrifice your piddling magic?"

Someone tapped him on the back. He wheeled about to find Chapotetini scowling.

"Because of your sons and daughters. Because of your wife. Because of your father on his ornate seat in the marketplace. Because of the city and the gardens and the empire your people have carved out of the sea-ringed world. All of it will come to naught, all will be razed and burned and thrust into the void if the Luminous succeed. We are indeed willing, should no other path be found, to lessen ourselves to stop this cataclysm. But understand: the Luminous were created by the Enemy of Both Sides as a foil for us, and they may just as easily vanquish us as fall beneath our waning might."

For a moment, Achitomal was again a child, shivering in the dark of an eclipse as his grandmother told him of the monstrous Tzitzimimeh that even now sought to swallow the sun before descending to devour the world and all who lived upon it.

"Our lives depend," she whispered hoarsely into his ear, "on the might of the dead warriors that accompany the sun, aided by the souls of hunchbacks and cripples sacrificed today to combat those demons. Let us pray our defenders gain the upper hand, or this evening we wander bereft, shades in the bowels of Mictlan."

As a man, he had grown skeptical of such portents. But this was a day for easy belief.

"You hesitate." Chapotetini scrutinized him.

"You cannot keep me here, is that not so? When I raised my bow at you, you stopped me, but that was to defend yourself. None of you could ever hold me, force me to comply."

"No."

A smile played across the merchant's face. "Excellent. Then I have the upper hand in the haggling."

The leader of the Hidden crossed her arms over her chest. "Haggling? What do you mean?"

"Do you not see? This is *trade*, my dear *tzapatzin.* I aim to seek a very high price. Make an offer."

Chapotetini recoiled as if in disgust. "Price? Offer?"

"You have need of me. What do I receive in return?"

"The continued existence of the earth suffices not?"

Achitomal shrugged. "No. It in fact does not."

"Very well. To begin with, we will be rendering you impervious to dark magic. We can make this a permanent trait."

"That seems a worthy beginning. What more?"

Her fist spasming over her lodestone, the elfin woman gave a frustrated sigh. "What else have we? No jewels hewn from naked rock, no riches that one of your ilk would covet."

"Yet you wield magic. Think, Chapotetini. What skill can you bequeath me that I would find profitable?"

A moment passed in strained silence. Then one of the other Little Folk called out in their jangling tongue, and Chapotetini's face lit up.

"Do you know of the giants, Achitomal? Those monolithic men and women of the First Age of the world?"

"Of course I do."

"We will give you the talent bestowed on that mighty people by the Feathered God himself in the mists of time—the gift of languages. No matter the tribe or species, you will understand and be understood. Is that price dear enough, merchant spy?"

His mind reeling with the implications of such ability, Achitomal shrugged his carrying frame from his back and unwrapped his *maccuahuitl*, a sturdy wooden sword edged with razor-sharp obsidian blades. He whipped it through the air in a complex pattern, grinning like a madman.

"Sold. Take me to the Luminous, to this Ezmeya bitch. I will gladly remove her head from her shoulders for you, Little Folk."

3

The sun was low in the West behind them when the group reached the end of the vast flood plain. Chapotetini called a brief halt to their march, sending four of her folk into the brush to forage.

"If you crave meat," she called to Achitomal, "you will have to hunt it yourself. The Hidden consume no animal flesh."

He nodded and took up his bow. Having spent much of the day dumbfounded at his new skill, harkening close to the muttered exchanges of centuries-old beings, the merchant was now glad of the time to focus on his looming task. The ceremony had been simple—the Little Folk had surrounded him, their lode stones had glowed brighter than the sun, and then their power had thrummed along his thews and soul, transforming him in ways he only began to understand.

As the thrill of this metamorphosis had faded, the reality of his trade grew starker. He learned that the specific rite Ezmeya had torn from the elder Hidden required the sacrifice of four hundred men and women, whose deaths would release enough divine energy to awaken Itzpapalotl, the Obsidian Butterfly, cold and inhuman queen of the Tzitzimimeh. Once that Great Old One had spread her black-taloned wings and ripped through the very fabric of the heavens, she could rouse her slumbering siblings to enact the end of the age.

Through magic and deduction, the Hidden predicted this ritual would begin at moonrise that night, six hours after sunset. There was time for a hasty meal, and then the group would be on the move again.

As Achitomal scanned the landscape for a likely covert, he thought back to his training at the *telpochcalli,* the military academy where he had been prepared for manhood. He relived his encounters on the battlefield, seizing captives during the Flower Wars to be sacrificed at the Great Temple. He reviewed each stratagem he had later used as a merchant spy to gain the upper hand when faced with dubious odds. Fickle fortune, the unknowable gods or his own wiles and strength had always served him well. This mission was no different.

By the time his arrow pierced the heart of a quail he flushed from a copse of mesquite, Achitomal felt certain of his chances, given the aid of his companions.

Tonight he would save the world and walk away from the encounter richer than ever.

"The lair of the Luminous lies just beyond that grass-crusted dune, at the heart of a vast alkali flat, the bone-white and salty remains of some ancient lake. We can go no farther with you, Achitomal, lest we risk alerting the Luminous to your approach. But we shall not leave you without succor. We have made you proof against their spells, but behold! We now prepare your flesh as well."

Another of the Little Folk approached with a gourd brimming with what appeared to be blood—a thick, viscous fluid that glinted red-black beneath the bright stars. Chapotetini took the bowl in her hands and lifted it to Achitomal.

"Drink deep, merchant. This is *teoayotl,* sap from the roots of the World Tree. It will amplify your strength and endurance well beyond that of mortal men."

Tangy and sweet, the god-broth spread like fire from his gut, lambent along his limbs, sparkling in his eyes. A force like the divine rushing wind that had set the sun in motion at the beginning of the Fifth Age swept through his very soul. Trembling with energy, Achitomal snatched up his weapons and rushed into the night.

Above, the milky stream of heaven was slashed by the ominous crevice of the Black Road. Stupefying, incomprehensible terrors awaited beyond, dormant but uneasy. Everything hung in the balance. If he failed, Achitomal knew he would watch the eldritch monsters tear through that gap in creation like unholy spawn birthed upon the world.

The moon had begun to peer over the horizon as the merchant reached the white expanse of the dry lake. At its center, thronged around a deep depression in the earth, stood four hundred men and women. Heightened senses revealed that the missing vanguard merchants swayed mindlessly among the crowd, subsumed deep in whatever sorcery held the group in place. Ranged around them were four dozen men and women, naked save for elaborate boots that protected their feet and legs, the only mark of their twisted nature the taloned hands that even now bared copper blades to the growing moonlight.

Apart from them, a gossamer gown of cochineal red clinging to her ample curves, stood the most haunting beauty Achitomal had ever seen, all fiery curls and ruddy lips, unblemished skin flushed with almost debauched glee as she chanted:

As untold eons reach their end,
And thick, rich ichor stains the sand,
Stir within your chrysalis,

Crack your shell and struggle free,
Spread your wings upon the void,
Mighty claws that rend the world,
Rouse your brethren, dead in sleep—
Teach the chattel true despair.

There was more, but Achitomal pounded the salt, hurling himself at her. With a howl of fury she lifted a stone scepter carved in writhing, tentacular shapes and sent a blast of sable force against him. The attack slipped over his flesh as harmlessly as water, and the berserk merchant leapt high into the air, swinging his sword with inhuman might. The obsidian blades bit deep into Ezmeya's flesh, sheering through sinew and bone, severing her head. As her body tumbled, blossoming blackened blood, the rest of the Luminous screeched in rage.

Achitomal, driven by blood lust and god-broth, fell upon them. He slit one Luminous from hip to breasts, unmanned another, hacked off limbs, sent heads tumbling onto the alkali crust.

Then, with a sickening wet sound, the remaining Luminous pulled away from their own legs, trailing phosphorescent ooze as their bodies sprouted feathers, arms became wings, faces lengthened into crooked, vicious beaks. Surrounded by auras of scintillating blue, the Luminous wheeled through the night sky as massive vultures and owls, diving toward Achitomal, raking at his face with talons that emerged beslimed from the gaping sockets of their hips.

Dropping his *maccuahuitl*, Achitomal unslung his bow and sent arrow after arrow winging into the star-dappled dark, crashing plumed monsters to the bone-white sand, their glow fading as they died. At last, however, his quiver was emptied, and a dozen shrieking predators fell upon him as one.

Overwhelmed, he dropped to one knee, slashing at them with his stone knife as they gouged his flesh. Through the deafening slap of wings and numbing pain of beak and claw, Achitomal heard human shouts. Then he felt some of the monsters pulling or being pulled away, and he stood, seizing the vulture that now pecked at his heart and snapping its thick neck with a vicious twist.

The four hundred victims were free of the enchantment and had taken up the bronze knives of the Luminous. Achitomal's three countrymen were slashing at low-flying enemy, while the Atenhuahqueh busied themselves hacking the beasts' abandoned legs to bloody bits. Some of the creatures managed to snatch their limbs away and soar off into the inky distance, but most were either slain or forced to abandon their mutilated extremities.

Their harrowing cries faded, replaced by the sobbing and hoarse shouts of the river people. The effects of the god-broth were also waning, Achitomal realized, though the worst of his wounds had stopped bleeding and were scabbing over.

The three vanguard merchants approached him, hobbling and clutching at gashes on their flesh. The oldest spoke.

"I recognize you. Achitomal, true? I am Mayahuin; my companions are Oton and Yaopol. You are well come, sir. But how is it you did not succumb to their magic? Whence comes this strength of yours?"

As if in answer, the Hidden emerged from the darkness, illuminated by their lodestones. Achitomal nodded at Chapotetini and grinned.

"Oh, from the same place as all good things, my friends. The marketplace."

5

Two days later, Achitomal watched alongside one of the local chieftains, Yaluklam, as the other three merchants guided the Atenhuahqueh across the river at a wide spot just before a meander. Achitomal had pulled a sturdy rope from his pack, and his countrymen had tied it to trees on either bank to aid the fording.

The merchant spy was telling the chieftain roughly how long it would take to meet up with his own retinue when Chapotetini stepped from the brush and approached, her presence prompting Yaluklam to back away in obeisance and join his people.

"So you are taking them after all," she observed.

"Yes. I admitted my purpose to you from the beginning. Do not regard me with such distaste. You had a fucking choice. You could have sacrificed your own power and kept them from me in the end."

For a moment the elfin woman said nothing, averting her eyes to stare at the slow-moving water and the mass of flesh.

"How did you convince them to leave with you, Achitomal? What did you tell them?"

"That the Luminous would no doubt return, furious and seeking vengeance. That I would protect them. That a better life awaits them among my people."

She gave a wry laugh. "And they believed you?"

"Why should they not? I speak their mother tongue as one born to it. Besides, my words are ring with truth."

"Truth? Come, merchant spy. What really awaits them?"

Achitomal stepped toward her, leaning in close enough to catch the sterile, stony scent of her skin. "A better existence than this, Chapotetini. Most will be sold into the service of nobles and will live long, happy lives. They will not hunger or want for shelter. A few will be selected for sacrifice, bathed and pampered, treated like the embodiments of the gods for a time. Then, yes, they will be sacrificed for the benefit of all."

"And none will be free. How can you call enslavement or ritual death better?"

Staring into the depths of those ancient sea-dark eyes, Achitomal saw no irony and no self-knowledge.

Suddenly he pitied the Hidden, though he knew so little about them.

"Ah, you poor, blind bastards. Can you not see that you and your kind are slaves as well?"

He walked off without another word. When at last he turned back, she had melted away into river, rock or reed.

HARD ROAD TO THE STARS

WINDS THAT STIR VERMILION SANDS

2370

Seven-year-old Rodrigo ben-David sat alone in the hovel, spooning the last bit of last Shabbat's *chamin* into his mouth and using a hard bit of crust to scrape the pot clean. The thin, cold wind rattled the aluplaz walls mercilessly. Winters in the Hellas Region were tough, and in Babulandia, one of the most notorious shantytowns on Mars, the lack of municipal infrastructure made it nearly impossible for the residents to keep themselves warm.

As he moistened the crust in some weak, tepid coffee and slowly chewed that soggy staleness, Rodrigo prayed his father would finally return today. The food was now gone, and the boy had already pushed the limits of his neighbors' meager hospitality well beyond their accustomed limits. Babulandia had accreted into existence during the exodus from religious oppression on Earth earlier in the twenty-fourth century, and its inhabitants, a jumbled-together pastiche of cultures and languages, were mistrustful and not particularly giving. Another day of being along and Rodrigo would have to strike out for Malacandra City, where he believed his aunt lived and worked, though he had never met her.

Isaac ben-David had left a week ago, returning to Nirgal Vallis, where he'd been scavenging a century-old, abandoned research station. Rodrigo's dad scraped out a living this way: hunting through what others considered junk, looking for bits and pieces that could be resold or repurposed. With the station, he claimed, he had finally found his *mina de oro*, his gold mine.

"*Las kozas van amijorarse, fijo. Ya topo algo,*" his father had muttered in Djidio before leaving. "I'm gonna find something good, promise it, and we're gonna be set, *muchacho.*"

Rodrigo had tried not to cry, but his eyes had gone damp, and his father had grimaced. "Hey, life of the *Sefardis,* no? First the *katolikos* run us out of Spain a thousand years ago, and now they run us off the whole planet, got to come to Mars—*el guerko ke se lo yeve*—and freeze our *kulos* off. But you and me, we adams are gonna laugh last, yes? So you stay put, light the menorah right before night falls. Shamash, too, so when I come home I'll see them burning through the window, yes? Come on, no tears. *Pasiensia Cohá, ke la nochada es larga.*"

Isaac had smiled broadly then and clicked on the holographic image of Rodrigo's mother, dead these five years. "Your mom would want you to be brave, *fijo*. And *el Dio Barukh,* he'll be watching over you."

And Rodrigo had tried, really tried, to be brave. He looked at his mother's face, flickering with the uncertain power source, and tried to remember her voice, singing to him. In snatches it came to him, overlaid with his father's rich baritone—the song of Avraham Avinu, newly born, miraculously singing to his mother, Amtilai:

Yo ya topo ken me alejasse
mandará del syelo ken me akompanyará
porke só kriado de El Dio Barukh

Wish I had someone to get me out of this shack, Rodrigo thought. *Wish* el Dio Barukh *would send me someone to keep me company.*

He had faithfully lit the candles, one more each night. The food had dwindled. He had gone out into the cold with his respirator to panhandle at noon, when people often tossed a few scraps to the *bakenekos* that infested Babulandia. Sometimes he had even kicked a dozen or more of the mutated felines out of the way to get at a couple morsels, his thick clothing and mask keeping him from their nasty claws.

Two days ago, a dark figure had followed the boy back to the hovel, slinking along the meandering way with what might have been bad intentions. Stopping abruptly, Rodrigo had drawn from his jacket an ancient pistol his father had rebuilt. Pointing it at the shadows of the narrow street, the boy had waited. The gun was enormous in his hands, and heavy. But there was only one projectile inside, and Rodrigo bit his lip so as not to shudder with fear. *Wish this was the staff of Moses, powerful enough to break open the street and swallow him all up*. The boy, of course, had no such forces at his command, but he stood as if he did.

After a few moments in which despair yawned like the grave, the presence had withdrawn. His heart pounding so hard he began to sweat despite the cold, Rodrigo had dashed the last few meters to his home and sealed himself within. Since then he had lived off the nearly nonexistent stores his father had left behind.

And now they were gone.

So Rodrigo lit the shamash and used it to light each of the other eight candles of the *hanukkiya*. He couldn't remember all the words his father would say, but he repeated what he knew as he dipped the longer candle to share its flame. "Like you protected them backadays, please protect me now. And bring Papa home."

He set the menorah on the ledge of the window, nine flickers refracted by the thick, transparent pane. Sitting at the table, he quietly spun a worn, lop-sided *sevivon* and waited. For his father. For the candles to burn out. For the darkness to overtake him. He was so utterly alone, so close to an amorphous nothingness that threatened to snuff him out like the tenuous flames. Exhaustion and hunger prevailed in the end, and he slumped onto the table, dropping into sleep like a silent stone released from a great height.

Hands were on him, pulling, pushing, grabbing. Someone snatched the pistol from his jacket pocket. He was thrust onto the bed. Rodrigo's eyes were open, but the candles had burnt out, and so it was as if he struggled with darkness itself, with some demonic entity congealed from the night. *The guerko,* he thought, shuddering to the roots of his being. He cried out, screamed. There was no honor in silence, now, nor cowardice in his weeping. Like an animal he thrashed against the swirling black around him, kicking, scratching, biting. With every blow from his assailant, who seemed desperate to rip off his clothes, Rodrigo's howl grew into a shriek that surely must have reached the ears of God himself.

A bang, and light streamed into the hovel. Rodrigo felt despair begin to rend him, for more of them had arrived, and soon they would truly hurt him in ways his young mind did not want to grasp. But then his father's voice thundered through the cold, darkling air.

"Get away from my son, damn you!"

And there came an unholy, low moan from his father's hands, silhouetted against the faint exterior light. He was holding something, and it was thrumming with the sound of a thousand angels' wings. Suddenly the air itself felt like it was cracking open, and the figure pressing Rodrigo to the thin mattress was hurled against the wall, though nothing appeared to have touched him.

Isaac rushed to Rodrigo and pulled him from the bed with one arm while gripping some strange machine in the other. As they reached the entrance of the hovel, Rodrigo saw through tears of anguish and relief that the device looked like nothing he'd ever seen. Its shape didn't fit his geometrical expectations. Its strange blues and greens seemed drawn from a spectrum alien to human eyes. Thin cables like tendrils twitched and wound themselves around his father's arm.

"What … ?" the boy began, hoarse. His father hushed him and led him to their battered transport. Activating its external illumination, he checked his son thoroughly.

"He hurt you? Son? Did he …"

Rodrigo shook his head. "No, Papa. No, you came just in time. I was … I was so scared."

"It's all right, *fijo*. Don't think he's gonna be getting up for a while now."

Rodrigo looked at the device. "You found it? At the vallis?"

"Yes. I'd just about given up. Saw a strange cave and felt, I don't know, drawn to it. Went inside, found this. It's our ticket, Rodrigo. I told your mama we'd find something like this someday. Something that changes everything."

"It, uh, it ain't human, is it, Papa?"

Isaac gave a strange smile. "You're a smart boy. No. I've seen just about every machine man ever made, and this ain't ours. So far beyond us that … well, it's a miracle, let's just say."

Vague intimations of power stirred a desperate hunger in Rodrigo, a yearning for safety and protection that made his chest ache.

"Can I … can I hold it?"

Isaac bit his lip, doubting. Rodrigo stared at his dad, watching the indecision.

Clearly ashamed of his near failure to protect his son and recognizing the boy's need to dispel his powerlessness, Isaac pulled the device from his hand and passed it to his son. "Be careful. Don't squeeze the rod. That activates it."

It was heavy, but not like the pistol. It was almost a living weight. The tendrils slipped around Rodrigo's thin forearm, and the rod slid easily into his palm. A great sense of peace came upon him then. *This is how Moses felt. Lifting his staff above the water. His enemies didn't scare him no more.*

The boy regarded the hovel in which he had huddled in fear, in which he had been attacked, in which he had felt despair. Inside was the darkness. The loneliness. Death. Abandonment.

Raising his arm, he squeezed the rod with all his might. A groan wrenched the night, and a ripple of nearly invisible energy *pushed.* The hovel crumpled like wet paper, smashed brutally into the ground and against the outcropping of rock that stood just to the west of it. His father gasped. "Rodrigo! What did you do, boy? Our home! That adam!"

The seven-year-old turned to his father. "Now you ain't got a choice, Papa. You got to take me with you."

Without another word, Rodrigo ben-David walked to the vehicle's door, cycled it open, and climbed inside to wait.

2378

As the rickety vehicle shuddered to a landing, Rodrigo ben-David bookmarked the physics text he was reading and set the pad aside. Climbing out of his sleep-nook, he walked the few steps to the cabin, where his father was already unsealing his safety harness.

"Why did we stop? I thought we were headed to Malacandra City to sell the generator we dug up."

Isaac ben-David winced and rubbed his temples. "Always you're asking the questions, *fijo*. Go get me a pill from the kit. *Me arguele la kavesa.*"

Grumbling in adolescent frustration, Rodrigo walked back to the head, palmed open the medkit, and scrounged around for analgesics, thrusting aside grafters, gauzes and creams. There was one last packet hidden behind the cauterizer, wedged into a crack in the cheap paneling. He snatched it free and stomped back to where his father was lifting open the trap to the storage compartment.

"Here. Now tell me what we're doing, Father. You know I hate it when you make decisions without consulting with me."

Isaac swallowed the pills quickly and made a scoffing noise. "Ah, *fijo*. 'Father.' 'Consulting.' You're sounding more like a book every day."

"Quit evading the question. *Para ke mos arrestamos*?"

"All right, all right. *Vos sos komo la mula de Cohá.*" He pointed at the opening at his feet. "I found a buyer."

Rodrigo's stomach tightened. "For that?"

"Yes, for that. And don't be starting, *fijo*. You maybe are fifteen, but I'm your papa, yes? For near seven years I've went along with your *kapricho*."

"Whim? You think I was acting like a little spoiled kid when I begged you not to sell it? What would the government do to us if you tried to sell it to them, huh? And who else is gonna pay what it's worth? The Brotherhood? The Qabdat Ar-Rum? Some other crime syndicate? Damn it, they'd kill us quick as spit, Father. I swear, it's like you're the child here."

"And what, you want we should just keep on using it to blast away sand and rock, scraping by on hardly nothing, just what we get for selling scrap?"

His heart hardening despite his love for the old man, Rodrigo shrugged. "That's the life you picked for me, Isaac. You left Earth with Mother, came to this cold, God-forsaken planet …"

"*El Dio Barukh* ain't forsaken nobody, Rodrigo. And what would you want me to do, eh?" Tears stood out in his father's eyes, and suddenly his face twisted in grief as he shouted. "They obliterated Israel! They scattered us! Again!"

Part of Rodrigo wanted to reach out and embrace Isaac, but he continued, implacable. "Then how can you say He hasn't forsaken us, Isaac? So you fled here. A new life for Jews, for *Sefardis*. But Mother died, didn't she? I spent my childhood alone in that shack in Babulandia while you eked out a miserable existence." Stepping closer to his father, whom he dwarfed by a good twenty-five centimeters, he dropped his voice to a quiet rasp. "That *device* is the only thing Mars ever gave us. The only thing God ever placed in my hand. If you just give me time to learn some more, I know I can crack it. The way out of this miserable life isn't selling the thing to some ignorant *kaseijin*. It's figuring out the technology and reproducing it."

Isaac dropped his gaze for a second, rubbed the dampness from his cheeks. For the past few years, Rodrigo had found it easier and easier to impose his will on the older man. A father's devotion to his son tended toward reverence at times, and Rodrigo had instinctively taken advantage of that weakness. But now Isaac's eyes grew flinty, and he thrust a bony finger at the teenager's chest.

"Ah, so you want to have it out, eh? Adam to adam, like equals. Well, let me make this clear. We just landed in Isana Singu, little fishing village on the coast of the Hellas Sea. In about ten minutes, a buyer is gonna show up. Renhou Jimi."

"Renhou Jimi? Really? Are you out of your mind? RenTek is basically a front for yakuza activity in Hellas, Isaac. You think he isn't going to have a couple of gunsels in tow?"

Isaac half-closed his eyes and spoke over Rodrigo's last words. "He's going to pay us twenty-five thousand New Yen, *muchacho*. Would take us ten years to make that much paras doing what we do. We're gonna take it, buy a little shop in Malacandra City, fix *makinikas* nice and calm. I see what it's doing to you, that thing. Every time you use it … it's like … I told you about your uncle Judah, yes? How the *katolikos* of the Nuova Pace Romana chipped away at him day by day till he converted? Turned his back on the ways of the *Sefardis* and el Dio Barukh. That's what I see in you, *fijo*. That device is changing you."

Rodrigo shook his head in disgust. "What's changing me, Father, is a very strong desire not to end up like you: a victim. And a willing accomplice to your victimhood. I don't think a tinker's shop is going to give you any power over your own life. I think you're going to have to pay protection to the yakuza clowns who're going to buy the device, and we're going to be tied to them and their corrupt, predatory ways for the rest of our lives. You're about to make a very big mistake."

"Well, the device is mine. I found it, boy. I hunted the caves of that vallis and found it, and now I'm gonna do whatever I think is best, you hear me? So that's it for the discussing."

With a dismissive wave, Isaac clambered into the storage hold and emerged with the metal container they kept the strange contraption in. Rodrigo gave an exasperated snort and sat at the dining nook. "Don't expect any help from me. If you want to make a stupid decision like this, you can handle it by yourself."

Isaac closed both hands into fists and looked at his son with barely bridled anger. "You do what you want, adam," he muttered in a tone he'd never used before with his son. Rodrigo felt a spasm of shame, but said nothing. When the older man irised open the lock, the teen stood up and followed him out, the two of them slipping on and sealing up thermal coats as they disembarked.

Outside, Rodrigo saw they had set down near stone piers that jutted into the ice-clogged waters of the Hellas Sea. The pylons had been fashioned from the same red andesite that made up most of the sand on this particular stretch of beach, and the effect was unnerving: a shocking crimson foreground against the pale white-rimed blue that spread across the horizon. A few battered wooden boats stood out in silhouette, black forms drawing nets from the sea. To the south, Rodrigo could barely make out the dilapidated shacks that presumably made up Isana Singu, one of dozens of fishing villages that clung tenaciously to the Martian soil at the edge of the vast southern sea, in fruitless defiance of the brutal, cold winds that shrieked shoreward from the floes.

Isaac reached back through the lock and dragged the metal box out, setting it on the red sand in front of them. As he knelt to thumb open the clasps, an ostentatious transport descended some forty meters away. Within seconds, four men exited, casting their eyes back and forth as they descended the gangway, three of them with weapons drawn.

Renhou Jimi and a trio of yakuza made-men, Rodrigo concluded. As they approached, Isaac stood to greet Jimi, a pallid, skeletal man with a constant, smug smile.

"Isaac-san," he barked as his companions arrayed themselves in a semicircle around the meeting place. "You have brought the device, yes?"

"Yes. Here." From his thermal coat he pulled a pad. "You can transfer the monies onto this."

Jimi accepted the thin, battered rectangle. "I'm gonna want a demonstration first, as agreed."

"Of course." Isaac went to open the box, but Rodrigo spoke up suddenly, compelled by something he didn't quite understand.

"I'll do it." He flipped the lid up with his left foot. Jimi leaned in to regard the demented, alien angles of the device resting within the box. If anything, it resembled some sort of nightmarish squid, nauseating blues and greens tapering to a shock of black cables that even now seemed to move of their own accord. His heart quickening, Rodrigo plunged his left arm into that squirming morass, wincing as the device gripped him almost eagerly. The trigger bar was warm against his fingers despite the biting cold.

Jimi took a step back. "So this thing, it can blow stuff up, yes?"

"Not really," said Isaac. "Like I told you, it shoves things. Don't know how. Maybe it messes with gravity or something. But, anyways, squeeze hard enough on the mechanism inside it and whatever you're pointing at gets … well, Rodrigo is gonna show you. *Adelante, muchacho.*"

Rodrigo turned toward the west, away from the transports and the men, and angled the device so it pointed at the ground a few meters distant. Then, with a grimace, he squeezed.

Gouts of sand and rock shot into the air in a violent, arcing stream. When the wind had shredded the dust, a large hole was left in the beach. Rodrigo and Isaac were not at all surprised; this was how they'd made a living for years now, using the device to uncover salvage that other scavengers couldn't get at. But Jimi and his companions were visibly excited and wary. Two men moved closer to Isaac with deceptive casualness.

"Good, that. What's the range? You could, I don't know, hit one of yonder pier pylons?"

It was farther than they'd ever attempted, but Rodrigo shrugged and moved away from the group, his back to them as he regarded the ice-rimed sea. One of the piers seemed to be in disrepair, and he aimed at it. Closing his fist around the bar with greater violence than he'd ever used, the teen sent its imperceptible force thrumming through the air. The pylons were ripped from their moorings and cast into the water. A nearby pier also collapsed and a wave some five meters in height rose and shattered itself against a distant floe.

Rodrigo stood for a moment, awash in the power he had unleashed. The fishing boats nearly capsized. Faint shouts of terror wafted toward him on the gelid wind.

The muzzle of a gun pressed into his neck.

"Turn slow." *One of the yaks.*

Rodrigo did as he was told. His father was kneeling on the vermillion sand. On either side of him stood a mobster, lazgats trained on his graying head. Tears were in his eyes. He shook his head slightly in warning.

Behind Isaac, Renhou Jimi was still smiling.

"Thanks for the demo, *bozu*. I'm gonna need you to hand that thing over now, yes? Otherwise, my friends here are gonna be forced to kill your o-pops. Don't want that, yes?"

Black strands tightened along Rodrigo's arm. He felt he might vomit. The ice, the wind, Jimi's eyes … all cold and flat and inhuman.

With a horrifying snap, all warmth left Rodrigo's soul as well.

"You're going to kill him no matter what."

Jimi's smile broadened. "Say again, *bozu*?"

"There's no way you're going to let either of us live. You've decided there's too many potential problems, us being alive. Complications for whatever plans you're making right now. So if I give the device to you, my father's dead. I'm dead."

The man behind him pushed his gat deeper into the flesh of his neck, twisting it so the sight bit at his skin. "You're dead if you don't, *kusobaka*, so might as well cooperate with Jimi-san."

The weight of his entire existence pressed down on Rodrigo's chest for the briefest of moments, a black, bloated hand that squeezed the trigger of his mind. And the young man understood that he was a weapon in the blind grip of history.

"*Te kyero bien, Padre*," he whispered, and dropped to one knee as he lifted his arm to fire. The four men were torn to pieces in a bloody, groaning gale that caught the edge of Isaac's transport and sent it tumbling down the beach. Rodrigo jerked his head away from the devastation in time to see the fifth man bring his gun to bear. The teen swung around to fire, but the lazgat sizzled to life first, its purple beam cutting deep into Rodrigo's bicep and nearly severing his arm. Brain-numbing pain trammeled his entire body, pushing him toward the darkness, but black tendrils whipped from the device and anchored his limb to his shoulder.

Then the device swung itself up without his help and shoved at the last mobster with pulverizing finality.

Rodrigo could stand no more. He fell into the black, unmoored from life and love.

Three weeks later, he stood beside the rough men and rude women who had nursed him back to health, cauterizing his wounds, carefully removing his severed arm from its snare and packing the alien device away in the metal case. They had buried the bodies, hidden the transports, said nothing to the regional authorities. The fisherfolk of Isana Singu had no love for government or yakuza, and they stoically aided this teen whose powerful arm had lain to waste some of their oppressors at the cost of his own father.

They called him *Urakaze*, the cold sea wind. He claimed no other name.

When they had stood beside the unmarked grave of the young man's father long enough, he motioned them away, back toward their village. Then he thumbed open the case and slipped the device over his remaining arm. Walking unsteadily to the broken hills that shaded into mournful dunes, he found a scarred monolith from which he carved a massive plinth, a cube of red and gray granite, shot through with black webbing. Carefully he used the alien tool on his awkward right arm to nudge the stone across the sand until the monument rested atop Isaac ben-David's shattered bones.

"God," he muttered bitterly, at last able to speak, "since you never gave a sign that you cared, I'm leaving this sepulcher on your behalf. My father lived his miserable, pointless existence, weakened by his faith in you. I'm not saying you don't exist. It's just clear now that you're not going to help the way people want you to. Maybe you already did, but Isaac just didn't understand what your help looked like. But, you know, that's fine. Because I'm ready to help myself.

"No one is ever going to hurt me like this again, do you hear? I swear it on your name. You've put this staff in my hands. I've bought the right to use it with blood. So here's what I'm going to do. Are you listening? I'm not Job. I'm going to use this tool. I'm going to figure out how it works. Not so I can just avenge my father, but so I can bring the justice everyone keeps waiting for you to dispense. Either you want me to do it, or you simply don't care. Whatever. Just keep out of my way."

It was enough. Nothing remained to be said. He turned toward the village and saw his people watching him, like grains of sand awaiting the wind.

UNDOCUMENTED

It's snowing when we reach the border, and ice floes clog the Río Grande.

"We stay away from the camps," the coyote hisses in the evening darkness, jerking his hooded head at the rows upon rows of orange tents, refugees desperate for a Mexican work permit. "You can't get processed, boy. Got it? *Que no te procesen.*"

"Yeah, yeah. I got it."

"Tell me in Spanish, *chamaco.*"

"*Ya capté, viejo. No voy a dejar que me procesen.*"

He nods, scratches his beard. "*Eso.* Almost sound Mexican, *pinche pocho.* Remember, as far as everyone's concerned, you're a *nacional,* Pablo. Keep telling yourself that. Only way you're going to make it if someone chats you up."

I don't say anything. We're waiting for the guards to sweep this area before running down toward the water. There's about a five-minute lull between trips.

"I'll never get used to this shit. You don't remember the way it was, huh?" the old man mutters. "Before."

"Nah, I'm sixteen, man. I was just a toddler in Chicago when the Loop failed. I just barely remember the first eruption."

"So not an ice-ager, but close enough, huh, *escuincle*?"

Before I can make a sarcastic reply, the guard hovers past, infrared sensors swiveling in a circle, and it's time to run. We crunch along the frozen sand, zigzag silently between the tents. At the wall, there's a moment when I think it's over, that this old man is going to get my ass killed, but no. His devices open the maintenance portal and we pass through to stand at the river's edge.

"Órale," he snarls, and I quickly strip down to the thermal suit, stowing my clothes in the bag along with my food, equipment and employee chit. He does the same, leaving his outer garments in a pile on the concrete, then turns to inspect me. Nodding, he pulls the hood over my head, tucks a stray lock of hair inside. Then he checks the seal on my bag, thumps it into my arms, and pushes me toward the water. Pulling down the infrared goggles, I clench the rebreather between my teeth and slip beneath chunks of ice, the cold burning at my face.

We swim at an angle across the slow current, not coming up till we reach the far side. We have to walk half a kilometer upriver before we come to the nearest maintenance portal. It's shinier and more high-tech than the American one, and the coyote takes longer to trick it into opening. My thermal suit has dried by this point, and I pull on my clothes and parka.

"Remember, the hardest part is the frontier strip." The old man gestures broadly. "Goddamn *guardroides* are everywhere. *Está cabrón pasar*. Follow the GPS, and blanket yourself the minute you hear the beep, eh? Once you're through to Nuevo León, *no hay pedo*. You'll be good. Act normal, 'cause you ain't got documents beyond that chit. But they're pretty cocky. Figure their perimeter defense keeps all intruders from Gringoland out. You got this, *chamaco*."

The crossing is as far as our money has bought his help. Guidance through the strip would have been another $10,000. My '*buelita* already sacrificed everything the family had to get her grandson to this point. She's living in a government refuge in Louisiana, not a cent to her name anymore. So I'm going it alone from here. My gut twists in fear, but I step through the portal without a word.

Clipping the GPS to my suit and plugging it into the converter, I drape the Mylar blanket over my shoulders and start trudging through the drifts. I glance up at the sky often, on the lookout for drones and *droides*. The clouds have thinned a little, and a sliver of moon peeks through. The red blip of Mars is near it, and my chest hurts a little as I think of my uncle up there. Last we heard, La Ermandá had taken over the shantytown he was living in. Piece of shit gangsters. No choice but to join them, serve them, or get your ass killed by them.

With that option off the table, '*buelita* said there was no choice. She contacted the coyote she knew, got everything lined up for me. I'm smart, a quick study, so I learned the basics of the job in no time. Coyote thought my age would be a problem, but I look older, nineteen or twenty at least, with top marks on every secondary learning module. He had his contact add my biometrics to the system. Now I've just got to get down there.

The GPS beeps and I drop to the snow, pulling the blanket over me. It doesn't block my body's warmth completely—even with the cold, that would be a dead giveaway, a thermic black hole on the landscape. Instead, it filters my heat signature to be the same as the surroundings, which it mimics in color like a chameleon. But even with my suit helping to regulate, temperature will build up and eventually leak out. I've only got a couple of minutes. If the robotic sentinels in sky or on land hang around much longer, I'm dead.

There is a faint hum overhead. Then the light on my GPS fades and disappears. I stand cautiously, but the drone is gone. No more time to rest. Got to keep moving. I have forty-eight straight hours' worth of walking ahead, and little more than sixty hours left to reach my destination. There will be plenty of time for sleeping once I've made it.

Over the next hour I have to duck down three times. On the third, the *'droide* slaloms so close it could touch me. I almost throw up what little rations I've been able to eat. Inside my suit, I'm sweating like freaking crazy.

But in the end, it isn't the robots that nearly kill me.

I am nearing the edge of the frontier strip. What passes for dawn in the year 2220 struggles up the horizon to my left. I undrape my blanket and begin to stow it when a low growl makes me spin around.

On a shallow ridge stands the biggest mountain lion I have ever seen, clearly a bespoke beast made in some government lab—saber teeth, shaggy pelt, broad and vicious paws. It leaps on me, pushing me through the snow and grinding me against frozen soil. Its hot breath comes in gusts as it snatches for my throat through the snow that's collapsed in upon us. I can only move my hand, the one that's still inside my bag. My mind is a frantic blank. Fear jolts me with adrenaline, but I am powerless. I realize I'm about to join the one billion who have died in the cataclysms of the last decade. My death won't even register for anyone, except *'buelita.* This is it. Lost in snow and ice, *como mamá y papá, como 'buelo Moncho …*

Then my grasping fingers find the laser welder, the one I've been practicing with since the deal was made. With a surge of hope, I pull it free, thumb the power on, and shove it upward, right into the jaw of the massive cat. The bespoke beast doesn't even have a chance to yowl—the laser penetrates its brain and all three hundred kilograms of the bastard collapse on me, twitching and dead.

It takes me a while to scramble free of its weight. "*Pinche puma de mierda,*" I grunt, giving its carcass a kick. I shove the welder into the right pocket of my parka, wanting it handy in case another bespoke beast attacks.

No time to recover. *Probably tracking its movements and vitals.* I start to run. The snow is thinner here, and soon I reach the ice-glutted Marte R. Gómez Reservoir. The idea is, again, to use the insanely cold water as a way past the sensors at the edge of the strip. With rebreather in mouth and clothes packed in the bag, I dive and begin to swim, passing a good meter beneath the buoys.

Halfway across, I feel strange turbulence nearby. Going completely still, I blow all my air out as I've been trained, allowing my body to drift and sink. Once I'm near the bottom, I reach out carefully, grabbing some hardy plants and pulling myself into the muck. A sentinel sub passes just meters above me, pinging the depths. For a second I know I'm busted, on my way to a detention center and then to deportation. But the automated ship moves on, and I am able to suck on the rebreather in relief.

I emerge ten minutes later. The pale sun glows uselessly through scraggly clouds. Wind off the lake freeze-dries the water droplets on me. I brush them off and pull my clothes back on.

I'm getting pretty hungry by the time Comales comes into view. It's hard not to gawk at the wealth and orderliness, the goods displayed in windows and on digital signage, the modern vehicles parked along clean, broad sidewalks where men and women in warm, fashionable clothes walk fearlessly. The Chicago of my childhood was a frozen, violent hell compared to even this small border city. Gangs of scavengers ready to mug, rape or kill anyone daring to exit their ice-crusted hovels. Tasteless rations, and not much of them. A government in ruins and no longer even pretending to help. Escaping had cost us so much, so many lives, corpses lost in the blinding white of the glacier-packed plains.

Getting to the government refuge was madness. It almost broke 'buelita and me both. But me, standing in Mexico, in this paradise of freedom and plenty? That's a freaking miracle.

A couple of people have noticed me, stock still and dumbstruck like a stupid tourist.

Move.

I make my way along the busy streets of Comales, avoiding the drifts thrown up by *barrebots*. A transit cop cocks his head at me, maybe curious, so I duck into a restaurant. A waitress hands me a menu. My eyes swim at the abundance. So much goddamn food. Feels almost sinful. She clears her throat, so I quickly order *tacos mañaneros*. Lots of hot sauce. A steaming cup of *café con leche*.

"Not from around here, are you?" the waitress asks in Spanish.

"No. I'm from Río Bravo. Going to Los Ramones to live with my uncle." It's the cover story I concocted. My grandmother has distant relatives there.

She nods and sets down a squeeze bottle full of green salsa. My heart slows its thudding. I fit in. I'm believable. After all this worrying about being made for a *pocho*, a US-born Mexican, I'm pulling it off.

The cop is gone when I leave the little hole-in-the-wall. I take to the countryside again, slicing through wire fences, deactivating ranchers' substandard sensors. Dusk sets in by the time I reach the state line between Tamaulipas and Nuevo León.

Last body of water, I think, staring at the San Juan River, exhausted. I go through the ritual, cross over undetected.

I haven't slept in like thirty-something hours, so I find a little hillock and dig myself into the snow, wrapping myself in the blanket and setting my GPS to wake me in four hours, which is all I can afford. I'm not even halfway there yet.

The rustling of wings startles me awake. I throw off the blanket and a crust of snow.

The sun is out! I look at my GPS. I have slept ten hours.

"¡Puta madre!" I scream, startling the magpies who have settled on the hillock. "Of all the goddamn luck!"

My muscles cramp, but I start to trot and then to flat-out run. Options whizz through my whirling mind. I realize that I'm going to have to do what the coyote told me not to do under any circumstances. There's no other way to make it.

It takes me all day to reach the city of China. I wash up at a truck stop, have a meal in the diner and watch the truck captains. I finally see a guy with a trustworthy face. He's nice to the waitress without being a pervert, leaves a decent tip.

I catch up to him as he's heading toward his rig.

"Excuse me, sir?"

He turns, works his toothpick to one side of his mouth. "Yeah, kid?"

"I was wondering if you might give me a ride. I need to get to the city of General Terán. My grandfather's ill, and I'm supposed to help out at his body shop while he's in the hospital."

I don't know whether I went too far with this story or not, but after a moment, the captain nods. "Sure, why not?"

"Thanks!" I stretch out my hand. "Pablo Maldonado."

"Nelson Gutiérrez, at your service. Come on, let's get in the cab. It's damn cold out here."

We clamber up to the module above the mammoth front wheels. I slump into one of the seats, and he powers up the rig, double-checking the AI and sensor array before engaging autopilot. The truck hisses out onto Highway 40, the computer communicating with satellites and the transit network to ease us into traffic with no incident.

There are six hours left. I'll be in General Terán in less than an hour, and then another three hours to walk to the site. Going to make it.

Captain Gutiérrez talks to me about his family in Galeana, how he got into the business, his plans for expansion. The smooth drone of the truck and his voice lull me, and soon I find myself nodding off. Seems to be no harm, so I drift into a light sleep.

Hands fumbling at my bag, reaching into my jacket. I jerk awake, find the captain drawing back from me. He's got my chit in his hand.

"That's what I thought," he says, almost purring. "Spent some time in the States before the Loop failed. I hear the English in your voice, kid. You hide it well, but ..."

He taps his ear with his free hand.

"Give that back to me," I demand.

"A *pocho* with this sort of a chit," he jerks his head at my bag, "and that uniform. How much did your family pay, kid? A hundred thousand? What are you willing to pay *me*?"

"Damnit, I don't have much. About five hundred, in Reformed Pesos."

Captain Gutiérrez laughs. "Five hundred *refritos*? You've got to be shitting me. All right, let's see. Maybe with a little something else thrown in."

He eyes me up and down, and I know he means sex.

"Forget it. I'm not for sale, you son of a bitch."

"Oh, yeah? Too bad, punk. I know the chief of police in General Terán. I can call him right now, have a patrol car waiting for your illegal ass at the truck stop. Your call, Pablito."

I hug my bag to my stomach, glaring at him. The words of *'buelita* echo in my ears: "You're the last of the Maldonado men, *m'ijo*. Your uncle's probably dead in some vallis on Mars right now, victim of *la mafia*. You've got to live, ¿entiendes? You got to keep the family name alive, teach your children and grandkids who we were and what we did. No matter what, Pablo. No matter what."

Dropping the bag, I nod.

"All right, bastard. You've got my back against a wall. To hell with it. Let's go."

I pull off my parka, but my hand reaches into the right pocket.

Gutiérrez laughs, unbuttons his shirt. "Come on to the back. Little sleeping cubicle where we can be more comfortable."

I nod, walk ahead of him, clutching my fist to my pants as if unsealing them. When I reach the bunk, he puts his hand on my shoulder, gently turns me around.

My eyes blurring, I slice his arm off at the elbow. He screams, clutches the cauterized wound. I twist away, kick him onto the thin mattress, hold the sparking blade centimeters from his face.

"Shut the hell up and don't move."

He babbles a stream of obscenities and groans, but he does what I tell him. With my free hand I undo his belt and cinch it around his ankles, then I shred the pillowcase, using it to tie his remaining hand to a climate control vent on the wall and to muzzle him.

"If you get free and screw with me, Gutiérrez, I'll take your other arm. You're not going to ruin this, bastard. You don't know what we ..."

I choke back a sob, turn and iris shut the compartment. I have to spin immediately toward the head. I vomit up everything I've eaten and more.

Fifteen minutes later, the truck hisses to a stop, the AI announcing arrival at destination. I palm the door open, drop into a soft pool of light, and quickly walk away. By the time they check this berth in the morning, by the time the cops scan for DNA and start to look, it'll be too late.

My GPS guides me to the Pilón River, but this time I just walk along its banks, heading generally southwest, my destination lost against the peaks of the Sierra Madre, black and shapeless in the night.

Dawn comes at last, and my future looms before me. I strip off my clothes and the thermal suit, pull on the jumpsuit with the Diarca corporate logo, shake out my parka and slip it back on. I chuck the discarded items into the river and head back to the highway, walking toward Montemorelos.

I can't get in an autocab or self-serve bus without a government ID, but someone sees the color of my jumper and gives me a ride to the gate. A dozen corporate security guards question me and examine my chit, scan my retina and check my prints, but it's okay. The coyote wasn't bullshitting us. My biometrics are in the corporate database.

"You'd better hoof it," one guard tells me. "Last maintenance group is due inside in ten minutes."

At my exhausted look, he sighs and shuttles me down to the pad. The sheer amount of private security is staggering: tanks, mechas, trenches, laser turrets. Getting into Mexico was a snap compared to the prospect of penetrating this corporate fortress without documents.

The ship towers, impossibly huge. Built on earth because of piracy concerns, *el Sexto Sol* contains some ten thousand Mexican citizens, mostly upper middle class or technocrats of some sort, all now in d-sleep. It could be centuries before the generation ship finds a new home, awakens them to rebuild our ancestral civilization.

But I won't be one of them. Even the sale of every single thing owned by an entire extended working class family couldn't buy me a spot in a hypostasis tube.

The guard stops at the maintenance ramp, calls to the group leader. "Got a straggler here."

"Well, hurry up, man! We're at T-6000, and I need to get everyone squared away in their sections."

I rush up the ramp into the bowels of *el Sexto Sol.* My chit goes through the scanner, my equipment is inspected, and I'm shunted into a lift along with another five men and women. We look at each other openly, contemplating the future. We will live our entire lives together and die before the sleeping ever awaken. Fear and hope clouds our eyes.

We're taken to the solar sail deployment section and led into a cramped living space, three stacked bunks on either side of a narrow aisle.

"Strap in," our guide barks before hurrying away. My new name is etched on the top bunk on the starboard side, and I climb up, sealing myself into the g-sheath.

Taking a deep breath, I look across the aisle. A woman, not much older than me, looks back.

"Hey, there," I say. "I'm Carlos Borromeo."

The new name feels strange on my tongue, but it fits me somehow.

"Ana Carranza. Nice to meet you."

The rockets start to rumble. Several of my crewmates gasp.

"Kind of cramped in here, huh?" I say with a smile.

Ana shrugs and seals herself in. "Yeah, but pretty soon we'll have the run of the whole ship, won't we?"

The thought fills me with such unexpected joy that I laugh above the building thrum.

"Yes, plus a lifetime to explore it …"

She laughs as well, her eyes bright, and her last words are lost in the stress of thundering lift-off.

The burden of tragedy, loss, humiliation, my harrowing journey—it seems part of the brutal, indifferent gravity that crushes me into the mattress now as my new home struggles to break free of the dying embrace of the old.

Then, like divine mercy, the weight is gone.

FLOWER WAR

Chimalmah Papalo looked out the windows of her office in the Ministry of Science building atop Chapultepec Hill, her skin prickling in awe at the moon-silvered expanse of Lake Texcoco. The steel pylons of the causeways blurred into mist and gentle waves so that the handful of predawn motor vehicles seemed suspended on a magical skein of quicksilver and light as they drifted toward the scintillating skyscrapers of Tenochtitlan, the business district at the heart of the imperial capital.

The moon hung fat and full, like a frangipani bud ready to burst. Chimalmah lifted a finger and touched the glass where its bright circle appeared to float.

"We're coming," she whispered, pausing for an almost worshipful moment before returning to her desk. Sipping at her steaming *texatl*, she reviewed the latest telex reports. The Soviets had backed down from their untenable rhetoric after the Emperor's speech to the League of Nations. The British Crown had gone so far as to applaud Cemanahuac for its space program, though the queen's use of the politically insensitive word "Aztecs" made Chimalmah cringe.

In the early morning hours, Imperial Intelligence had picked up encoded radio transmissions from Buckingham Palace instructing the presidents of both North American dominions to redouble their efforts while also showing diplomatic restraint and respect.

In essence, though the race into space wouldn't be definitively won until the landing itself, most heads of state had admitted their defeat.

But foreigners had never really been the problem. The biggest obstacle to space exploration was right here in Cemanahuac: the superstitious mire Chimalmah had spent two decades trying to climb out of, the primitive mindset that would keep all Cemanahuacah clinging to the earth like a rafter of fat, domesticated turkeys.

The plan is working, though, she reminded herself. *The next few hours will be the hardest. After that, there will be no turning back for any of us.*

Dawn was already flushing the peaks of the mountains to the east when the door to her office opened after a perfunctory knock.

"Madame Director? They've arrived."

Chimalmah looked up at the thin, graying form of Mimich Zollan, her assistant director of operations. The accustomed European cut of his suit was balanced by a more traditional cape of raven feathers and conical hat. It was a monumental day, after all, that required nods to one's culture.

"Good. Let's walk them to the platform. Is *Xiuhcoatl* ready?"

Mimich nodded as she gathered a few documents into a leather portfolio and fitted her quetzal-down cap in place with pins.

"They're prepping the turbines now."

Together they took the lift down to the ministry's receiving area, where two figures rose, flanked by entourages and Imperial Eagle Knights temporarily tasked with their protection. Chimalmah had met with both on several occasions. The man—decked out spectacularly in turquoise robe and scarlet cape, long silver-rimed hair twined with flowers and feathers, glittering nose and earplugs bespeaking his position, cotton sandals cushioning his every step—was Omaca Nepantlah, High Priest of *Tohuentzin*, the state religion of the Empire for centuries before the reforms of Tizoc III. Contrasting with his ostentatious display was Anantli Yohualli, an elderly woman clad in a simple white robe. She was the chief priestess of the goddess cult known as *Inanyotl,* an offshoot of the older tradition.

Securing their public support for the moon mission had taken several years and many concessions. Chimalmah's intimate knowledge of both faiths, whose adherents made up more than seventy percent of Cemanahuac's citizenry, had been key in reaching that agreement.

Today, however, was a day for science, and the director could barely contain her irritation at having to once again hold the hands of these purveyors of fantasy.

But still she smiled.

"Good morning, Your Eminence, Reverend Mother. It is, as always, an honor to share some of your valuable time in the service of Cemanahuac."

The high priest gave his traditional half smirk. "All we do is in the service of the gods."

"Oh, don't be so ornery, friend," Anantli Yohualli chided with a smile. "Bringing humanity closer to the heavens serves both patriotic and divine purposes."

Chimalmah simply nodded, though she wanted to shout the word *science* again and again into their pious faces. "Indeed. And now, if you will kindly follow me, we can head for the terminal and board one of our most treasured new marvels."

Led and trailed by black-clad Eagle Knights, the group made its way down broad, vaulted corridors to a platform where the turbine train was thrumming in wait upon glittering rails. As technicians slipped off the bright green and red metal skin, the protective forces arrayed themselves throughout the various cars, and the diplomatic party settled into a richly furnished and roomy compartment.

Chimalmah gestured around her with pride. "We named this cutting-edge transport *Xiuhcoatl* after the fast and fiery serpent used as a weapon by Lord Huitzilopochtli."

Omaca Nepantlah lifted one eyebrow and twisted his lips in a grimace that suggested grudging approval. "As the animal form of the god of time, this is an auspicious name for a locomotive."

"Chosen by the Emperor himself. And you're right, Your Eminence. The train is amazingly fast. We should reach the coast in a little over four hours, without the noise and discomfort of an air transport."

At her request, everyone found a seat on the various couches bolted throughout the compartment in order to ride out the initial thrust. The Eagle Knights, of course, simply stood where they were, betraying no evidence of strain. Once *Xiuhcoatl* was smoothly running along seamless rails at cruising speed, each party relaxed and fell into quiet internal conversation. Mimich brought regular updates to Chimalmah from the on-board telex, sobering reports that thrust her deep into serious contemplation.

Absorbed by the precarious details of the momentous day's numerous moving parts, she did not at first hear Omaca Nepantlah address her.

"Madam Director? Dr. Papalo?"

Chimalmah's head emerged from the sheaf of paper. "I'm sorry, Your Eminence. What was that again?"

Fingers slowly stroking a small obsidian mirror, the high priest repeated his question. "Over the past two years, you have been very respectful and accommodating of our faiths. But you have said little about what you yourself believe. I was just wondering why that is."

Her gut tightened up as a jolt of indignant adrenaline quickened pulse and breath. "Well, Your Eminence, I am a scientist and functionary of Cemanahuac. I've always imagined that serving the technological needs of an elective, executive, constitutional monarchy meant setting aside personal creeds and focusing on the rights and well-being of the citizens of the Empire."

"Artfully dodged, Madam Director. However, I will be straightforward. I suspect you have no *creed*, as you carefully put it. It is no secret to us that your father was Acaxel Papalo, priest of the Quetzacoatl temple in the town of Tochpan, and you yourself were an acolyte to a priestess long after his fall from grace. But you abandoned the houses of the gods, did you not?"

"She found comfort in the bosom of the Goddess, as you already know." The eyes of the high priestess were bright with what might have been sadness.

"For a time, yes. But before long she left your white temples, as well. Tell us truly, Dr. Papalo—do you still believe in the gods, whether the vast pantheon embraced by *Tohuentzin* or the emanations of the goddess that

Mother Anantli here adores? You have spent many months convincing us that Tlacaelel XII respects the old ways and will work to preserve them, but you are his representative in this moon business, and I would know your heart."

Biting back the desire to hurl a bitter answer, furious that they had dug into her personal affairs, Chimalmah instead looked down at the papers in her lap and took one up. "Trust me, it's not my beliefs that are an issue here. They don't matter at all. Let me read something to you both.

"'Life on earth is bitter and fleeting. Death should be our only goal. And most glorious of all is death on the battlefield, flesh reaped like blooms by the scythe of the Lord of the Near and the Nigh. We promise a great conflagration, a great flood, a Flower War the likes of which this Fifth Age has never seen. The foolish Emperor soils his throne with these Eastern distractions from the Mexica Way, these sacrilegious attempts to scale the World Tree and touch a holy face. As the *Book of Utterances* says of the perverse ruler, *Certainly he has become brazen, wishing to belittle holy things. He acts as he wills, lives as he wants, thinks as he desires. May he learn to fear you, Mocker of Men. May he merit some reprimand from you, whatever you would give him: punishment, illness, dishonor, destruction. Throughout the world your true followers abide—choose one of them, instead, to replace this crazed and evil king. Crush him with your fist of rage!*

"'Ah, and *we* are his Fist of Rage, brothers and sisters of Cemanahuac, ready to rip the impious from his throne. We will remind you of the chaotic might of Tezcatlipoca, of Lord Huitzilopochtli, of the Tzitzimimeh themselves, fierce avengers from the heavens. Today we will don the flayed flesh of our enemies. Today Cemanahuac returns to her former glory!'"

Chimalmah crumpled the sheet with disgust. "It's signed by Ehcatzin Toyolca, leader of Zomalli Imacpich, the 'Fist of Rage,' bloody-minded terrorists with fervent faith. A dozen attacks on government and scientific targets in the past two years. Scores dead, yet rising popularity. Those are the 'old ways' you want to preserve, aren't they?"

Nepantlah's face grew red. "You know very well, woman, that we do not condone the violence of that group of extremists!"

It was all Chimalmah could do to not leap to her feet and scream at him. "Woman? Ah, yes. You reveal yourself at last, Your Eminence. As a *woman*, I tell you that your church *has not done enough*. You issue milquetoast condemnations, but you don't silence priests who align with extremism in their temples, and you've done nothing to adjust church doctrine to support civil rights, science and progress."

"Church and state are separate in our Constitution," the high priest spat. Amantli Yohualli looked on in beatific calm, making no attempt to halt the argument.

"Ah, when it's convenient, you bring that up. Otherwise, you'd love to have someone on the throne that would return Tohuentzin to its privileged place as state religion." Indignation stripped her normal reasoned reserve away. "You know, since you're so damned interested in my beliefs, since you have stuck your ample nose into my affairs, let me tell you my story, High Priest.

"Yes, I was presented to the temple as a baby, consecrated to the calling of priestess. After my mother died, my father was even more determined that I fulfill that role, taking up my mother's mantle. And I *believed* in what I did. I found comfort in service to Xochiquetzal, tending her gardens, feeding her birds. I buried my grief in the feathery green of her robes.

"My father's 'fall from grace.' Yes. His faith wasn't enough to deal with the bereavement he felt, and he became a drunk. Siphoned off temple funds for his vices. But I felt compassion for him. I didn't blame the church, either. But gradually I began to look around. Many gods, but who did we mainly bow down to? Tezcatlipoca and Huitzilopochtli, violent and bloody figures who imposed morality but didn't live by it. Every night, looking up at the sky, I couldn't help thinking of how Huitzilopochtli had dismembered his sister, hurling her head into heaven to become the moon. When it came time to say my vows in Tenochtitlan, I visited the bas-relief disk depicting her broken body at the foot of the Great Temple and thought of all the women who had been hurled down those steps to lie lifeless upon her."

"There has been no human sacrifice in more than three centuries! Smaller personal offerings shed with holy spines suffice. Bah! I waste my words. You clearly have no understanding of the Great Mystery, the price mankind must pay to keep the wheels of the cosmos turning."

The high priest appeared ready to launch into a speech, but Chimalmah cut him off. "Oh, I understand it, all right. It's just nonsense. Blood has no *teotl,* no magical property that feeds the universe. It's just water and minerals and protein molecules, themselves formed from atoms, made up of subatomic particles."

Anantli Yohualli finally spoke. "And beyond that, my daughter? What lies deeper than your quarks and bosons?"

"Ask the Japanese," Nepantlah growled.

Chimalmah refused to take the bait, realizing she was going too far. She had been ordered to keep these two from suspecting anything, and her outburst might have already jeopardized the project.

So she bit back her indignation, ignoring the dig with a slight smile and focusing on the chief priestess's more sanguine tone. "We don't know yet. But for the first time in human history, we have the tools for finding out. Look, I joined your religion hoping to find a new perspective on womanhood, one that valued love and nurturing above conquest and blood. And I did. It was peaceful and healing, Reverend Mother. But in the end, it was all based on fairy tales.

"Think of the struggles required to garner support for this mission: you first quailed at the idea that the boots of men might trample divine flesh. For you the faithful, the moon may not be the decapitated head of a rebellious goddess, but you *do* believe it is the fire-transformed body of an arrogant god. Despite centuries of telescopic observation, you believe that the craters on its surface are the tracks of a rabbit hurled against him to dim his light and teach him humility. That, ultimately, is why I left you as well. I wanted objective truth, not a web of lovely stories."

"So you turned to science." The words were ugly on the high priest's lips, as if he were accusing her of prostitution.

"Yes. And today it triumphs."

The three of them looked at each other in silence for a time until their various attendants drew them aside with whispers of inconsequential matters that would hopefully distract them from what seemed unbridgeable chasms diving each from each.

It was nearly 10 a.m. when the train slowed to a stop. The party disembarked slowly, treasuring the view. Before them spread the Jade Gulf, sparkling green-blue beneath the late spring sun. And upon those waters, just a few hundred rods from shore, lay Victory Isle, where the invading Spanish had been driven definitively from Cemanahuac in the final battle of that attempted conquest, some four hundred and fifty years before. The desolate sands of the former place of sacrifice were now home to a sprawling launch complex, established after the Second World War by the Imperial Agency for Space and Flight. From here the mighty Tlacahueyac rocket program had taken men into orbit for the first time. Now Project Citlalloh would take them to the moon.

Chimalmah finally saw the hordes of visitors, news trucks and reporters as the Eagle Knights led them past the terminal to where government transports awaited. Beyond the barriers, in fact, people swarmed the beach as far as the eye could see. A wooden platform, draped with flags and feathers, had been erected for this very moment. She and her two guests ascended the steps and took their places.

Her heart quailing for a moment at dark premonitions, Chimalmah scarcely listened as the religious leaders pronounced a few ambiguous and vaguely supportive words to the cameras. In her memory, the Emperor's words echoed with ominous import: *They won't understand, Dr. Papalo. They will be furious and frightened. And they'll demand answers from you. Just be firm. You know the cost of letting those bastards win.*

Then the closing prayer of the chief priestess died on the summer wind and it was time for the director to address the throng herself.

"I stand here with you, fellow Cemanahuacah, awed by this event, which for the first time takes human feet to the soil of another world. Like High Priest Nepantlah and Chief Priestess Yohualli, I salute the daring astronauts, the wise scientists and the able technicians, as well as, more broadly, the people of Cemanahuac and our Emperor for this undertaking, which, until now, only had precedents in the realm of imagination.

"Our nation's very own emblem—its traditional seal—with the eagle and the serpent, already embodies the double destiny inspiring humans since their remote origins: the serpent symbolizes the Earth and all that holds us here; the eagle represents flight, undaunted and far-seeing, a fearless pilgrimage that makes it possible for the legacy of the centuries to reach ever-broadening horizons. Far from contradicting each other, both images are complementary and together reflect our temporal, earthly, nature and the visionary aspirations that nurture scientific progress.

"It is the Emperor's sincerest hope that this human accomplishment will result in a renewed unity of the citizens of Cemanahuac, that it will prove beneficial to humanity in general, and that all the peoples on Earth will recognize through its scope their common destiny, for the development of this new stage does not offer power nor riches nor spiritual fulfilment, but instead a deepening of our unquenchable thirst for enlightenment and an unyielding faith in the supremacy of reason and justice as a way and an inspiration for human conduct. Thank you!"

Ignoring the barrage of questions and camera flashes, the IASF director allowed herself to be herded into one of the vehicles with Mimich Zollan. As the caravan crossed the bridge that spanned the narrow bay, she glanced out the window again and again, scanning sky and wave.

"I doubt anything will happen just yet, ma'am," the older man said, touching her arm lightly.

"I suppose not. Someone would give us a heads-up if they were moving sooner than anticipated."

"Indeed. Well. You, uh, certainly declared your allegiance back there. Are you sure it was wise to be that strident?"

Chimalmah sighed. "It'll all be over soon enough, Mimich. There will be a shitload of other things for people to worry about. My implied dismissing of religious faith will be lost in the avalanche."

Within minutes they had reached the parking area behind the squat, muraled bunker of the Ilhuicamina Flight Center. Though nearly a hundred notable men and women filled the stands of the open-air VIP viewing area, Chimalmah's party was escorted to the visitor viewing room at the back of mission control; some fifty other dignitaries were already seated there, from local municipal and provincial leaders to members of parliament, ambassadors, businessmen and other assorted guests of the Emperor.

Chimalmah took a few moments to greet key individuals, most of whom asked her the same question: What about the Emperor, his cabinet, the leaders of his party? None of them was present. Had there been an unannounced delay?

Show time. She gestured to a technician and asked him to shunt the room's internal audio and video to the press feed and loudspeakers in the stands.

"Ladies and gentlemen," she called out, raising her voice to answer this concern definitively for all involved. "This is Dr. Chimalmah Papalo, Director of the Imperial Agency for Space and Flight. Because of repeated threats from the terrorist group Zollan Imapich, Imperial Intelligence has requested that the Emperor and his staff not view the launch from this site. Instead, His Imperial Majesty will address the nation shortly after takeoff from an understandably undisclosed location."

While this mollified some, others began to grumble to each other heatedly, concerned for their own safety. But as Eagle Knights deployed along the walls and the calm voice of Mission Chief Cilimi Machico began wrapping up pre-launch activities over his headset mic, everyone became infused with the excitement of the moment. Looking out over the various flight system specialists at their consoles, the group could see the massive Citlamitl rocket looming beside the complex stack of umbilical scaffolding, its towering length emblazoned with a colorful image of Ehecatl, wind god aspect of Quetzalcoatl, a riot of rippling feathers that even now gave the illusion of flight. Screens above and below the windows showed different camera feeds, including one of the base of the launch tower, where the astronauts were at last disembarking from the newly arrived transport van.

The half-dozen men strode magnificent despite their bulky orange spacesuits, features distorted into mythic blurs by the sunlight glinting off the thick plastic of their helmets, from which ceremonial quetzal feathers emerged like tapering rainbows. As the cameras tracked their movement toward the lift on the launch tower, someone in the viewing room muttered into the silence:

"They seem taller today, somehow."

Then chaos was unleashed.

Cement exploded at the men's feet in chunks, throwing up fragments and dust. Whining thuds overwhelmed the remote microphone till only crackling static could be heard. One of the astronauts was lifted into the air, spinning, while another one dropped to the ground, his helmet splintered and red. The other four crouched, reaching back into their life-support backpacks and pulling out machine guns with which they opened fire at something off-camera. At the same time, a squad of Shorn Ones exploded from the transport van, their bright yellow uniforms causing the monitors to distort. The elite fighting force began hurling grenades at unseen foes as their single braids coiled madly around their shaven, painted skulls.

The battle moved away from the camera in a matter of seconds, though Mission Control attempted to follow the Imperial soldiers as they pursued their attackers, throwing up different camera feeds on the main screen.

The visitor viewing room had erupted into panicked pandemonium, sobs and arguments and angry demands. The Eagle Knights prevented anyone's leaving, despite the indignant protests and commands of the various functionaries.

"Those were not astronauts at all, were they?" came the voice of High Priest Nepantlah at her elbow. "What have you done, Dr. Papalo?"

Before Chimalmah could reply, someone screamed. On the monitor, a flash of light was dying, and they could see the launch tower beginning to collapse.

Please. Please work. Don't let this have been for nothing.

"Now, you sons of bitches!" shouted Mission Chief Cilimi Machico. "Launch it now!"

Flames burst from the Citlamitl rocket, pounding against the ground with such force that Chimalmah's very bones began to thrum. Pulling away from the umbilical connections that joined it to the tower, the motley-hued cylinder lifted into the sky just as the massive stacks of rigging toppled onto the rocky sand.

Silence fell.

"But," someone muttered in confusion, "if the astronauts never boarded, then why did they launch it?"

The monitor followed Ehecatl's image as he rose higher, higher, higher …

… and began to curve in a steep parabola.

"Mother of the Gods," came a strangled sob. "It's going to crash!"

Chimalmah turned and looked with as much dispassion as she could muster at the shock and despair on their faces.

"No," she simply said. "No, it isn't."

Nearly ten minutes later, every loudspeaker and video monitor crackled back to life. In seconds, the voice and visage of Emperor Tlacaelel XII commanded the attention of all in attendance, his chiseled features stern beneath his ceremonial headdress of quetzal plumes and emeralds, his turquoise cloak of office draped regally over a black suit of European design.

"My people, you are no doubt alarmed and perhaps even frightened by what you have just witnessed. Let me assure you, however, that you were at no moment in mortal danger.

"For months now, Imperial Intelligence has been tracking the internal communications and movements of the terrorist group that calls itself Zomalli Imapich, responsible for the deaths of 213 citizens and some one hundred million tepoztics in damages. We discovered, through covert infiltration of their network, their plan to attack today's historic launch.

"I must now share certain state secrets with you, my friends. Early on in the brutal campaign of the so-called Fist of Rage, it became clear to me that a second, clandestine launch site might be required for the safety and success of our lunar mission. So, with the cooperation of the governor of the Commonwealth of Yucatan, I used my executive discretion to establish one on the Empire's southernmost Atlantic shore.

"Furthermore, I issued the summary judgment that, should any group of citizens attempt to kill our astronauts and destroy this launch, their entire organization would pay the ultimate price for this treason. You yourselves, only moments ago, bore witness to their violence, their flouting of our laws.

"Punishing their crime would be complex, requiring extreme measures reserved only for the direst of situations and most dastardly of foes. Once we knew for certain of the impending terrorist attack, once we had ascertained the details of that plot, once we had mapped in meticulous detail the stronghold of these ruffians in the foothills of the Chichimec Desert, then did I put a difficult plan into motion, one to which only a very few could be privy to catch the enemy off-guard.

"Today, you have not witnessed the launching of the Citlalloh VI mission. That will occur tomorrow at the secondary site.

"No, the rocket that took to the skies moments ago bore not a landing module, but a low-yield atomic weapon, a smaller version of the bomb we used to destroy Tokyo and end the war twenty years ago. Just before I began this address, the missile impacted against the headquarters of Zomalli Imapich, utterly obliterating that destructive group. Members of the group on missions elsewhere have been rounded up and executed as traitors.

"I have exercised my Constitutional powers to accomplish this. I have been tasked with the enforcement of our nation's laws, and that I have done. No band of terrorists will ever be allowed to hold captive the future of Cemanahuac, to impede our scientific progress. We move ever onward, ever outward, to the moon, the planets, and the stars beyond.

"*That*, dear brothers and sisters, is the true Mexica Way. May the heavens shower us with blessings, and may we ascend to them on the wings of genius."

The screens went black.

Despite the questions on everyone's faces and lips, Chimalmah raised a hand to extend the silence a little longer. Turning to Mission Control, she signaled a technician, indicating that she wanted her voice broadcast again.

"Invited guests and VIPs, this is IASF Director Papalo again. Though I understand your desire to interrogate me about the particulars of the Emperor's daring strategy for ensuring the scientific ascendency of our nation, I should inform you that in an hour's time, two passenger planes will arrive on the nearby airstrip. Transports are standing by to give rides to any dignitary who wants to attend tomorrow's launch. The Emperor is providing for your accommodations in the Commonwealth of Yucatan at his winter estate in Tulum.

"If you are interested, please indicate this to an Eagle Knight, displaying your valid pass, and you will be escorted. Thank you."

She motioned for the connection to be cut.

The room was nearly empty of visitors an hour later. The grilling had been brutal, but Chimalmah had remained calm. In the end, she knew, her nation's long tradition of executing traitors would calm most people's initial shock. World opinion would be scathing, sanctions might be imposed, but the Emperor had proven his mettle in the global arena. The technological advances and vast petroleum reserves of Mesoamerica were too tempting, in the final analysis. Cemanahuac would be reprimanded, then forgiven.

Only High Priest Omaca Nepantlah and Chief Priestess Anantli Yohualli remained, flanked by their entourages. His face was livid and clammy, hers distant and sad.

"Well?" Chimalmah asked. "Are you coming?"

Nepantlah walked toward the doorway where she stood. As he drew close, he muttered for her ears alone:

"I cannot. But tell him I understand. There will be no further opposition while I remain."

When he had left, Anantli gestured for her people to wait outside. She embraced Chimalmah for a moment, and then she shut the door as if for privacy.

"So. Deceit and violence. Interesting. I got the distinct impression you couldn't stomach either."

"It's not the same. We did this to continue our search for truth, to promote progress, to protect the people. There were larger issues than ethics at stake."

Anantli placed her hand on Chimalmah's head, like one would a child. "Oh, my daughter, we are more alike than I had imagined."

"Don't be ridiculous. What are you talking about?"

The high priestess gestured at the door. "What do you think he and I have done all these years? Indeed, what is religion itself if not the loving deception of others as we tirelessly search for truth?"

For a moment, the old apprehensions squeezed at her chest, the foolish ghosts of dread, revenants of belief that retribution awaited. Then she saw her mother, dead in the temple, unaided by Xochiquetzal or any other god. She saw her father, drunk and then jailed, abandoned by his order, his religion.

And she remembered the first image of an atom she had seen, at university, all that dancing, wobbling perfection, answer to so many questions on which the gods had been silent.

"The difference, Reverend Mother, is this: our deception is brief and our answers are tantalizingly close. We already have the means to find them. You, however, refuse to admit the tools even exist, and you will never shatter the illusions you've created."

Three days later, the Imperial cabinet and key IASF staff watched on a monitor in the Emperor's audience chamber as astronaut Ahcopa Michin crossed a crater and planted the eagle-and-snake deep in the lunar dust. There were cheers and toasts and ecstatic embraces: the Emperor was hailed, and he passed tobacco tubes around to celebrate.

Chimalmah, not a smoker herself, slipped out onto the balcony and stared up at the waning gibbous moon, hanging bright as a petal from a Funeral Tree in the clear summer sky.

We reached you. Set our feet upon you. Soon outposts then cities will rise on your silvered sands, and from your bosom we'll hurl ourselves out into the awesome night.

Ehcatzin Toyolca, whose bones spread pulverized in a smoking crater far to the north, had written of Flower Wars, those ancient staged conflicts in which both sides had taken sacrificial victims captive. Rather than fear death on these terms, the warriors of old had deemed it an honor to be seized by the enemy and offered up to alien gods.

Chimalmah thought of scythes and blooms with a shudder of epiphany.

Though she had reaped the enemies of progress, heaped them high and set them alight with a nearly holy fire, she felt no remorse.

They had found the glory they sought.

So had she.

HOUNDS OF HEAVEN

JEALOUS SPIRITS, THUNDERING GUN

Sometime during the first week of April, 1870, amid a late-afternoon spate that soon tapered to drizzle, Philip Kindred crossed from Texas into the territory of New Mexico. His Andalusian, Moctezuma, picked its slow, careful way among the desolate, increasingly rocky terrain, and Kindred knew he would soon need the services of a good farrier to shoe the horse. Near dusk they forded a small arroyo, and the former ranger dismounted near a stand of mesquite, unsaddling his horse, rubbing down the sweaty sheen of its black flanks, and hobbling it to graze on buffalo grass nearby. Once he had gotten a decent fire going, he set to boil some pinto beans that had been soaking all afternoon in the clay pot that dangled by a thong from his saddle. Tossing in the last bit of salted pork from his now meager stores, Kindred, thin from long lonely months spent meandering the Llano Estacado, stirred the mixture till he figured it was ready to eat. After supping and washing up in the arroyo, he sat in the dirt, back propped against his saddle, and watched the darkness thicken, his mind an earnest blank.

Eventually the sky cleared, and the moon gleamed its lurid light through the chill air; Kindred stoked his fire and decided with a resigned insomniac sigh to finally begin reading Longfellow's translation of the *Inferno*, which had spent the better part of a year buried neglected in his saddlebags. Dropping deeply into the story, he immediately identified with Dante, a man adrift, purposeless at the midpoint of his life. *Then chosen. Set upon a road he would never have elected of his own free will. Just as I was.* But the hellish visions in the medieval parable paled beside the horrors Kindred had witnessed during his struggle, more than seven years spent fighting twisted agents of darkness. Across the Union, people slept in relative peace each night of this post-war reconstruction, unaware of how close they had come to the final conflagration for which the Civil War had been but a façade. Shoulder-to-shoulder with other, greater warriors, Kindred had battled to stave off the eruption of Hell itself across the continent. But disaster had been, for a time, averted. They had fought, that band of reluctant heroes, and they had won.

However, now Kindred was alone, completely alone. And as he reached the eighth canto, he shuddered at the vicious, indignant cry hurled at Dante from upon the walls of Dis, Hell's capital:

More than a thousand at the gates I saw
Out of the Heavens rained down, who angrily
Were saying, "Who is this that without death
Goes through the kingdom of the people dead?"

Who indeed? Why do I live, while they have died? While she *has died? And why am* I *permitted to see that which so few can*? But he had already learned that there was no answering that sort of question, and so he simply shut the book and huddled under his saddle blankets, the cold, starry darkness silently nudging him into somnolence and dreamless sleep.

The next morning, as sunlight struggled bloodlessly to mount the Staked Plains, Kindred packed his gear and set out on Moctezuma toward the West. *Head west.* That had been the command, and his bereft heart had little else to guide it. The gold disc at his back rose higher in the sky, its light attenuated slightly by wisps of cloud on a northwesterly breeze. Beyond that, the universe was utterly still. *Holding its breath*, he mused. *Waiting to see what comes next.*

A low hill, and then the sullen, dingy white of an adobe mission. He would have ridden by briskly, giving the cemetery a wide berth, but the throng of black-clad souls and the ululating sounds of grief compelled him inexplicably, and he nudged Moctezuma toward the funeral. Though he tried to focus on the priest, whose monotone Latin became more intelligible with each forward surge of the horse, Kindred could not but see the grim shades that clung dumbly to most gravestones, slack faces staring into nowhere, incorporeal hands clutching uselessly at wilted garlands of yucca flowers. As he passed, those empty visages turned dead eyes on him, quickened for a few moments by the power he had been granted, but he knew their silent vigil would continue once he had moved beyond them, no release in sight.

It seemed that an entire town was in attendance, some three hundred souls, most of them weeping as a small casket was lowered lovingly into the earth. Dismounting, Kindred flipped the reins of his horse around the lowest branch of a stunted pecan. He stood quietly as the service ended and in small groups or one by one the parishioners walked northwest, into the chilly breeze and presumably toward the town. The priest glanced at Kindred, exchanged a few words with two men wielding perfunctory shovels, and entered the mission. Kindred started to follow him, only to have an inner urging turn him back to his saddlebags, from which he extracted a rectangular wooden case. Holding it gingerly in both hands, he headed toward the mission.

Inside, the priest was kneeling before the altar, his shoulders shaking with silent sobs. Kindred pushed his slouch hat back, its stampede string tightening slightly against his larynx like a thin leather noose. For a moment he hesitated, respecting the sanctity of grief, but the same impulse that had made him bring the case pushed him forward, and he called to the genuflecting figure.

"*Padre, ¿puedo hablar con usted?*"

The priest stood, his back still to Kindred. "*Dime, hijo mío.*"

"*Acabo de ver como habéis enterrado a una criatura. Habéis asistido todos, el pueblo entero. ¿Qué es lo que ha sucedido?*"

The priest turned and seemed surprised to see Philip standing there, a dusty white man in his forties, with one holster empty and death in his eyes. "You are American."

"Yes."

"Your Spanish, it is very good, but not at all Mexican. Not even *novomejicano*. Very … Peninsular. Very … *¿erudito*?"

"Erudite."

The priest nodded, taking a few steps toward him. "I can hear the university in your tones. I am from Italy, learned Spanish when in seminary. You too have … studied this? You are a man of books?"

"I was, yes. Things … changed. I became a Ranger, then a soldier."

"And now?"

Kindred looked down for a moment, shrugging weakly. "I'm not sure I can explain what I am now, *padre*."

The priest seemed to weigh this odd response in his heart. "I see. To answer your question, the town entire came to the funeral because this is the ninth child which it dies in the last four months here in Santa Inez, and the people are confused and frightened and desperate to find the other missing children."

A wrenching in his gut dimmed Kindred's vision and buckled his knees with such violence that he had to lean heavily against a rough-hewn pew. *Missing children. Santa Inez.* "Inez?"

"Yes. This town. Name for Saint Agnes." The priest's reddened eyes narrowed with genuine concern. "This name, it affects you, yes?"

Kindred shut his eyes for a moment, perceived the glow of faith that limned the priest's form. He focused on that glimmering outline, used it to keep the pain of his many bereavements at bay. "My wife was named Inés. I … lost her. She died, eleven years ago." *And then I lost her again, when she moved on forever. My beloved Beatrice, my guide, gone.* He could still see her gossamer smile, the nearly intangible brush of her angelic form. *Head west,* she had said as the wind pulled her ghostly image to silken shreds, *until you hear my name. There you'll find your destiny.*

Gripping the oaken case with determination, he opened his eyes to the physical world and straightened. "But it's not just her name. The children … I am …" He groped for words, trying not to picture his son, trying not to remember those feelings of impotence. For he had power now, yes he did. Power to halt the darkness. "*Padre*, I need to understand what has happened here. I think I'm meant to help."

"Very well. As a man of learning, you perhaps can have some knowledge that it will help us. Come with me, to the friary. It is there that I live. I will explain so well like I can the events of this year."

Across a dusty square that weeds sought vainly to invade stood the whitewashed friary, and inside the priest invited Philip Kindred to rest in a comfortable chair beside a clay hearth at the center of the northern wall of the main room.

"To begin, my name is Sandro Bronzino."

"Philip Kindred."

Father Bronzino muttered the name as he served Kindred some water, as though mentally translating it into Italian or searching for some hidden meaning. Handing the simple clay cup to his visitor, he nodded sharply and began.

"I only have been in Santa Inez for around three years. I came to the territory at request of Bishop Jean Baptiste Lamy; many of my Jesuit brethren, they came with me, most of us from Italy. I request this specific parish, for it remind me of my home. Everything went well the first two years, the normal cycle of life in the small town. Then it began, the sickness. Many little children, they suffered tremors, fevers; their little faces, some of them, became twisted. I did what I could. A doctor from Santa Fe came, only to confirm what had the local experts already said: the children's illness had no medical explanation.

"Soon, two occurrences. Many of the older townspeople, they claimed that the illness was the work of phantoms that roam the night, searching for victims. Also, many men came to confess me of strange, sinful dreams in which beautiful women came to them. In the mornings they would awake feeling weak and looking pallid. At first, I suspect a simple hysteria at the illnesses, but then several men … *se volvieron locos* …"

"They went mad," offered Philip, leaning forward expectantly.

"Yes. Then some of the sick children … they disappeared. We searched and searched, but nothing. The town was so tense, so desperate. Many accused to the mad men of having done something, but no evidence was found. A group secretly lynched one of the men. It seemed all would go mad soon, and I send word to the diocese for help.

"Then children start dying. Babies, in their majority, under four years of old. And the rumors of phantoms, they became a loud cry. The people demand to me, to the bishop's representatives whom came at my word, that we exorcise the town. But such a thing … unheard of, yes? And the oldest among them, they said to us, 'No, not demons. Ancient warrior women, spirits of those who they die giving birth. Driven by jealousy. *Cihuateotes.*'"

Philip could stay seated no longer; the anxiety that had been building in him as Father Bronzino told his tale now thrust him to his feet.

"Cihuateteoh," he corrected in a horse whisper.

"You have heard before of this myth?"

Kindred shook his head. "It's no myth, padre. Cihuateteoh … means 'divine women,' you know. Nahuatl word, Aztec. They are also called *cihuapipiltin*, 'princesses.' Vampiric warrioresses, agents of chaos and destruction." For a moment, shuddering, he saw in his mind's eye a death-white harpy swoop down and rip off a soldier's head, one of his more gruesome memories of the war. "They won't leave until every child here is dead or gone. We must act as quickly as possible. When was the last death?"

Father Bronzino simply stared at Kindred, fingering the crucifix that shone silver against his black habit. "I think you should leave, Mr. Kindred. Thank you for your concern."

Kindred's brow creased with irritation. "I don't understand you, padre. I can see that you believe: your faith shines strong and steady. Would it help you if I called them demons … *succubi*? Is Latin more palatable for you than Nahuatl, is that the obstacle? No, the problem is that you don't believe in *me*, is that not so?"

Suddenly burning with the empty anger of so many fruitless months, Kindred slammed the wooden case he carried down upon the rough-hewn dining table to his right. Flipping the latches up, he swept the top open to reveal the hefty weapon contained within. "Come over here, *padre*. I want to show you something."

Bronzino stood his ground, obviously frightened, but trying with all his might to conceal his fear behind indignation. "*Mejor guarda tu pistola, hijo. No hay necesidad de violencia. Sólo dime qué quieres.*"

"*Basta*. I'm not going to shoot you. Please, just come look closely at this gun."

Timidly, Bronzino approached the table. Kindred watched his eyes fall upon the pistol, tracing the strange Islamic vegetal patterns engraved upon its gold and silver-plated double barrel, abstract swirls broken by tessellations of crosses, stars and *aums*. Then his gaze was drawn to the word faintly carved into the ancient wood of its softly curving grip, and he leaned in as if to make out the letters.

"Its form is based on the Le Mat pistols the Confederacy used. Probably constructed in New Orleans when the first batch was being manufactured, though I don't know by whom. It's a .42 caliber, with a nine-chambered cylinder that rotates around a tenth chamber, .65 caliber. Ten chambers, perfect number. But that's not what's so special about it, *padre*.

"Are you familiar with the writings of Gregory of Tours?" The priest's eyes indicated he was. "Gregory uses two terms extensively: *sanctus* and *virtus*. The meaning of the former is pretty transparent, but *virtus* ... well, he employs it to mean the mystic potency that emanates from sacred people or things. Think of it as supernatural energy, a contact between the physical and the spiritual worlds in which the former, being an inferior reality, must always yield. *Virtus* derives most naturally from absolute faith and deep love, and it can transfer from spiritual beings or enlightened humans into inanimate objects. *Virtus* has its opposite, of course, as all things do, a destructive supernatural force born of great hate, anger and greed."

Kindred indicated the pistol with a jerk of his head. "This is a weapon of *virtus*, designed to counter decay, destruction and chaos. Listen. The barrels were forged from puissant metals: one of the nails with which Christ was fixed to the cross was melted down to shape them." The priest's eyes narrowed, and Kindred decided against mentioning how the blades from one of the Prophet Mohammed's scimitars and from the Sword of Laban made up the bulk of the pistol's frame. "The plating? Drawn from the sheathing of gold around one of the poles of the Ark of the Covenant and from the silver procession cross St. Augustine bore when coming before Ethelbert, king of Kent." Grasping the double barrel, Kindred lifted the weapon from its resting place and brought the right-hand side of the grip up to the priest's eye level. "What do you see engraved in this wood?"

The priest, a bit disconcerted, hesitated, then read aloud. "Rex."

His eyes lifted, and Kindred's gaze held them. "Rex. 'Et inposuerunt super caput eius causam ipsius scriptam hic est: *Iesus rex Iudaeorum.*' Matthew 27:37."

Bronzino's breath caught for a moment in his throat. "You are expecting for me to believe that the handle of your pistol is from the *titulum* the Roman soldiers nailed above Our Lord's head?"

Well, half of it. The other half is wood from Buddha's bodhi tree. But let us proceed slowly. "I don't expect you to believe a thing, *padre.* I am perfectly willing to make you see for yourself." Flipping the gun around, Kindred pointed it at the priest. "Move over to the window, the one that looks out over the cemetery. *Now.*"

Trembling with obvious fear, the priest reluctantly complied. Kindred stood beside him and holstered Rex. Spitting into his right hand, the former ranger ran his left index finger along the windowsill until it was filthy with dust, and he mixed this with the spittle to form a small quantity of muddy paste. Quickly, not allowing Bronzino time to jerk away, he smeared the mixture across the middle of the priest's forehead. Leaning close enough to smell the other man's acrid breath, he whispered a single word:

"*See.*"

Turning to look out at the tombstones, Kindred watched the gloomy shades move without purpose around their graves. The priest beside him, seeing now what the American could always see, what he could never close his eyes to, gave a weak cry of shock and terror.

"The purposeless dead, Father Bronzino, trapped in a limbo of their own making. You asked me what I am before … I am their keeper. And yours. I'm the one who staves the darkness off just a bit longer." *How long I resisted, yet how easily the words now roll from my tongue.* "The universe is like an onion, and I've just peeled back a layer for you. But there are deeper levels to this world, crawling with black creatures I hope you never need face. Such a monster is preying on the children of this town, and you *must* help me to stop it, tonight, before another innocent is taken from you."

For the briefest of moments he saw his son astride a piebald mustang, long hair plaited, scalps dangling from his belt, cruel words barked in the Comanche tongue streaming from his lips. *Taken, like he was. Taken and twisted. I cannot allow the same to befall the children of this town.*

"¡Basta! No quiero ver más. *Te ayudaré en lo que pueda*, please just take this vision from me, Mr. Kindred!"

"Shhh." Philip covered the priest's eyes with his left hand, rubbing the mark away with his right. "You are blind again, *padre*. Be glad of it."

A few moments later, once the priest had regained his composure, the two stood shoulder-to-shoulder at a municipal map the diocese had commissioned some years earlier. Bronzino indicated one by one the homes from which children had disappeared or in which children had recently died, and Kindred marked each spot on the map with a cartridge from his Model No. 3 American.

Bronzino inhaled deeply. "I see a trend toward the edge of town, yes? Toward the western edge?"

"Yes. The cihuateteoh follow the descent of the sun, heralding the night, the darkness." He regarded the procession of cartridges, each a little further southwest than the previous. His mind imposed an arc across the sites, and the pattern clicked for him. "It's a parabola … following the sun's azimuth at different times during the afternoon and early evening. And look, what do you notice about the houses? Look closely at the streets."

Bronzino leaned in closer. "I am not … wait, I understand. They are at crossroads, each of them."

With his finger, Kindred followed the arc in the air above the map, moving past the last marker and only stopping when his hand hovered above another intersection. He tapped a shaded rectangle sharply. "Who lives in this house? Do you know, *padre*?"

"The family *Fernández*. Juan José and his wife Teresa; they have four children. The youngest is a boy of about four years' age."

"I need you to take me there. Now. We must talk to them and get ready."

"Get ready? What will you do, Mr. Kindred?"

Kindred's hand went instinctively to Rex's ancient, well-worn grip. "I will do what I do, *padre*. Vanquish the monsters."

The house, a flat-roofed adobe structure like most in Santa Inez, was warm and inviting despite its humble size and furnishings. Crucifixes adorned the walls near niches that contained vaguely pagan *santos*, and the colorful kitchen was festooned with dangling *ristras* of garlic and chili peppers. With the priest at his side, Kindred stood in the doorway and made his case. Juan José Fernández, fear in his eyes balanced by the composure of his stance, immediately agreed to Kindred's offer of protection. He and Teresa did all the American asked, encircling their children's bed with sharp metal objects and salt, whispering comforting words to the startled young ones as Kindred looked on with an aching heart. They ate a silent supper together, a simple but nourishing meal of beans and maize tortillas. Everyone's eyes flitted over Kindred as if trying to size him up, a bit intimidated by his strangeness and the unearthly power he assumed they could sense in him. Bronzino blessed the house and each of its inhabitants after they had all eaten; when the children had been put to bed, Teresa approached Philip one last time.

"Don't let them take my children, sir," she whispered in Spanish, acute worry giving her eyes a haunted sheen. "For the love of God, do all you can to keep them safe."

Kindred almost broke then, but he tightened his hands into fists by his sides, twisting his emotions aside for a time. "I swear to you," he rasped between clenched teeth, "that not another child will be taken. Tonight, it ends."

She nodded without a word and ducked her head in respect, turning to sit watch with a Bible and a crucifix at the foot of her children's bed. The three men went outside to sit upon a low bench on the *portal.* In hushed tones as the twilight deepened from purple to velvet sable, Juan José and Father Bronzino explained more fully the events of the past few months, confirming further for Kindred the nature of their aggressor. Juan José went on talking, describing what he knew of the founding of this pueblo, its history under Spain and Mexico, the few changes that US citizenship had wrought.

Finally the two men had no more words with which to fill the tense evening air, and they looked expectantly upon Kindred, obviously desperate to learn more about him. He sighed. *Why can I not simply fight their battles for them? Why must they insist on understanding why I do so?*

"All right. I suppose you deserve to know what you're up against." He gestured at the night, at the domain of their enemy. "The *cihuateteoh* are the ghosts of women who have died during childbirth. The Aztecs thought them warrioresses, due the same respect given a fallen soldier, as they had battled with their unborn children and lost. Truth is, they are vicious harpies, the shades of women warped by bitterness and hate, women whose own evil complicated their pregnancies and cost them their lives. Their abode is just beyond the limbo I have shown you, Father Bronzino, but their hate, anger and covetousness is so powerful, for some of them, that they can cross into this plane. And this they do, wandering the night sky like clouds, drawn to crossroads where they prey on innocent children in morbid mockery of lost motherhood. Sometimes they attempt to seduce men, deluded into believing that somehow they may again conceive ..."

Juan José looked deeply into Kindred's eyes. "But why, sir, is there such passion in your voice? My wife and I are forever grateful that you would defend our home, but why? Why do this? Why risk your life to battle demons? Priests I can understand—they are married to Christ. But you ..."

Kindred pulled his gaze away, toward the east, toward the gossamer clouds that robed the waning moon. "It would be easy just to say that I must, that I was chosen. But again, you deserve more than that, you and your whole town. You see, I ... I lost my wife and son to the dark forces of this world years ago; my wife was sacrificed to facilitate their vile machinations ..." his voice hitched, and the priest softly touched his arm. "And though I finally recovered my son, he was broken. Spiritually. I had to give him over to those who may … rehabilitate him, in time. So my quest was fruitless in terms of its original object—my family remains lost to me. But I gained something, nonetheless: the gift of sight, the ability to manipulate *virtus*, and … a vocation." He paused for a long time, the words slowly building up in his mind till they forced his lips open and he hoarsely proclaimed the most profound of his motives. "Above all, gentlemen, I learned to *believe*, to have *faith*. That, I assure you, was the greatest miracle of all."

A jingling and scuffled footsteps in the street brought Kindred to his feet of a sudden, his right hand tightly wrapped round Rex's grip. Juan José quickly stayed his arm with a hesitant gesture. "It is only Doña Chela. She is a *granicera*, a healer and medium."

Bronzino frowned. "She is mostly a fraud," he muttered. The elderly woman making her slow way down the dusty street was almost completely masked by the accoutrements of her trade—ristras of herbs, several satchels, a half-dozen crosses and talismans—and the crocheted shawl draped over her moon-white hair. Though the three men were sitting deep in shadow and darkness, she stopped as she passed in front of the Fernández house, turning to gaze at the portal.

"Come out where I can see you, stranger. The whole town is buzzing with the rumors of your visit, and all that saves you from a mob of inquisitive ignoramuses is their fear of the *cihuateteoh* you have come to fight. You would be surprised at how rapidly news spreads through a small village like ours."

Kindred smiled to himself, taking an immediate liking to Doña Chela and her no-nonsense frankness. "I'm but another *granicero*, like yourself, *doña*. Lending my small talents to the protection of the innocent." He noted happily that she seemed pleased at his self-deprecation rather than annoyed by it. A toothless grin bisected her wrinkled face, and she cackled softly. "I wonder whether you are as handsome as your voice hints."

But as Philip stepped into the moonlight, her expression changed abruptly, and she ducked her head in an awkward curtsy. "Forgive my forthright babbling, Holy Messenger. I had …" she shivered, almost as if with fear. "I had no idea."

Here it comes.

Father Bronzino walked out into the street with them. "Chela, whom do you believe this man to be?"

"Man?" she whispered, eyes widening. "This is no man, father. Arcángel San Miguel, that's who he is."

Bronzino grunted. "The angel Michael? Nonsense, woman. He has power, that I will admit you. But he is no angel."

"I'm definitely *not* an angel, doña."

Chela dared to raise her eyes and stare nervously at Kindred's amused but worried smile. "No? Then, can you explain this?" She fished around, fumbling, in a satchel around her neck, finally extracting a *bulto*, one of the rough wooden *santos* common to the territory. "A santero sold this to me in Santa Fe three months ago. Arcángel San Miguel, trampling the old dragon underfoot."

Kindred took the holy object from her hands, its virtus pulsing tangibly in his grip. This particular icon of Michael had Kindred's own sandy blond hair and blue eyes, was dressed in the pants, shirt and rough jacket of a common cowboy, and sported a slouch hat thrust back on his head. Under his booted feet, a creature resembling more a reptilian coyote than a dragon twisted in exaggerated pain, and Michael's outstretched hand held not a sword, but a pistol.

"You had this made," Father Bronzino accused, "when you heard of Mr. Kindred's arrival and his decision to fight the demons."

Before the old woman could reply, Kindred shook his head and muttered in English. "No. No, she didn't. But it doesn't mean what she thinks. I swear to you that I'm not an archangel or any other heavenly messenger, Bronzino."

Chela, who had apparently understood, leaned in and asked as well as she could, "Then, who you be?"

Before he could assay a response, the *cihuateteoh* were upon them.

There were two of them, wheeling like desert-bleached psychopomps in the sky above the Fernández house. Even from a distance of some fifty yards, their hideous forms curdled one's blood: ragged white dresses whipped about their emaciated frames, long black hair trailed and billowed about them as they jerked to and fro in the air, skeletal faces were frozen in a rictus of frenzied despite, and needle-sharp talons on hands and feet seized at emptiness with horrible desperation. The air thrummed with the low, demoniac cry of their unnatural envy.

"Run," Kindred managed to say, his blood pounding relentlessly in his ears. "Run!" he shouted when he saw how the other three remained motionless, enthralled. "Run or die!" he screamed, and the priest shook himself, grabbing Chela and Juan José by the upper arm and bodily dragging them into the house.

Kindred took several deep but ragged breaths, and then stepped more fully into the crossroads. The plaintive cry tugged at him like a siren song, turning sweet and seductive.

Come to us, love. Come and forget your grief. We will ease your bereaving. We will teach you oblivion. What have these done to deserve your protection? Why should you wander, alone, friendless, loveless? Turn your back on this undeserved penance. Come to us instead.

Kindred felt the call but heeded it not. For a moment, the scent and voice of Inés filled his senses, and he closed his eyes, seeing her upon a hill outside San Antonio, veiled by a thousand butterflies. That vision was enough to immure him. The cry turned angry and violent once again, setting the very earth beneath his feet to rumbling. *Very well. Die, you self-righteous dog.* A sound like the fluttering of a dozen flags in a gale. A startling drop in temperature. And, suddenly, silence.

Then Philip Kindred, once biologist, once professor, once entrenched skeptic, shuddered with the weight of lonely faith. "I believe," he whispered, opening his eyes as one *cihuateotl* rushed at him with a banshee's lunar-white, sepulchral cry. "I believe. I *believe*. I BELIEVE!" Rex fairly leapt from its holster. His hand rose in its practiced arc, cocking back the hammer and taking aim with otherworldly precision. A monstrous grin spread across the face of the hurtling apparition as she saw the weapon; then Rex roared his smoky, metallic shout, and her face twisted in unexpected, impossible pain. She veered aside, her flight faltering; Kindred raised his other hand to fan the hammer as he squeezed the trigger with his right, pounding the demoness with four more lead bullets, cast from melted absolution crosses he had dug up from consecrated graves and dipped in holy water. The *cihuateotl* hit the ground with a grating thud, and Kindred turned on his heel just in time to avoid the talons of her sister, who instead of ripping off the American's head merely sliced open his left shoulder, showering the dust with blood that looked almost black in the moonlight.

"Damn you," he muttered, grimacing with the excruciating pain that threatened to overwhelm him. "That's what I'm about to do. Damn you to the outer darkness, the thirteenth realm." His shoulder was ablaze with toxicity, but he could not afford to focus on it. "Come to *me*, and I'll show you *true* oblivion!"

This one was quicker and forewarned; she tacked this way and that, trying to dodge his gun's sight, moving faster than his physical vision could follow. So he closed his eyes and let his inner vision guide him, sensing the black void before him created by her presence. His arm stopped moving and the darkness moved closer; suddenly, he knew where she would be next, and Rex jumped to the left and fired three times in rapid succession. A horrible scream went up, and Kindred opened his eyes to see the second *cihuateotl* hit the ground a few paces from where her sister was struggling to get back up.

Kindred moved in closer, cautiously. The *cihuateteoh* managed to dig their hind claws into the clay-rich earth and stand together, wounded but furious beyond human comprehension.

Come, dog. Come closer and feel our vengeance.

With deliberate calm, Kindred used his thumb to rotate Rex's firing pin to the central chamber. He lifted the weapon slowly, taking careful aim.

"Oh, I *am* a dog—no denying that. But guess whose dog I am, you thieving, murderous bitches."

Thumbing back the hammer as two began to rush him, Kindred blasted them with powerful scattershot: bits of silver, steel and garlic soaked in holy water. As the projectiles struck their unholy forms, the *cihuateteoh* bulged obscenely, as if finally pregnant after years of fruitless despite. Then they exploded in a conflagration of blue fire that faded, leaving no trace of their ever having been in Santa Inez.

No trace beyond the tombstones of their victims.

Gradually, the dusty street began to fill with townspeople, first the Fernández family with their priest and Doña Chela, who sought to dress Kindred's wounded shoulder as he knelt silently in smears of his own blood, then neighbors who had been peering with temerity through their narrow windows during the battle. Finally, the word spread, and the entire town seemed to converge on the intersection, silently milling about, trying to get a glimpse of their strange savior.

Slowly, timidly, several weeping women approached Philip and knelt beside him. One of them spoke in soft Spanish, introducing herself as María de los Ángeles García de Herrera. "And our children? Those that were stolen? When can you retrieve them?"

Philip's eyes burned as he shook his head. "I cannot. They are … lost to you now, I'm afraid."

"What?" The woman's face went from imploring to indignant. "You have killed those demons, but you cannot rescue the infants? What kind of salvation is this? My little girl was taken only two weeks ago! Surely there is some way, some incantation, something!"

Bronzino touched her shoulder, but she shrugged his hand away. "Better you had never come, *Americano*. Better you had not given us even a moment's hope." She spat at his feet and stared at him virulently as silence fell upon the crowd. Doña Chela moved toward her then, an indignant expression on her face, but Kindred gestured for her to hold.

Reaching down, he scooped up the spittle, along with his own blood and the reddish dirt. He stood unsteadily and anointed the bereaved mother, smearing a maroon *X* across her wrinkled brow. She started at his touch, and a thin man in the crowd, presumably her husband, made a weak gesture of warning. Kindred ignored him.

"No, María. You are wrong. Your loss remains, but other losses are averted. What else is there for the bereft but to prevent more bereaving? Now," he leaned close to her trembling face, smelling her anger and her fear, "you must *see*. See. See."

Her eyes widened, horrified, and she whimpered incoherently. Kindred recognized her emotions, had felt them himself. It was not easy, being chosen. But he had seen in her soul a black seed, and he knew that her virulence could signify a possible return of darkness to this town. Short of shooting her, there was only one way he knew of to stave off her descent.

"You believe yourself purposeless, without hope. But I give you a new charge. You are now this town's guardian, ma'am. You must let Father Bronzino or Doña Chela know if ever you see the agents of darkness walk its streets."

Bronzino cleared his throat nervously. "And you? Will you not stay, show us how to protect ourselves?"

Kindred considered a moment. "For a time. Until my shoulder heals. Eventually, however, I must move on. There are of course some lessons that I can teach you, but your own faith, Sandro, is your best protection. The tools your faith has given you will suffice, I swear to you. Just take them seriously. Use them well. And open your mind to other weapons," here he nodded at Chela, "that you have previously discounted."

The crowd eventually began to disperse. Leaning on Juan José, Philip began to make his exhausted way toward the Fernández home. *Stay for a time, yes. Feel the comfort of human company. But then …* the tugging on his heart had not subsided, though it felt unencumbered again, for the first time in nearly a year. *So this is my destiny? Protecting the defenseless? But that can't be it. I've already spent years protecting them in Texas. Where does it end? Where do I take my final stand? And will I be alone?* There were no answers: his master was as silent as always. Pausing at the *portal,* Kindred glimpsed the moon, setting in the West.

Head west. That's all there is. I suppose I'll have to make the rest up as I go along. He remembered something Inéz had said when first they had met, in San Antonio so many years ago. "The odd thing about life, Mr. Kindred, is that we know where the journey ends. How we get there, however, is entirely up to us."

Smiling at the remembered sound of her voice, Philip stepped inside the warmth and renewed happiness of the adobe home, greeted by the sweet music of children's laughter.

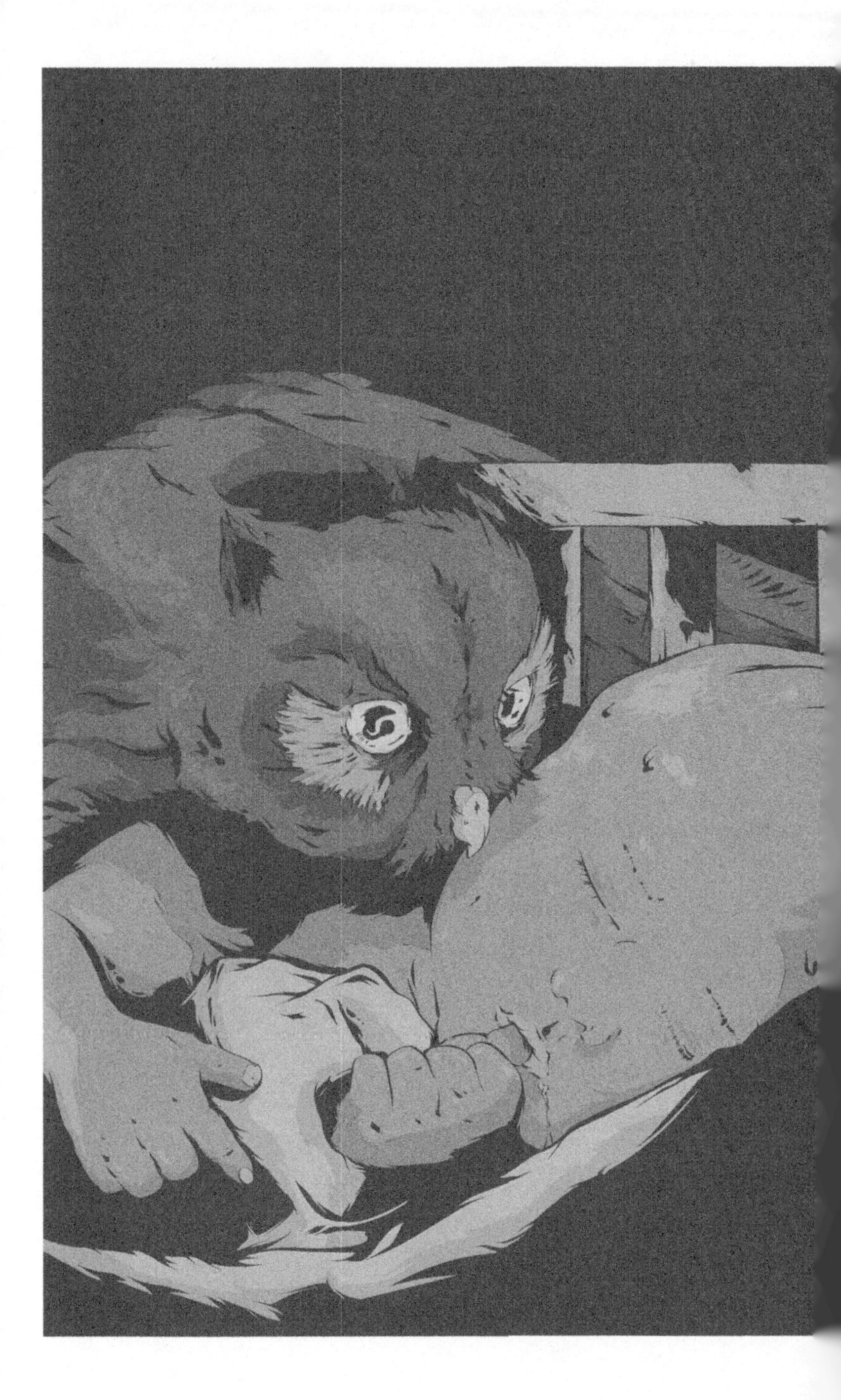

ANCIENT HUNGER, SILENT WINGS

Nicolasa Sandoval Murillo had not quite reached her thirteenth saint's day when the hunger came upon her, sudden and sharp like talons round her gut, in the middle of the night. She crept wincing but quiet to the kitchen, where her grandmother's clay *olla* of beans cooled slowly upon dying embers in the wood stove. Snatching up a cold tortilla someone had left on the roughhewn table, Nicolasa uncovered the jar and began shoveling the spicy mixture into her mouth. Soon she found herself gagging—the beans, normally delicious, tasted of ash and bile. With a frantic lurch she stumbled out of doors and vomited onto the mucky street.

The door opened behind her, and a figure emerged with a petroleum lantern: it was her grandmother Florencia Murillo—Mamá Lencha—and in place of anger or concern, a look of resigned understanding smoothed the woman's wrinkled brow.

"It is the hunger, yes? It awakened you."

Nicolasa nodded, her empty stomach too queasy for speech.

Lencha sighed. "I had hoped to put an end to this, leaving Tlaxcala with your mother and aunts, coming north to this territory of New Mexico. But the curse is in our blood, as my own grandmother assured me."

"What … curse?" Nicolasa shivered at the late autumn chill beneath the clear night sky, and Mamá Lencha set down the lantern to wrap a shawl about her thin shoulders.

"Once every fifty-two years," she whispered, embracing Nicolasa, sharing her warmth with the frightened girl, "another woman in our family becomes a *Tlahuelpuchi.* A drinker of blood."

The stars above wheeled in dizzy spirals. Nicolasa's mind quailed as if an abyss had opened before her. She shuddered, crossed herself, shook her head in denial. "No. No."

Lencha stroked her hair, tried to calm her. "I fear it is true, Nico. I was only ten when the hunger flowered in me, more than half a century ago."

Nicolasa struggled to grasp the implications. A girl on the cusp of womanhood, she was scant years from forming a family of her own and weaving her existence into the weft of her community. She wanted this night to be a dream, for Lencha to be a liar, but she trusted her grandmother more than anyone in her home, in the town of Las Vegas, in the entire world. There was no avoiding the truth of the revelation.

"So … you are a vampire? And now … I have become one, too?"

"Bah, vampires. No, we are nothing like those undead monsters. We live, we work, we eat and sleep. At the end of our divinely allotted time, we die. But once a month … well, once a month we must feed."

An electric thrill rushed along Nicolasa's nerves at the words. "We must feed? On … blood?"

Lencha leaned her weathered forehead against her granddaughter's, her milky eyes glinting strangely in the late November moonlight. "Yes, my love. On blood. The blood of the innocent. We feed, or we die."

The following day, Lencha announced to the family that Nicolasa would be sleeping with her now, affording the three older sisters more space in their cramped quarters. Miguel Sandoval Luna, Nicolasa's father, objected weakly, pointing out that Maria, the eldest, would be marrying soon and that there was no need for the move. But the house belonged to Mamá Lencha: she was the family matriarch. Wisely, Miguel fell silent and let the women manage the household affairs. His wife Fidela gave him an appreciative nod, and the two of them ducked into the workshop that occupied the front room of the house, the family millinery and cordwainer's that sustained them economically. Lencha, meanwhile, oversaw the transportation of Nicolasa's meager belongings to her room.

All day the hunger coiled inside the girl like some ancient wyrm, thrumming in her veins, setting her hands to twitching and legs to wobbling. She could eat nothing, and her mother fretted over her while her sisters glared with suspicious envy. Nicolasa tried to imagine what it would be like now to gossip with her cousins and neighborhood friends, but the gnawing need inside her muddled all fantasizing. When she thought on Abelino Castillo, the young man who stared at her during mass and whose gangly, angular body had visited her dreams more and more often in recent months, she could not help but imagine what his blood would taste like, hot and salty and rich like her mother's beef broth. By evening, the girl was dizzy with shame and anticipation.

Finally night fell, and Nicolasa sat on her grandmother's bed, her heart galloping, fearful but voracious. Lencha shut the door, latched it, and mumbled a few unintelligible syllables. Then she turned to her granddaughter.

"Now we begin. First, let me share what I was told before I first fed. None of us knows how the curse arose. Some say the old god Huitzilopochtli thus damned the daughters of his sister, Malinxochitl, who tried to lead the Aztecs astray when they left Aztlán. Others claim that the blood thirst was born of the betrayal of Malinche, she who helped Cortez conquer Mexico. A few insist that Spanish wizards cast a heinous spell upon mestizo women when all this land was part of New Spain. Those of us from the state of Tlaxcala wonder if our condition might be the price the descendants of Tlaxcalan Indians pay for standing against the Aztecs.

"None of that matters, of course. You simply need to understand what is required. Once a month you must drink the blood of a child. To do this, you will transform."

Nicolasa sat up straighter. "Transform? Into what? How?"

Her grandmother knelt to unlatch a copal-wood chest beside the bed and began rummaging around. "Each of us is born with a *tonal*, an animal soul. Few of us ever see it, and only a handful can bring it forward. A tlahuelpuchi can."

Turning, she handed Nicolasa a feather. The girl took it, ran her fingers along the shaft. "A bird? Am I to become a bird?"

"Yes. A large, predatory bird. Likely an owl. We will open this window, transform, fly to a nearby house with an infant child, pass over it in the sign of a cross to lull the family to sleep …"

Nicolasa's skin prickled in horror and something akin to delight. "And we will go inside to feed, yes?"

Lencha nodded solemnly and stood, her old joints popping. She put her hands on the girl's shoulders, stared into those anxious eyes.

"But we only sip. Enough to calm the hunger. You must never drain so much of the child's blood that it dies. The consequences …" Her voice hitched, and a strange cloud of misery shadowed her features. "The consequences are unspeakable."

Relief took some of the edge off of Nicolasa's anxiety. "Oh, thank the Virgin! I had imagined such terrible things. But it is just a little blood, after all, no? We sip and we fly home. Everything returns to normal for another month.

"In essence, yes." Lencha reached for the lantern on the bedside table. "There is, however, a catch."

Half an hour later, they both sat naked on the packed dirt floor. Nicolasa grimaced as Mamá Lencha, mumbling the word "nodiyetti" over and over, pressed the lantern against first one thigh and then the other before passing it to her granddaughter. Wincing with the pain of it, Nicolasa did the same. Her legs, weak all day, went completely numb.

"The creature you have felt curled up within you for hours, child?" whispered Lencha. "That is your tonal. Grip your feather and release the beast. Give way. Let it take hold."

With an appalling sucking sound, Lencha abruptly pulled her hips away from her legs, trailing sticky strands of some translucent pink sludge as she dragged herself toward the window. From the gaping holes below her buttocks, talons began to emerge, wriggling.

"Oh, Holy Mother, I do not think I can ..." Nicolasa began, her voice edging toward hysteria, but then she felt an odd tugging at her groin and an uncontrollable urge to be free of her legs, like yanking at a loose tooth or picking a scab. Looking down, she saw she had detached herself as well. Gibbering the nonsense word she had learned minutes ago, the frightened girl held tightly to her feather and began pulling her truncated body toward her grandmother.

Lencha was trembling wildly upon avian legs, outstretched arms sprouting feathers, her aquiline nose hooking into a black beak. She was wreathed in an eldritch glow, a faint blue phosphorescence that limned her form against the darkness.

Every inch of Nicolasa's body ached and itched. Her *tonal* squirmed in the depths of her viscera, struggling for freedom. The girl gave a weak groan and set her consciousness aside, turning control over to the beast. The change was immediate: her taloned feet scratched at the black earth, her face twisted and stretched, her young flesh blossomed with hundreds of feathers. In moments she was transformed. A massive screech owl, golden plumed and magnificent, she twisted her head around to regard the great vulture perched on the windowsill, the trunkless legs sprawling useless in the dirt.

And then, without a word, they leapt into the night air. The owl's wings beat effortlessly at the cold, snatching at currents, wheeling higher in pursuit of the vulture. The simple adobe homes of this older part of town spread quilt-like below, and soon the vulture dipped toward one of the larger residences. Don Rigoberto. Owner of a grocery. Young wife recently delivered of a plump baby boy.

The owl mimicked the pattern set for it by the vulture: north to south, then east to west, soft hoots punctuating every swoop. Then drop to the wood sill of the high southern window, work open the shutters with tip of black beak, flutter in to perch beside a mother curled protectively around her baby.

A chilly shudder: feathers retracting, revealing human flesh. Two naked, legless forms upon the quilt, like double-amputees from the War. The smell of the baby: sweet, tantalizing, vital.

Lencha touched the mother's brow, whispered her nonsensical word, and then gestured at the infant. "Gently, now. Lips to his neck. Your teeth will protrude, puncture. Then you suck, slow. You will want to hurry. Do not. And when I touch your shoulder, stop."

The taste was indescribable. Warm, living, mineral, salty-sweet. Nicolasa groaned with a bliss she had not expected, every inch of her body and soul alive as never before. Awakened. When she felt Lencha's hand upon her shoulder, she wanted to refuse, to prolong the exhilaration. But she obeyed, pulling away, and her grandmother dipped her head to sip as well, the shimmering blue haze that blurred her form growing brighter with every swallow.

Then the flight back, every sight and sound a heady, tangible experience for heightened senses. Shifting back, easier now, then scuttling to forgotten legs, watching in dumfounded admiration as pink tendrils resocketed bone, knit flesh-to-flesh. Finally, nightgowns and woolen blankets, the warmth of another damned soul sharing a bed in the deep dark night, formless dreams that tumble from high cliffs and swoop endlessly over nothing.

The hunger was gone in the morning, and life continued spinning through its eternal cycles as if nothing had changed. But Nicolasa could not look upon the world the same any longer. She began accompanying Mamá Lencha as she delivered the family's famed hats and shoes to the wealthier area of Las Vegas, where the ranks of two decades of American settlers had been swollen by another ten years of post-war pioneering. As Lencha stood at doorways, on porches, under porticoes, conversing easily in lightly accented English, Nicolasa found she was herself picking the language up, more quickly than ought to have been possible. "It is due to the curse," Lencha explained. "We learn the speech of the birds and the beasts with ease."

When the hunger came upon them again in December, they soared across the river through light flurries and fed on a two-year-old Anglo girl left alone in a crib. In January the victim was a newborn suckling at its sleeping mother's breast while they sipped at its rich blood. That February Maria Sandoval was married, and they feasted on the chubby twins of a visiting relation.

During mass each week at Our Lady of Sorrows, Nicolasa felt torn, worried. It was clear she could not confess to being a tlahuelpuchi and to drinking the blood of infants. She had no need of Lencha's warnings to understand the danger of such an admission. But taking God's body and blood into her mouth (*nothing like blood, none of that hot sweetness*) in such a state was a horrible violation of all she had been taught in catechism. To block this train of thought, she took to watching Abelino more and more often, until he caught the hint and approached her on the steps of the church one Sunday in early spring. For weeks they exchanged mere pleasantries and brief gossip, leaning against the red sandstone of the bell tower in full view of the congregation. Then Abelino spoke to Don Miguel and got permission to visit with her on a Saturday evening. They sat on rough wooden seats far from each other, with Lencha as chaperone and the giggles of Nicolasa's older sisters punctuating Abelino's attempts at romantic declarations.

As friendship turned to courtship, Nicolasa insisted on feeding separately from her grandmother, arguing that within a year or two she would probably be married and needed to practice dealing with the curse on her own. Lencha reluctantly agreed, with the condition that she still decide which homes would be visited and which children would be victims.

Nicolasa's first solitary feeding was sheer ecstasy. She was able to drink more deeply, waiting until the infant began to struggle weakly before releasing it. Fire raced along her veins, and when she caught her image mid-transformation in a mirror upon the door of an armoire, her feathers seemed to glow like burning bits of sulfur.

Over the next few months, emboldened by the surge of power from so much innocent blood, Nicolasa realized that her gifts extended beyond the time of feeding: she could lull people into a trance for about a week afterward and make herself fade into the darkness at night, skills she used mockingly against her sisters and to sneak out for innocent trysts with Abelino. The boy's kisses were nowhere as blissful as the rush of warm red from a sleeping child, but they awakened other, more human hungers in her. Her grandmother, who always seemed to be keeping a watchful eye on her, warned Nicolasa repeatedly that she was rushing into power and womanhood with little understanding of responsibility, and though the girl feigned compliance, she continued to do as she pleased.

This growing independence filled Nicolasa with conflicted notions of the universe and her place in it. When Father Shiffini mentioned original sin in his homilies, the curse brought upon mankind by Eve's disobedience and Adam's foolish love for her, Nicolasa felt nauseous. Doubly damned by God. A young woman, she shouldered a larger portion of the blame for humanity's fallen state. But who railed against the men, against their mismanagement of households and nations? Where was the sermon condemning the slaughter of thousands during the War? Disgusted by the judgmental arrogance of flawed men, Nicolasa reveled with even greater abandonment in the exhilaration of her undeserved punishment.

Then came the night that she swept out of a high window in delirious stupor and saw a child wandering alone along the narrow streets. Swiveling her strigine head, she detected no one, and her *tonal* fairly howled with greedy desperation. Dropping to a mesquite branch in deep shadow, she called to the sniffling waif with a sweet mother's voice, luring him away from the houses.

Then falling, eternal arc, talons on his flesh, a feathery embrace, the shuddering change, gripping him through bootless struggle, sinking teeth deep and taking heady draughts, heart beating against her naked breast, slowing, stopping. The taste of life's final drops upon her tongue. Warm summer air like a caress, her *tonal* screeching for joy within her, leaping into the sky, higher than ever, riding the wind shear, jet currents ruffling the plumes of her crown.

There was no going back, and no waiting for the feeding night. Once a week, shamelessly mesmerizing her own mentor, she would slip out and quest. Seldom did she find children out of doors, so she would enter homes at random, fading into darkness, and drain babies to their very deaths. Their empty eyes and motionless limbs haunted her dreams at first, but lust for power and bliss bleached away that vacant, broken staring until Nicolasa felt not a twinge of regret.

By September of 1874, the town was abuzz with fear. Something evil was ripping infants from the bosoms of their mothers, ending their lives. Lencha soon suspected Nicolasa and confronted her in the shop while her parents were out purchasing leather and fabric.

"You have become *ezzyoh,* have you not? Blood mad. Murderous."

"Mamá Lencha," the girl began.

"Shut your lying mouth. You have the audacity to put your own grandmother in a trance to carry out your hellish deeds? All those innocent children, dead, gone forever, trapped in Limbo because *you cannot control yourself like a true woman!* Do you not understand the danger you put your family in? The entire town suspects witchcraft. Those Jesuit priests that Bishop Lamy invited from Naples, Italy, to set up a boy's school in town? They have arrived, and rumor has it that among their number is an exorcist. Any day now men who hunt monsters like us could come smashing through that door and drag your mother, your father, your sisters, all of us away!"

Nicolasa felt her chest constrict with panic, but she remained outwardly impassive. "You just want to frighten me."

The older woman's eyes misted as she shook her head. "No, Nico. In the town where I grew up, Tzompantepec, there were two families with the curse. My best friend was an older girl from the other clan: Ana Lima, eighteen, beautiful. She went bloodmad like you. We tried coaxing her, restraining her, but to no avail. Death reigned in that town for nearly a year, until the leaders hired a *curandero* who tracked Ana's movements and burst into her home with a posse of angry men. They discovered her legs and burned them, condemning her to that bird form forever. Then they lynched her entire family, even her little brother, not quite eleven years old. I remember watching them swing, tree limbs creaking … Is that what you want? The two of us trapped in feathered flesh? All the rest of them dead?"

The sudden waves of guilt were too much for Nicolasa. She began to sob. "I am so sorry, Mamá Lencha! I swear I will master this. Just … help me, please."

The old woman softened after a moment and gathered the teen up in her arms. "Shhh. Your sisters will hear this scandalous wailing of yours. Of course I will help you. But we fly and feed together from now on, yes?"

Though her *tonal* snarled in protest, Nicolasa nodded weakly against Lencha's chest.

A moment later, someone knocked on the door. Rubbing her eyes with the backs of her hands, Nicolasa pulled away from her grandmother and answered. At the entrance stood an American in his mid-thirties or so, wearing a simple brown suit, boots and a battered slouch hat that he doffed politely, loosening grey-rimed blonde hair to tumble down above his pale eyes.

"Good morning," he said in Spanish, his accent so perfectly Castillian that Nicolasa wondered if he might be a Spaniard and not an Anglo. "I have come to see about getting a new pair of boots made. And a hat," he added waggling his old one pointedly.

"Oh, I do apologize," Lencha broke in before Nicolasa could speak, "but my daughter and son-in-law are not here at the moment. This is their shop, you see. Perhaps if you returned after noon ..."

He looked at them both for just a few seconds longer than was respectable, and then he smiled. "Of course. If you will just tell them Dr. Kindred dropped by. I will be teaching at the new school, not far from here, really. When I inquired after the best shoemaker in Las Vegas, I was informed in no uncertain terms that Sandoval was my man. So I will most definitely return."

There was the slightest twitch in his cheek as he gave a small bow, replaced his weathered slouch hat, and ambled away.

"Odd man," muttered Nicolasa as she shut the door. Her grandmother's face was drawn with worry. "What is it?"

"The way he looked at us."

"It bothered me, too. Strange clothes, for a priest."

"He is no priest, girl. Perhaps a layman. Or perhaps ..." She shook her head absently. "Forget him. In three more days the hunger will be upon us. We need to discuss which home we will visit. Care is required now that your foolishness has alerted the entire town."

Lencha decided at last that they would feed in the poorest part of West Town, and she kept Nicolasa close to make sure her student attempted no further solo outings. Then the hunger came—monolithic, impossible to flout—and both women stripped themselves of clothes and nether limbs to answer the harrowing shriek of their need.

Riding fall currents into Upper Las Vegas, adobe *jacales* huddled tight against the sable wood, drifting on a downdraft toward a garden muddy with autumn rain, then the vulture seizing a denuded limb to halt its flight, grackling a useless warning as the owl wheeled about and saw the glittering black circle, suspended in a tin washbasin, drawing her down, reflecting her eyes in its mirrored surface, eyes that filled that glistening obsidian disk till her *tonal* poured forth and was trapped, outraged and howling, and the legless girl went sprawling naked in the mud.

Twisting, Nicolasa turned frightened human eyes on her shifted grandmother, but a dark figure hurled a *rebozo* across the great vulture, the tassled ends of the shawl tangling together, tumbling the bird to the earth. The girl dug her fingers into the mud, preparing to drag herself closer, but fabric fell across her shoulders and pinned her down. From the darkness boots came squelching in the mire: it was Dr. Kindred. The form that had trapped Lencha coalesced from night shadows as it stepped into the meager moonlight, revealing a three-cornered hat and robes.

The exorcist. She warned me. She glared at one and then the other. *Two men. It figures.*

"Saecula in eius semini et Abraham," declaimed the priest, brandishing a crucifix. "Nosotros patres ed est locutus sicut, misericordiae recordatus, suum puerum Israel suscepit."

Nicolasa recognized the Latin words: the *Magnificat*, chanted often in Our Lady of Sorrows at vespers. But the exorcist was reciting it backwards, and every syllable was like a blow against the thews of her soul. The bundle that held Lencha squirmed and buckled: the old woman struggled to retain her avian shape despite whatever magic was being worked upon her.

"Dominum mea anima magnificat!" the priest concluded with a shout, nodding his head at Dr. Kindred.

"Thank you, Pietro," the American said, and he knelt beside Nicolasa. "Greetings, Miss Sandoval. I am sure you remember me. This is Father Baccalini. The two of us … well, you might say we patrol the darkness. We rout the monsters. As you can see, we know what you two are. We know what you in particular, young woman, have been doing. Now, I frankly would rather not have to destroy you. Clearly your grandmother has lived with this condition for many years without killing, and I presume she would teach you to similarly master your passions."

Baccalini called out. "This one refuses to be held. She will be free soon, Philip."

Dr. Kindred nodded and closed his eyes. Lifting his hand, he traced a strange glyph upon the air. "*Tlāhuihpochtlé* ximonēxtih!" he whispered harshly in some ancient tongue, and the shawl covering Lencha was stripped away by an unseen force. There lay her grandmother, panting and streaked with filth, eyes downcast in defeat. Nicolasa noticed that the fabric on her own back had slipped down slightly, uncovering her arms.

"Are you ready to talk, Doña Florencia?"

The old woman nodded, tears in her eyes. "Yes, shaman."

Nicolasa felt a scream building within. Who were these men? What right did they have to capture her, humiliate her grandmother?

"I know," Dr. Kindred continued in his soft, impassive voice, "that you cannot go without drinking the blood of innocents. I do not ask you to lay down your lives in rejection of this curse. It was placed on you unfairly, on your distant mothers in another age. So I offer this compromise: there are those who can procure from willing victims, not children but men and women with no carnal knowledge of another, a pint of blood a month. Sufficient to sustain you, though your power will be weakened. No more transformations. No ability to fade or mesmerize."

Lencha's eyes widened with a sort of hope, but something dark twisted in Nicolasa's gut.

"And why," she spat, "should we agree to any such arrangement? Who are you? By the looks of you, an American. From the North? The South? What were you doing ten years ago, Dr. Kindred? How many boys did you slaughter on the battlefields? By whose authority do you force us into the mud like whores, offer us our lives while stealing our magic?"

"Be still, Nico," her grandmother gently called. "These are men of God, child."

"They are men, Grandmother, brutal and empty! And why should I give a damn about their God? Look what the bastard has done to me!" The young woman gestured at her hips, the sockets gaping dumbly. Beside her in its obsidian prison, her animal soul writhed and thrummed with violence.

The priest crossed the garden with heavy steps. "We know where you live, Nicolasa Sandoval Murillo. Where you have left your legs. Heed Dr. Kindred. His offer is not one I would make were the choice mine. Relent."

The young woman gave her head a savage shake. "To hell with you and your threats. I'm done submitting. I will never relent!"

Rage roiling within her like a tempest, Nicolasa flung out a hand and overturned the washbasin, burying the stone mirror in mud and freeing her tonal. With a heart-rending shriek, she shifted into the owl and hurled herself at the sky. She beat furiously at the autumn air, straining for greater height, numbed by hunger and indignation, the town of Las Vegas growing smaller and smaller, receding into the dark.

The owl spiraled ever higher as the men's feeble hexes were shredded by vast thermals that caught her golden pinions and bore her screaming into the unknown. She was not condemned, not a victim, not yearning for pity or absolution.

No. Though pushed to the uttermost margins—forced to leave behind family, humanity, wholeness—there aloft amidst the star-speckled clouds, Nicolasa found something more exhilarating than power.

Freedom.

IRON HORSE, MYTHIC HORN

They was all four of them sitting in a cantina in Lordsburg when I found them, the queerest group of heroes you ever seen: a white man, in his forties, wearing a battered old slouch hat pulled low over his clear blue eyes; a priest, looked to be Italian, Jesuit I reckoned from his robes and three-cornered hat; a shorter, stouter fellow with a pork-pie, probably the rabbi I'd heard tell about; and the Celestial, his braid and robes a familiar sight to me. A Mexican barman, probably the owner, too, looked up at me as I walked in, raised his eyebrow a touch. Can't blame him; after that strange crew, to have a Chiricahua Indian gal in Celestial get-up push through the batwings, well, there's only so much oddness people can just accept without stopping to wonder what the hell is happening in the world.

Me, I seen a few sights would make that bartender do more than just raise an eyebrow. Things that would drop any fragile mind in a dead faint and make even strong men run screaming for the hills. So I really didn't pay no mind to his staring. It was New Year's Day, 1881, and I had a magical creature to transport all the way to San Francisco.

Problem was, I needed protection. That's why I was in this small dusty town of the New Mexico Territory, a shabby chunk of desert kept alive by the new railroad—I had heard these gents was the best in their field.

I walked up to their table, and first thing, that Celestial bowed to me and muttered something I only half-understood. I thought my Chinese had gotten pretty good, but I was at a loss with him, and said as clear as I could in that language, "I do not quite understand you."

"Ah," he answered in words I knew, nodding. "You speak Mandarin, not Cantonese. Where did you learn it, if I may ask?"

Here the white man interrupted, in English. I was pretty sure he was the Kindred fellow of the stories I'd heard. "More importantly, ma'am, who are you? What's your business with us?"

"Mr. Kindred?" He nodded. "Y'all are the Hounds of Heaven, ain't that so? Ones who fought and beat the demon army over to Fort Union?"

"Well," said the Rabbi with his queer German-sounding accent, "they weren't demons, exactly, but yes. That's us."

The Jesuit muttered in Spanish to Kindred, and the white man smirked. "Well, you've found us, if you were looking for us. I don't figure you just wanted to 'see the elephant,' or you'd just be gawking at us like others have. So why don't you tell us what's on your mind, Miss …"

I realized I was bungling the job, and I felt my face flush. "Gosh, I'm sorry. Name's Katy Whitmore. I need to hire your services."

The Jesuit grunted some more Spanish, and Kindred answered kind of irritated, "*Ya sé*, Pietro." I knew what *that* meant, and now I knew the priest's name. I also knew that him and Kindred probably didn't always see eye-to-eye, and that the other two was less hot-headed. But now Kindred was talking. "Problem is, Miss Whitmore, our services aren't exactly for hire. We do the work that needs to be done."

"Oh, well I have a right unusual job, and y'all are about the only ones can get it done, I figure."

They just looked at me quiet, waiting. They made me nervous with those calm blank faces, and I swallowed heavy. "We are transporting some real important freight clear to San Francisco, but we expect problems of the sort y'all are expert in handling. Of a supernatural sort, if you get my meaning."

Pietro narrowed his eyes like with suspicion or doubt. "Exactly what type of freight you are transporting, Miss Whitmore?"

I took a deep breath and looked Kindred right in the eyes, knowing that he was the one I needed to convince. "I guess you'd call it a unicorn." Flicking my eyes over to the Celestial, I simply added, "A *ch'i-lin*."

His face stayed impassive, but it was obvious from him tensing up his body that I'd done startled him good. "Why," he managed to say with faked calm, "would a *ch'i-lin* be on this continent, much less this particular stretch of desert?"

"Well, it's not too easy to explain, but let's just say he come to stop the evil treatment of Chinese workers laying railroad track. He was accompanied by," I had to stop and think of how to say this in English, "by five, uh, *seng*?"

"Monks." His jaw was still tight like a coyote trap.

"Right. All *sigung,* uh, masters. From a temple in China. O-mei Shan."

"Shaolin monks, from the great school and library of the North. Here in America." There was like wonderment or something stronger in his eyes. I could feel him getting even more wound up. The air was shaking with it.

"Yessir. But they was attacked by demons 'fore they could even begin their mission. Only one lived, and the … the unicorn was hurt bad. We—I stumbled across them and helped them heal up—we been biding our time for nigh on five years now, but we got to get him back. He won't make it much longer in this country, that's what he says. *K'uei*, that's them demons I mentioned, are all over. Bad times coming. So I'm asking y'all … help us. Help us 'fore it's too late."

From the look the Celestial gave Kindred, I knew I had them.

An hour later we met back up at the train platform, where Kindred made arrangements with the ticket master for the transport of all the heaps of baggage them demon fighters had brung along. One crate was some nine feet long and took all four men plus a couple local boys to move onto the knotty planks. Dozens more boxes, carpet bags and valises were arranged around it, containing the accouterments, I guess, of their supernatural profession.

I knew all their names now: Sun Mu-pai was from China, expert in Tao magic; Father Pietro Baccalini was an Italian exorcist, real good at casting out demons and the like; Moshe Loew was a rabbi, though I didn't know for sure what his talents were. Master Sun made it real clear that their help was going to depend on them seeing the beast, but I wasn't too worried. My job was to get them to this point, and my master had assured me the rest would take care of itself.

Master Sun walked over to me as the stuff was being piled up. He give me curt bow, the slightest of formalities, then asked me in Chinese, "It falls to me to devise a strategy for repelling any attack that may be made on us. Please, clarify for me—the k'uei of which you have spoken ... are they full *jiang shr*?"

"No, sir. My master, K'ung T'u-yi, has told me of those drinkers of blood, but the thing that attacked the monks six years ago was pure spirit, not animated flesh. A demon, I am told, a revenant of some dead person's *p'o* soul."

"Such demons are typically hungry for justice, for revenge: how came one to attack a being as holy as a ch'i-lin?"

"We don't know, but the *Book of Changes* warns of a great number of these spirits, searching for us. We are blessed to have your protection."

Sun Mu-pai took his leave, musing on what I'd told him. Before too long, I caught the sound of the Rogers 4-4-0 engine, tooting its whistle as it come chugging toward us, coal smoke popping out in slower and slower bursts. My palms sweated and ached with fear, but I swallowed hard and focused like I was learned to do.

Once the train had stopped, my master disembarked. Before I could get to him to confide what all had been agreed, Sun Mu-pai walked up and muttered who knows what. My master thrust up the sleeves of his robe, revealing the mantis and crane burned into the insides of his forearms. The Taoist wizard seemed satisfied, bowing low. I was about to gesture him over before Kindred or anyone else snatched him up, but he glided toward me without any prompting. My heart started beating a little quicker. No matter how hard I tried to ignore it as disrespectful and ridiculous, I felt more alive when he was around.

"Wu Kai-tan," he said, addressing me by my celestial name with a smile in his eyes. "It is good to see you, *shigoo mei*. You have convinced them, I see."

"Yes, Master K'ung, though they insist on seeing the ch'i-lin before actually boarding the train."

"Understandable. Here," he drew a leather pouch from within his sleeves. "It served us well, but I am glad you found the Hounds of Heaven, as I doubt your small magic will suffice for the longer journey."

"I agree. Shall we begin, Master?"

I introduced him to the Hounds as quick as possible, and the porters set about loading all the gear into the car we'd set aside for us humans. Meanwhile, K'ung T'u-yi led us all to the other padlocked one.

"Y'all are about to enter the presence of something holy," I translated for him. "I imagine I ain't got to instruct y'all on your manners, but be aware. Step light; don't go disturbing the circle of salt and rice." At the mention of that barrier, the four of them looked at each other and gave approving nods. Seems my master had gone up a notch in their estimation.

He unlocked the door and slid it slightly open. A pleasant odor of cinnamon and cloves drifted out. One by one we squeezed in, me last of all. Ahead of me I heard the rabbi whisper all hushed and reverent, "Truly a *re'em* such as the ancients described. I've held that horn to my lips many times, but I never thought to see beast itself." No idea what he meant, but I figured *re'em* to be some Hebrew word for unicorn. I reckoned I understood part of why Loew was so amazed. Hell, I'd lived near the ch'i-lin for half a decade now, and I was still overcome by it. It was about the size of a deer, with a shaggy tail and cloven hooves. Its fur was multicolored, a white ground with intricate runes and symbols swirling about in black, blue, yellow and red. As it looked on us with its golden eyes, burning and eternal like two suns, its small horn—not bone but something like cartilage—seemed to point into our hearts.

A sound like a thousand chimes seemed to fill the air, but I knew from experience that the music was just in our heads. It wasn't language, not really, not even pictures. Just feelings, like right now thankfulness and joy. I looked round at the men and was a mite startled to see tears on Kindred's cheeks. He nodded.

"Yes," he whispered, though it wasn't real clear what he was responding to.

Sun Mu-pai turned to Master K'ung and muttered something I couldn't catch. The Shaolin priest nodded his agreement, and the Taoist spoke to his fellows. "The monk and I will travel in here, readying a last defense if you are unable to keep the k'uei from entering."

"Good idea," Kindred nodded. "I'll bring your bags over in a moment." Reaching out to place his hand on Master Sun's shoulder, he added, "We'll do our part, my friend."

Not long after, the train got a-moving, and I found myself sitting in the Pullman across the aisle from Kindred. My window faced south, and as the train began to pick up steam, I stared out at the Peloncillo Mountains, trying to make out the distant purple peaks of the Chiricahuas where I was born. I guess I got a mite wistful looking, for Kindred spoke, yanking me from my reverie.

"I noticed the medicine bag, Ms. Whitmore. I take it you're Apache?"

"Well, yessir, but I wasn't raised by them. My real parents, far's I can figure, were part of Cochise's band. Seems I was born round about 1860. Sometime in the winter of '61 Cochise ordered women and children back up into the mountains while his braves and him dealt with some soldiers coming onto the band's territory. I must've got separated from my ma as a rancher found me huddled in the snow up to Apache Pass, not far from the Butterfield station house, this here pouch clutched in my little hands."

I had to pause for a moment because that maggot's face was leering in my mind, his broken teeth and draggling mustachios … A deep breath, my eyes closed. The shortest moment of *tso-ch'an,* and I continued.

"Man's name was Frank Whitmore. He took me back to his ranch, a spread near the Santo Domingo River, and his wife was just tickled to have her a girl, her own children being mostly boys 'cept for a daughter that had died of the smallpox.

"I remember my childhood as mainly happy. Ma Whitmore learned me all sorts of domestic skills, made me dresses and dolls, read the Bible to me. My 'brothers' were considerable older than me, and when I was little, they give me candy and treated me like a princess. But along about my tenth year, all that commenced to change. The boys was all men; they went off to find their own fortunes down Tombstone way or to marry or fight the Indians …"

Kindred gave a sort of grimace. "A bit ironic, that last occupation."

"Yeah, well, didn't hardly nobody think of me as an Apache, not when I was just a wee thing. But as I got older, Frank Whitmore started a-cursing me for a red-skinned devil and whatnot. He for sure saw me as an Indian … among other things."

Kindred's eyes went soft, and I could kind of feel what was coming next. I didn't expect pity from him nor nobody, to be honest, but his look of compassion was sincere, and I could see the Buddha-nature my master had learned me about shining through the illusion of his flesh.

"He tried to rape you, didn't he?"

I ducked my head, feeling shame color my cheeks. Didn't have no reason to be ashamed, but there was the feeling anyhow. I had struggled long and hard to clear my heart of the desire to harm him, once I learned how craving such things, craving anything, in fact, kept me a slave to my suffering. But the shame … I couldn't be rid of it. "He didn't just try, Mr. Kindred. But you can bet I didn't stick around for more of that horrible life. No, sir. I high-tailed it out of there. Wound up in the Sierra Diablo—you know, the Black Mountains, a ways north of here—and that's where I come across my master and the ch'i-lin, both of them wounded."

For a moment, Kindred glanced toward the other end of the railcar, where Baccalini and Loew were readying their odd gear with practiced silence. They seemed to feel his gaze, and they looked up.

The priest asked, "What they were doing in the Black Mountains?"

"Well, like I said, the monks brung the ch'i-lin across the ocean so it could stop the horrors being perpetrated against Celestial railroad workers. They'd heard all the way to China about how they was being made to work in real deplorable conditions. What struck them as most worrisome was the many deaths and the way the bodies was just being buried in shallow, unmarked graves, without the proper rituals and with no one to remember those poor souls. Sure, lots was dug back up and shipped home for respectful burial, but too many was forgotten, left behind, with no one to ease their passing—a surefire way to create demons, though white folks be too ignorant to know it. So the monks, they come on a boat to Mexico, planning to cross the New Mexican border and head northwest into Utah, far's I can tell. But up in them mountains, they was attacked by a k'uei; I reckon the p'o soul of some dead worker that was drawn to the ch'i-lin's magic. What it was doing so far from the railways, I still don't understand."

The rabbi cleared his throat and broke in. "A *dybbuk*—k'uei—looks to attach itself to a live person. It had probably followed prospectors who came into New Mexico on the rails but then had taken wagons south to hunt for silver in the mountains. We've been hearing about similar attacks for some seven years now, but we've not experienced any activity first-hand."

Kindred sighed. "None of this surprises me, however. More than a hundred thousand Chinese workers have entered this country over the past decade, and despite the fact that our present ease of travel has been purchased with their lifeblood, we continue to treat those men and woman abominably. President Hayes has just signed the *Chinese Exclusion Treaty*, which reverses the open-door policy set in 1868 and places strict limits both on the number of Chinese immigrants allowed to enter the United States and on the number allowed to become naturalized citizens. In fact, Congress is considering a complete moratorium on Chinese immigration. In essence, the US has used the Chinese to build its railroads, but doesn't want them to stay, and certainly doesn't want them to have its gold or silver. That the tortured souls of dead Chinese want revenge is to be expected, as far as I'm concerned. But the ch'i-lin and its guardians must be protected, as must be any person innocent of the destruction of those lives."

"Amen to that. After five years of living in those mountains, the presence of the ch'i-lin drawing more and more k'uei to us, Master K'ung and me realized that protecting the unicorn meant getting it away from the US. So I got us a rig at Silver City—where I also heard bout y'all's outfit—and we split up, my master heading to Deming to ride the rails, and me taking a shorter route through the mountains to catch y'all in Lordsburg. And that, as they say, is that."

"I see." Kindred pulled out a wooden case, unclasped it, and pulled a strange pistol from within. He pored over it real careful, checking the mechanisms, taking it apart piece by piece.

"You don't mind me asking," I put in, "How'd y'all form the Hounds of Heaven?"

"Oh," he replied, "we didn't quite form anything, ma'am. Each of us was doing similar work in his own part of New Mexico, particularly in the area of Las Vegas. Trying to ameliorate the evils that our people had brought to this land or to struggle against forces that had amassed themselves long before our arrival. We were drawn together, you might say, again and again over the course of the last decade. Finally we came to realize we were a team. A group of warriors, staving off the darkness."

"Hounds of Heaven."

Kindred smiled, but he didn't say anything else, just took to cleaning his odd pistol, looking over at me from time to time with kindly eyes. I was all sorts of tuckered out, so I pulled down one of the beds and clambered up into it, pulling the curtain part-ways closed. Maybe 'cause nary a one of these men batted an eye at me being Indian and all, my mind wandered onto the figure of the Sixth Patriarch, Dajian Huineng, who my master had talked to me about a lot, given that he also was a poor person of a disrespected race, like me. Eventually all China, Master K'ung told me, learned to respect him, but when he first come upon Huang Mei Mountain, the Fifth Patriarch like to run him off. Called him a barbarian. Huineng allowed as how he surely was a barbarian, and unschooled, but he told the Ch'an leader, "Our physical bodies may look different, but our Buddha-nature is the same." Hearing them words was my first step toward freedom from my earthly situation, from the pain of my past and the confusion of the present.

My master, he would recite to me some of the more famous *kung-an*, cases that us students is supposed to reflect on as we move toward enlightenment. As I laid there, waiting for sleep, one case that had to do with Huineng come to mind, and I pondered it a spell:

The wind was flapping a temple flag, and two monks started an argument. One said the flag moved; the other said the wind moved. The two of them argued back and forth but they couldn't reach no compromise.

Huineng said, "It ain't the wind that moves; it ain't the flag, neither.

"It's y'all's minds doing the moving."

The two monks was awe-struck.

Meditating on the implications of that case, I drifted into a dreamless sleep.

* * *

A few hours later, a voice pulled me from the near-Nirvana of slumber.

"Ms. Whitmore. We've stopped for coal and water. It may be a good time to stretch your legs and so forth."

I pulled back the curtain and was greeted by Kindred's gentle smile. He gestured with a tilt of his head toward the door at the far end of the Pullman, and feeling the call of nature, I slipped out of the bunk, folded it away, and headed into the cool twilight air. Sign on the platform indicated we was at Cochise, and I give a little smile at the irony. A depot agent, frowning mightily at the need to talk to a Chinese-dressed redskin gal, pointed me in the direction of the privy, and after dealing with my various necessities, I washed up at the pump beside the depot.

The last thin rays of sunlight had left the sky by the time I climbed back on board. The three men were moving about the car, affixing to the windows yellowed strips of paper with what looked to be Chinese characters and some other squiggles, maybe Hebrew writing. I can read English well enough, and my master had been trying for years to get me to learn his people's queer pictographs, but whatever was on them slips was beyond me. Didn't matter none; I knew they was wardings of some kind or another.

The car lurched as the train begun to move again. The priest and the rabbit pulled two heavy stone tablets out of a box and dragged them to either end of the car, right in front of the doorways. I recognized the *pa kua* inscribed on them, the eight sacred symbols, all arrayed geometric-like around a yin-yang circled.

"Taoist magic," I muttered to Kindred, who'd been checking the vents or whatever-they-were that run across the top of the coach's walls, just above the folded-up beds. He had been anointing them with something, maybe holy water or oil or somesuch.

"Yes, ma'am. This sort of revenant can be formed after the death of a person of any creed, but it helps to use the symbols in which the dead had faith when living. Likely the poor workers whose energy was twisted in this way were believers in *feng shui* and other Chinese manipulations of *ch'i*. As much as we can, we'll use those systems to keep the revenants at bay."

"But each of you has his own particular sets of weapons, ain't that right?"

"That we do. Our ability to manipulate *virtus* is dependent to some degree on our own faith, and our tools reflect the roots of that faith." He touched the handle of his revolver. "Rex here, well, I … my people taught me to believe in the strength of firearms, so you could say that Rex has fallen to me as a result. There are times when that fact shames me, but I am what I am. The religious training of Pietro and Moshe has afforded them less violent means for combating chaos. Mu-pai falls between these two extremes, having both ritualistic and aggressive means of manipulating *virtus*."

"You keep saying that. 'Manipuating virtus.' What's *virtus*, anyhow? Is that like *ch'i*?"

"Exactly. Every culture has its own term for the energy that imbues the universe, that flows from love, understanding, creation, knowledge … all the positive actions that build rather than destroy. Your own people—the Apaches, I mean—call it *diyí*. The Comanche use the word *puha*. The Maya called it *ch'ulel*. But this energy, *virtus, ch'i*—it can be blocked, distorted. The Navajo, who call virtus *hozho*, term this distortion *hochxo*. Chaos. Entropy. Destruction. And there are forces that would marshal all the *hochxo* they can in order to see our world sundered to its roots. I suspect that the attraction of the k'uei to the ch'i-lin is driven by those forces."

The rabbi, dusting off his hands and beginning to deck himself out with the fancy doodads of his position, made a sound of agreement. "Yes. No other explanation for the desire to hurt a *re'em*—dybbukim should be reluctant to even approach such a powerful, holy creature."

"I reckon that must be so. I have had to run off a passel of them demons, and it ain't been easy."

"You used your pouch?" asked the priest, also draping yokes of cloth and rosaries and such about himself.

"Yessir. It happened by accident, really. First attack that come, my master was chanting and so forth, and I was so scared that I just clenched my hand 'round my medicine bag, closed my eyes, and begun whispering the only words in Apache I still could recall … something my mama must've sung to me when I was itty-bitty. I felt a cold, dark, angry force try to butt itself 'gainst my soul, but I kept clinging to this here pouch and saying them words till it went away. Later I found that I could put my hand on another and keep him from being attacked, as well. So it's only good for protection."

"That is sufficient," the priest told me with a smile. "We shall take charge of the rest, my child."

As if on cue, the Pullman rocked a little. Any other time, you might've sworn it was the wind, but I knew it weren't. Through the window I could see how dark forms flitted 'cross the stars, blocking them out from time to time. We were under attack.

Communicating with little gestures and glances, Lowe and Baccalini stood together at the center of the coach, back-to-back in the narrow aisle, lifting up their respective books of scripture. At precisely the same moment, the two commenced to read, one in the harsh but angelic sounds of Hebrew, the other in cold and liquid Latin. The combination should've been frightful ugly, but it weren't. It was comforting and harmonious, and despite the looming danger outside, I felt transported for a second, hearkening back to when I first come 'cross that cave in the mountains, me all emptied out from the desert and the endless sky, faced with them two strange beings, one of them chiming like a cherub in my mind while the other went on reciting the *Lotus Sutra* in his transcendent voice. Even though they was wounded and far from home, I felt safe for the first time in ages.

And I felt safe now.

Kindred didn't say nothing; he just stood beside me, his hand on his pistol grip, his hair all unruly as if was glad to be out from under that slouch hat he usually had on. The coach was buffeted something fierce—the windows rattled so hard they like to pop right out—and a horrible, raspy moaning come from all 'round us, the sound of hundreds of animal souls—the human spark long gone to another loop of rebirth—clinging blindly to the night air. Those driven bits of spirits rocked that Pullman back and forth so hard I figured we'd be throwed off the track any second, the train crashing into the rocks and sand, ripping open the other car and exposing the ch'i-lin to all them groaning scraps of darkness.

I squeezed my medicine bag tight in my right hand, feeling the bits of turquoise, shell, feathers and bone that rested there since I was a wee child. Hesitating a mite, I joined my voice to the protective clamoring of the two holy men, reciting words I wasn't sure I understood no more, repeating what I heard my mama's voice croon in the deepest parts of my memory: "*Gòdìt' ó' bàsxà' híljìj tc' ìndí; gòdìt' ó' bèbìk' è nà ìst ' ó tc' ìndí; hí tsát ' ùl bìt' ùl 'á lzà tc' ìndí.*"

Kindred pressed his face against the glass of the door that looked out on the other car, where I reckoned the two celestial masters was struggling to keep the k'uei from busting in. He shook his head and turned back to us, a harrowed look upon him. I could see through the tall window beside the door how the silhouette of the boxcar was wavering wildly.

"I'm going out there before those damned things derail the other car and kill us all. Keep her safe."

Drawing his strange pistol, Kindred stood on the stone tablet and opened the door. He stuck his head out, pointed at angle toward the sky, and fired. A blood-curdling, spectral scream split the air, and I reckoned whatever special ammunition he was using had gone and hit its target. Then he was out the door, and I could see his worn boots through the window, climbing the ladder up to the roof of the Pullman. I scooted down the aisle till I was in front of the door. From above us come shot after shot, and the howls of k'uei beat at my ears like the flailing arms of a drowning man.

The shaking of our coach stopped pretty soon; the rabbi and priest stopped their recitation, and in the silence a nerve-wracking squeal come, and I saw what seemed bits of flame leaping through the darkness. Kindred commenced to shooting again. The others come up beside me, and we all three saw in the muted light of muzzle fire and winter stars how the wheels of the other car come up off the track on one side, then slammed down onto the rail again in a shower of sparks and that agonizing squeal.

Baccalini looked at Loew. "I think that you should get your *shofar*, my friend. His gun is not the answer this time."

"Is it ever, really?" the rabbi responded as he hurried to the other end of the coach to retrieve whatever-the-heck a *shofar* was. He come a-running up the aisle again, unwrapping cloth from 'round an object. When he tossed aside the cloth, I recognized what he held in his hands: the horn of a ch'i-lin, shiny and ancient and hollow.

"Time to climb, Pietro. Are you going to be okay?"

Though the priest went a mite ghostly-looking at the idea of climbing atop the coach, he nodded. "Ms. Whitmore," he said, a bit shakily, "probably you should remain here."

"Probably. But I ain't going to, Father. I done faced these here things enough times that I might as well be there at the end."

Neither one of them argued with me, which was a surprise. Loew opened the door, and we stood on the small deck right outside the coach, the cold January air flapping at our clothes. Part of me wanted to cross the planking between the Pullman and the boxcar, see if I couldn't lend Masters K'ung and Sun a hand, but the black wraiths were all over it, thick as fleas, howling and writhing and pushing like a force of nature.

One by one we climbed up the iron ladder to the rooftop, where Kindred was reloading his gun. The train was chugging along at about twenty miles an hour, and the wind pulled at you like an insistent child. I crouched low, my stomach queasy with fear of falling. Kindred and

Loew was exchanging words, but I just kept looking at the boxcar, yanked to and fro by them crazed revenants, and I suffered because I could not bear to think of K'ung T'u-yi dead, though I put my own enlightenment at risk by my overwhelming desire that he live. Then it come to me: *it ain't the k'uei that's moving; it ain't the car that's moving—it's my mind that's moving.* It weren't clear to me how that could help my master, but it eased my pain some.

Unexpectedly I saw the door on the south side of the boxcar slide open a bit, and Masters Sun and K'ung swung themselves up onto the roof. Smoke—most likely from strips of paper they'd wrote their spells on and then burned in the Taoist way—clung to their robes and curled through the opening they'd left. Each of them yielded a sword: my master one of pale wood, probably peach, lent to him by the wizard, I reckoned; and Sun Mu-pai himself one of metal that glittered with the sparks, revealing seven stars etched into its blade. They commenced to hacking away at the k'uei; my master's blows ended in a curving arc, sending the demons into clay jars that I could just make out, lined up inside the boxcar.

But when Master Sun's blade sliced into a k'uei, the demon would burst into ebony fire and disappear.

"Destroying them isn't the answer," I heard Kindred say, though I didn't know if was talking to anyone in particular. I turned a little and saw the rabbi lift the shofar to his lips. He begun to blow, and the deep, clear sound washed over me like some kind of balm, cleansing my soul and clearing my mind. Loew continued to sound the shofar in a kind of rhythm or pattern, and I could feel how it was directed at the k'uei, forcing them to release the boxcar and be still. Kindred lowered his pistol; the masters sheathed their swords. Hundreds of k'uei slowly drifted toward us, held by the music of the unicorn's horn. As they neared, I was able to make out the familiar features, etched in ghostly gray 'gainst the black miasma—the face of beasts, each with horns and claws and a single leg that tapered off into nothingness.

Loew lowered his shofar and spoke. "Lost souls. You are clinging to a life that is no longer yours. You are attacking those who can help you find release. Turn from this course of action, now. What you have become is an abomination."

The k'uei seethed, silent but unwilling to heed nary a word.

Kindred touched Loew's arm. "You're the Baal Shem, Moshe. Use the Name."

The rabbi sighed and nodded his agreement. "You are revenants, nefesh or *p'o* souls. I entreat you to release your rage and indignation so that you can be guided to your ruah, your *hun*, that vital, human part of you for which you so violently yearn. In service of the Creator I entreat you by his secret Name, *Yehavoah*. Yield!"

For a moment, the k'uei seemed to fade, their fury subdued, but some commenced to snarling and hissing, and soon the entire legion of them turned all enraged and dove at the boxcar. I could hear the voices of the masters trying to reason with the demons, telling them in Chinese that they didn't want no more violence, that the k'uei should let them help ease their suffering and whatnot. The demons paid no mind; they just went swirling around the car, preparing for a final onslaught.

Then the sound of chimes filled my head, and I knew the ch'i-lin was trying to communicate with me. It sent images to me, one after another, quick and insistent. My eyes teared up as I realized what it wanted. "No," I muttered. "No, better to destroy them all."

But it was one of the five sacred animals, and when it sent feelings of disappointment into me, I begun to openly weep. It reminded me how the clinging of them k'uei to this world was the root of their suffering and that Dharma directed us to help such creatures let go and move toward enlightenment. Finally, the ch'i-lin revealed to me its own Buddha-nature, reflected in my own heart by the same. "All right. I'll do as you ask. But these men ain't gonna like it."

I stood, bracing myself against the dizziness, and called to the demons in Chinese. "I hear you, displaced spirits. You demand to possess the ch'i-lin. You want it to surrender itself to you. And I understand why, even if you do not. This is the sacred earth beast, and your need for proper burial draws you like fireflies to a flame.

"So heed my words. The ch'i-lin cedes to you, on a single condition—each of you will fly to it and enter it, passing through its horn. Within its flesh, you will find the peace and rest that was denied to you."

Master Sun, who I never seen show any extreme of emotion, crumpled like a bereft child on hearing my offer, his head in his hands. With a dark, oily laugh, the demons went streaming into the boxcar, a river of black hate that I couldn't hardly bear to watch. Kindred shouted, lifting his gun, but I stepped in front of him.

"It's what the ch'i-lin wanted," I muttered, touching his trembling arm. "And it's what Dharma demands. You'll understand in a spell."

I felt the train begin to slow, heard the hollow piping sound that announced a coming town. As the last demon slipped through the door, we all looked at each other with somber expressions, and then we climbed down the ladder and gathered in the Pullman. K'ung T'u-yi had gotten a hold of himself again, and he very calmly asked me to explain myself. Respectfully and quietly, I did, while the others put the coach back in order.

Once the train fully stopped, we descended. It was nearly 9 p.m. We'd reached Benson, Arizona. A good twenty-four miles to our south lay the town of Tombstone. All around us stretched the desert, strewn with forgotten bones.

After some instructions to the depot workers, we shuffled solemn-like to the boxcar. Master K'ung pulled open the door, and there stood the ch'i-lin, turned to clay, like the terra cotta statues I hear they used to bury the emperors of China with. A smell of cinnamon lingered in the air, mixed with the ashy stink of sated rage. When I got a whiff of that, something in me twisted. I was still just a young gal, after all. I could understand with my mind that none of this was real, that the ch'i-lin had plumb dispelled the illusion that there was a difference between it and the k'uei—when in reality the demons and the unicorn and the Hounds was all one. But in my heart, the ch'i-lin was the magical beast that had taught me how to live again, to raise me up above all them bad things I experienced as a child. And I couldn't hardly breathe because of the sorrow that squeezed my chest.

"We got to bury him," I explained to the Hounds of Heaven through gritted teeth. "We'll wrap him in hexes and spells and bury him deep in the desert sand. He holds them all inside, y'all understand. It's the only way to give them the proper rites. Over time they'll start to let go, and finally the ch'i-lin will crumble and melt into the earth, returning to where he come from.

"Do y'all understand this?" My heart was like to break at any moment. "He's gonna share in their shame at dying in this land, far from home, unable to receive the respects of their families. He'll keep them from harming the people of this nation, but that's the cost: the last ch'i-lin will lay there, in the desert, forgotten, like the bones of the railway workers."

Kindred without warning climbed up into the boxcar, put his arms around the clay unicorn, and muttered, "We will not forget." Then he wept, baring his grief while we stood watching. After a couple of minutes, the others went to him, touched his shoulders silently.

But I didn't want to comfort him. In that moment, I figured he just would have to bear the blame, even though he was never involved. His people done the crime, and he was the kind of man what would try to make amends. That, it seemed to me, was justice of a sort.

A couple hours later, we'd unloaded everything from the train, got the Hounds squared away at the hotel of this brand new boomtown, and rented a wagon from a sleepy hostler to ride about an hour's journey to the north, where we buried the ch'i-lin deep, warding him with every bit of magic we knew. We all stood round the grave, for that's what it was, quietly reflecting on the events of the day.

Kindred finally spoke. "What did it tell you to do next?"

I wiped my hands on my robes, but I couldn't be rid of the sensation of ground-in dirt. I imagined it would be there a long while yet. "Said for me and Master K'ung to search for another sacred animal. Said it sensed another group of masters that was likely sent after the monastery didn't hear back from the ch'i-lin's guardians. They brung a phoenix with them, a fire beast more appropriate to the task of stopping injustices done to the living. Whatever forces stopped our team's mission ain't gonna hesitate to interfere with theirs. So Master K'ung and me, we're gonna have to bid y'all a fair adieu. We're heading south, to Mexico."

"Did it say anything about us?"

I felt Kindred's gaze search my face, but I couldn't bring myself to look him in the eye, afraid of seeing his Buddha-nature and wanting to show him compassion. "Just that y'all should do as your conscience tells y'all."

Kindred looked questioningly at his three companions, and each of them made a sign of agreeing to whatever silent request he was making. He slung his spade over his shoulder and adjusted his slouch hat a little more snug on his head.

"In that case, though we've been heading steadily west, I think it's time we went north. It's my understanding that Chinese workers in gold and silver mines are being mistreated up in those territories. Though it's not completely our line of work, there is a debt to be paid here. Perhaps we can, uh, lessen the task your phoenix needs to do. At the very least, we will protect whomever we can."

We rode back to Benson together, and at the hostler's we shook hands and embraced. Kindred's hug was gentle, and he whispered two words close to my ear: "I understand." As we pulled apart, I give him a little smile, just to let him know that with time my sadness would fade. If we met up again to fight off the dark, I reckoned, we needed to be on decent terms.

Finally the Hounds walked away, toward the hotel, and Master K'ung and me, after buying a pair of mares from the hostler—who liked our gold more than he disliked our race—rode south into the deepening night.

As we all went our separate ways, it come to me in a flash: they wasn't separate ways at all. We are all walking the same path, though it ain't some road scored in earth or sky or sea. It's the path of easing suffering, both ours and that of others, and we walk it till ever creature stands free of pain and lies, in unity with truth and peace, at last enlightened and made whole.

ACKNOWLEDGEMENTS

- "Bloody Feathers" was originally published in the January 2013 edition of *Out of the Gutter*.
- "Wildcat" was originally published in the May 2015 edition of *Apex Magazine*.
- "Winds That Stir Vermilion Sands" was originally published in Issue 3 of *James Gunn's Ad Astra* and reprinted in the June 29, 2015 edition of *Strange Horizons*.
- "Ancient Hunger, Silent Wings" was originally published in the 2015 Kraken issue of *Devilfish Review*.
- "Jealous Spirits, Thundering Gun" and "Iron Horse, Mythic Horn" were originally published in *The Seed: Stories from the River's Edge* (2011).

ABOUT THE AUTHOR

David Bowles is a Mexican-American author from deep South Texas, where he teaches at the University of Texas Río Grande Valley. Recipient of awards from the Texas Institute of Letters, the American Library Association, and the Texas Associated Press, he has written several books, among them *Flower, Song, Dance: Aztec and Mayan Poetry*, *The Smoking Mirror*, and *Border Lore*.

Additionally, his work has been published in venues such as *Rattle, Strange Horizons, Apex Magazine, Metamorphoses, Asymptote, Translation Review, Concho River Review, Red River Review, Huizache, Out of the Gutter, The Thing Itself, Eye to the Telescope*, and *James Gunn's Ad Astra.*

Made in the USA
Las Vegas, NV
19 August 2022